Black Desk Publications Presents...

William Codex
Knight of the Silver Sword
Book One of the Initiative Series

I0675663

By
Brian Raif

To the one woman who could possibly make my mother wait
for the second book's dedication page.

Nancy Joyce Kimbrough
1929-2010

Thank you for the stories Grandma.

In the piney woods of East Texas it's not often that you encounter what most people in the world would call real cold. Most years we don't even see weather that those north of the Mason-Dixon would even call winter-like. Instead we have this season that runs from late November until late February where the air carries traces of a demented little frost that likes to creep slowly into your fingers and nose lulling you into a false sense of numb security that you barely notice, before suddenly striking with a gust of wind that shakes you to your core. It doesn't even have the decency to happen often enough to require a coat for all but the coldest weeks of the winter season.

I have always preferred a real cold. You can prepare for real cold. Real cold is a demon that can be fought unlike these short unpredictable bouts with the twisted little East Texas "winter" chill. One moment everything is comfortably numb and the next you are trying desperately to cover your face as a thousand tiny needles of ice carried by a gust of wind drive into your face only protecting yourself in time for that gust to die off in mocking laughter at your attempt. That is why I don't understand how more people down here don't understand the benefits of wearing a good scarf.

As a man in this part of the country I have caught a ridiculous amount of crap over the black wool scarf that I always have at hand this time of year. Not that I have ever really cared much about the thoughts and opinions of others on this subject. It really is a surprisingly functional garment.

The scarf has kept my face from falling off on mornings such as this. Not to mention all the other times it has come in handy. In my book, that was worth the occasional sideways glance or chuckle from someone with a face burnt red with winter chill. Still, it never made sense to me that in this area of the country where, in most other cases, function is normally valued over form; that a good scarf's function is over looked and instead seen as a mark of pretentiousness or femininity.

Then again mine is just one opinion of many. This time of year, in this part of Texas, I am far from the only one walking through the woods at five in the morning. Thousands of hunters are starting up their day in the woods walking isolated trails. Some are even in this very forest. Each of them are preparing to brave the elements and embark on one of man's oldest rituals: the hunt. But, none of them have to do it in business dress code, and hopefully none of them are stalking werewolves. Not that my scarf has anything to do with werewolf tracking; but, if a garment is field tested and approved by a monster hunter, that should stand as a strong seal of approval.

And yes, you heard me right. I said Werewolves.

Just east and south of Lufkin, Texas on highway 69 in the Upland Island area of the Angelina National Forest Reserve is the hunting grounds of the largest of the five registered werewolf packs in the state of Texas and one of the largest in the country. They, like most packs, roam deep inside the federal forest far off the beaten path in order to keep themselves and those they share the land with safe. It is especially important this time of year. As a rule the werewolves go out at night and hunters only hunt from a half hour before sun up and a half hour after sun down. Even then, legal hunting only happens during a small part of the year.

However, there wouldn't have to be laws if there weren't violations. Rogue wolves, who have either lost control of their gift or started disregarding the rules for more malicious reasons, have become violent toward humans in the past. Hunters disturbed while camping have attacked when they felt threatened. Worse yet there are always poachers who have no concern for the laws and traditions in place to protect both hunter and prey from threats both known and unknown. And that is just a few of the things that can go wrong with werewolves, who are just one of many different types of supernatural creatures that live in the world around us.

Needless to say, it isn't a perfect system but it is the best we have for now. When laws are broken or boundaries get pushed aside, that means someone like me gets a phone call at a totally indecent hour and is sent out to go walking through the woods at far too early o'clock while grumbling about the early twilight sun and a distinct lack of coffee. Most of my work involves night shift hours so I'm not exactly a morning person.

Just then, a gust of wind whipped through the forest about me. I grabbed on to the end of my scarf and tossed it over my face avoiding most of the chill's vicious bite. The scarf and my lack of fashion consciousness win again. I glanced over the edge of the wrap of black wool toward my watch to find out that it was still about ten minutes on the wrong side of six in the morning. Normally I only visit each of the packs twice a year, after one of their monthly runs, just to check on things. I usually only mildly dislike how deep in the forest the pack insisted upon meeting. It was worse today considering that I had just walked this path a few months ago to make my normal check in. Early visits are rarely a good thing in my line of work, and today was no exception.

About three hours ago I received the call from my handler that one of the wolves in the pack had been found shot shortly after midnight. It didn't take long for the other members of the pack to call in the attack. Meanwhile, a two hours' drive away, I had just managed to get done with an issue involving some local leprechauns. By which I mean I bribed them out of causing trouble with the latest in Xbox games and a couple of six packs of Guinness. And when incredibly powerful beings that have lived for thousands of years offer you an evening of video games and beer, you don't incur their wrath by turning them down; especially when they have the mentality of fourteen year old boys.

All in all, between the nature of the call out and the late hours I'd been keeping, the natural beauty of the land about me was lost for the most part. This portion of the reserve, several acres of reclaimed forest known as Upland Island, normally had a kind of a haunting charm to it in the light of the early morning. Muted blues and grays seemed to lay over the entire world in a thick blanket of fog keeping the land locked in a kind of dull haze for a bit longer before the sun fully awoke to burn the distortion away revealing the glory of the emerald evergreens that were so common in this part of the country. The endless rows of planted pine trees that give this area of the state its name, stood forever tall lost in the morning fog like an infinite hall of pillars stretching out in all directions across the earth as well as forever into the sky. I'd grown up surrounded by forest not unlike this one actually. Some of the most peaceful moments in my life have been spent in the pine forests of East Texas. As I looked about the forest I could almost start to feel that part of my brain awaken. But, too many things had my love of nature, the moderate affection it is, locked beneath the surface of my perceptions this morning.

I hadn't slept and my coffee cup was empty for the last twenty minutes of my drive. None of that really mattered. You don't have time for snooze buttons or refills when you're responding to this type of call. A person, granted not a being that was traditionally brought to mind with that word, had been shot. Someone, whom I had sworn to watch over and keep safe, was dead. I didn't have time for a second cup of java or to stop and smell the proverbial roses this morning. I already mentioned that I normally have something of a love for nature, but I have a much stronger, much deeper hate for early mornings. I've always been nocturnal and, in most cases, it comes in handy with my line of work. But, emergency or not you do everything you can to only visit with a werewolf pack in the early morning. Like myself, wolves-including werewolves, are nocturnal. Visiting them while it is dark is out of the question if you are looking to have a good conversation. Right before sunset isn't the best idea either. You'll get to talk to someone sure, but it leaves you walking through the woods in failing light knowing that a pack of wolves on the hunt is roaming nearby and you were the last non wolf they got a good smell of. Simply put, one just doesn't agree to walk miles into secluded forest in failing light, meet with a whole pack of one of man's few natural predators, and walk out under the light of the full moon. You suck it up, drink some extra coffee, if you get the chance, and you head out into the woods in the early morning after they have gotten the hunt out of their systems and shifted back to their "normal forms".

Even in human form a werewolf isn't entirely human. Pound for pound they are about twice as strong as a human and with all the extra speed and agility to match. Their wounds heal at the kind of pace that inspires comic book characters. Also they still have most of the increased senses and instincts of a born predator thanks to the way lycanthropy rewires the human brain upon infection. You see, higher brain function is more or less left unchanged. They can communicate, problem solve, and remember just like anyone else, but the difference is in the lower brain: the instincts. Down in the brain stem, neural pathways get rerouted and entire sections of the brain are re-purposed.

Human beings are part time predators on the food chain mostly by technicality. We are capable of taking life and of eating meat by benefit of omnivore evolution. We are a kind of an animal kingdom jack of all trades. A wolf is a carnivore plain and simple. They live and die by the hunt and the kill. It is a whole different psychological makeup. They say a lot of the early bare knuckle boxers were were-creatures of one type or another. Then again I haven't ever seen reliable records on any were-thing other than wolves. However, I wouldn't be surprised if some of those mixed martial arts types you see on pay-per-view now days are as well. All of that considered, the last thing you want to do is go out to meet a pack unprepared.

A brightly polished silver pendant depicting a Greek cross on a chain wrapped about my wrist, a gift from an old girlfriend, was tucked up my sleeve. A good hard flick of my wrist could bring to bare quickly enough. The ring of silver around the equal sided cross was large enough that it made the cuff of that sleeve look bulged, but not so much so that it didn't comfortably fit in the clutch of my hand. The personal artifact packs a punch but I wasn't so esoteric as to only depend on it.

Clipped to my belt at the small of my back was my first choice in defense against werewolves. A SIG 2022 nine millimeter semiautomatic loaded with steel jacketed silver cored hollow point rounds. One round in the chamber and a full magazine was ready at a draw and trigger pull with two extra mags resting in a leather case beside the gun's molded retention holster. All the silver used to make the bullets had been gifted to me by a contact I had picked up on the job during one of my first solo cases.

It is a common myth that any piece of silver will do to kill a werewolf. The truth is that the silver has to be gifted. Not only that, but you have to be directly connected to the person that gave it to you for it to work for you. You see, like a lot of things supernatural it isn't so much the physical aspect of whatever you're using to hurt the creature that allows it to be harmed. It has more to do with the spiritual energy vested in it. After that, it all works by connections. Silver, in this case, is symbolically tied to the moon and the moon is tied to the werewolf. The sacrifice of giving a gift endows the metal with positive energies that can, upon use, follow that path of connections into the werewolf causing a severe allergic reaction that greatly slows their supernatural ability to heal. You could say that the silver acts like an electrical capacitor or battery holding energy until such a time that a connection is made and then it uses those metaphysical connections like a circuit path to dump its charge further down line, in this case down line is the werewolf. Also one needs to consider the exact nature of the gift. The greater the sacrifice made by the giver, the greater the energy vested into it, the greater the affect it has.

The silver to make the bullets was gifted to me by someone I helped with a problem a few years back. I work for a government paycheck and as such I don't charge people who have problems. The police don't charge when they investigate a robbery. I don't charge when I take care of a poltergeist. None the less, I got a letter in the mail one day about a year ago saying that little old Mrs. June had insisted that I inherit her silverware. Her will claimed that I could put it to better use than her children who received the rest of her millions. Thanks to Mrs. June I have the bullets on me, a couple of boxes stashed back at my office and about another two boxes of ammo worth still in original form in my silverware drawer at my house. It was a heartfelt gift but considering it was inherited the sacrifice involved wasn't very powerful. That made the silver perfect to be melted down into bullets. The silver had the required energy and connections vested into it that the effect wouldn't be spectacular. It was still enough however to slow down the wolf's healing powers and let a bullet do its normal job.

You also have to be pretty specific when you start playing with silver bullets. I normally carry something heavier than a nine millimeter in the line of duty, but it's a lot more expensive to make a silver bullet in forty five caliber than nine millimeter and you get almost as much bang for your buck. Also, the smaller faster round is a good thing to have when you are dealing with a supernaturally fast creature like a werewolf. Another important consideration is that a bullet made of pure silver won't work. The metal is too soft and will break apart and strip inside the barrel not only leaving you with an irregularly shaped inaccurate bullet, but also ruining the barrel of your gun at the same time. The steel jacketing over most of the bullet protects it from stripping and the fact that the round is a hollow point allows it to mushroom resulting in direct contact with the silver as it penetrates the werewolf. One more thing about bullets. The idea of one shot one kill is crap. You still have to put the bullet somewhere lethal and contend with a mad werewolf until it bleeds out and dies. The silver and the vested energy only slow the wolf's ability to heal.

If you don't have a silver version of anything that would kill a normal person on hand, anything that ends life instantly will work, but you try to decapitate a werewolf and let me know how that goes.

Fire can be effective but it is going to have to be hotter and they are going to be able to survive in it longer than most people could dream of. Silver really is the best way to go despite all the complications.

While we are talking about the specifics, the whole full moon thing is mostly bunk as well. A werewolf doesn't have to change with the full moon. Due to their ties to the lunar cycle the change is less painful and easier to perform on the full moon. Most newly infected can only change on the full moon for a few months. The issue with that is that a werewolf must make the change once every lunar cycle or the extra hormones produced by the wolf part of their brain will start having strong side effects on the human part of the brain. This usually causes deep bouts of depression or fits of anger. Most experienced wolves change every couple of weeks to take the edge off and keep themselves in check. Problems only start when someone goes too long between changes. That's the purpose of the packs. Most packs gather and change to run every month on the full moon. It's a camaraderie exercise. It helps build the pack mentality and keeps the wolves in check. More importantly for me, perhaps, is the fact that it ensures that every member of the pack is present and accounted for and is witnessed making the change at least once a full moon.

For the most part the packs police themselves on the month to month affairs and I make a trip out twice a year after one of their full moon meetings to check on the attendance records, gather a few statements, and make sure that the wolves and the surrounding humans aren't causing any issues for one another. Granted with this pack I would have used almost any excuse, except the current one, to make a trip down to the forest just for a bite of Sue's campfire breakfast. Sue is married to Brandon, the pack's alpha male, and has earned the title of alpha female of the pack in her own rights. She acts as a kind of teacher, grandmother and arbitrator for the pack. While I have to make sure to pay my respect to Brandon to keep everything on the up and up, Sue is my real contact within the pack. Don't misunderstand. Brandon is a good man, perhaps a bit rough around the edges but that is what makes him an exceptional pack leader. The tricky part for me is that the same traits that make Brandon a good protector of his pack and cautious of any threats from the outside world are those that make him a bit hard to deal with when it comes to all the official business.

Here is another little bit of need to know information about werewolves. You aren't going to sneak up on them when the pack is gathered together. A fact that I was reminded of as I saw a young man dressed in a gray sleeveless shirt and black runner's pants that stood a few inches under my own five feet eleven. Despite the fact that he couldn't have been five foot eight, or a day over seventeen for that matter, the young lycanthrope probably outweighed me by sixty pounds and none of it was soft weight either. I wasn't what most would call thin, but at nearly six feet and one side or the other of two hundred pounds, depending on the time of year, I wasn't going to win any weight lifting contest soon. The stern looking young man closing in on me with the close cropped dark hair certainly looked like he could, and knowing what he was I suddenly found myself thinking about those early bare knuckle fighters.

"You Codex?" he asked, keeping his tone intentionally gruff and deep, as he looked me up and down as if he was sizing me up for a fight, or a meal.

"Yeah, that's me. And you are?" I asked, trying to remember the young man's name. I'd gotten an email about a new wolf in the pack from Sue about four months ago that fit the kids description. Since He was still suffering severe hangover symptoms after the change the last time I was out, I hadn't gotten to interview him yet. Sad tale really, he was just at the wrong place at the wrong time during another newer wolf's uncontrolled change. Sue had also contacted me to let me know that, despite the normal setbacks, the "new pup" was a natural and was quickly finding his place in the pack. She must not have been kidding either. Generally young adult wolves guard the perimeter but only after years of growing up as a part of the pack.

"Phillip Gordon. Everyone else just calls me Phil." He said with a quick smile before hiding the relaxed expression back behind the gruff front the young man was putting on. Guard duty was serious business, especially now considering what had happened the night before.

"Well Phil good to meet you." I said extending my right hand allowing him to move in and close the gap between us. He'd almost jumped back as I reached out my hand, but once the human part of his brain took over he held out his own and grasped my hand in a bit too firm shake typical of a young man in his later teens who realizes he is stronger than the grown-ups now.

"Wish I could say the same. Wasn't supposed to meet you for a couple more months yet." He said fighting back that smile again before inclining his head toward the camp. "Keep with me from here on out I'm just..."

"You're just the outer guard around the ring of sentries close to the pack who are on unofficial kill orders all things considered." I stated for him with an understanding nod as we continued to walk through the woods. "Understandable with why I am here. Just be careful around something like a kill order from an upset pack leader. It won't protect you from the law." I reminded Phil as we walked.

"I thought being a werewolf protected me from that." Phil said with a sarcastic chuckle as he looked back my direction. "Not a jail around that can hold me the way I figure it." he said holding up his hand and miming the act of bending bars apart.

"You're right they can't. Not many prisons are equipped to hold a werewolf. That's why werewolves aren't normally sent to prison."

"Yeah? What do they do?" Phil asked before his eyes went wide and he started to speak again but I took over the conversation.

"I get a call and I drive in from wherever I'm staying. I try to find a peaceful solution in most cases, can't do it all the time. It's about the only type of call I hate more than the one I got this morning" I stated while I looked the kid over. His skin had actually started to pale as he realized what I was saying. Man, I can sell the "scary hero" face sometimes.

"You mean that if you can't find a solution ...you would come and...?" The young man started showing his age as he hesitated to finish the sentence.

"Not my favorite part of my job but it has happened before. Never with this pack." I said leaving the issue at that as I picked up the pace over the next hill where I was sure we would meet another set of camp guards. "Don't worry. You pay attention to what Brandon and Sue teach you and you're going to be fine Phil." I patted the boy on the back.

"You mean what Sue taught," Phil reminded me. As we topped the hill into the rising sun I could see that we stood directly in the path of another two young guards standing about ten yards ahead of us.

One was another young man of fifteen or so with ruddy hair and freckled skin. He had a noticeable scar over one of his pale green eyes. Patrick was one of the packs born children. Born of two of the pack's existing members, he had been making the change for that vast majority of his life. It showed in part in the slightly extended canines despite his current human shape. Something more of the wolf stayed with those who had been born to it rather than infected. In all honesty they grew up to be more powerful creatures and had even been noted to have greater control over the change than others. Odds were if Patrick could keep a good head on his shoulders into adulthood and stay in the pack's good graces, the position of Alpha could be his one day but that day was far off. Despite his feral stance and sharp teeth, his smile was still that of a child's, and as I topped the hill he waved his arm over his head.

The other pair of guards were an entirely different picture. Five years ago when I started this job, Stormy was a pretty little sixteen year old girl who I had just helped transfer to this pack. Starting about two years ago Stormy had gotten hard to ignore. Standing far enough over five and a half feet to be tall but not so much that she would be intimidating to anyone, Stormy was, to put it lightly, easy on the eyes. Long lean legs were encased in tight jeans that led up to the suggestion of a black hoodie style sweatshirt with red trim that just barely covered her midriff and clung tightly enough to impressive curves that the partly unzipped top made you take notice when she took a deep breath. Blonde hair fell down well past her shoulders and despite the fact that she had spent the last night in wolf form she'd bothered to re-apply makeup: bright purple eye shadow, too pink blush, and that ultra-glossy pink lipstick that just seem to make women look, willing. Pale blue eyes encased with a bit too much eyeliner and something on her skin that seemed to glitter. It all made Stormy that type of woman every man stared at, rather they really wanted to or not. Getting caught by a spouse or girlfriend would get them slapped and Stormy glared at.

"Will!" Stormy shouted as she half ran, an act that made her top do interesting things, toward Phil and I before standing on her tip toes and throwing her arms about my shoulders. "I don't like why, but I'm glad your here." she whispered before settling back down to the ground. "Things are really tense down in the camp."

"Thanks for the heads up." I whispered in response to the honestly unneeded tip off. "Could you give me a little bit more than that?" I asked as I politely returned the embrace with one arm.

"Sure Will..." The pretty blonde started before another voice broke in.

"Brandon says we aren't supposed to talk to anyone Stormy." It was Patrick who, despite his friendly demeanor, had stayed quiet until now. I'd known Patrick since he was ten. He'd always gotten along well enough with me, having grown up with someone in my post around. However, he was loyal to his pack without falter.

"Oh shut it Pat." Stormy quipped back shaking her head. "We aren't supposed to talk to any passersby. This is Will. He is going to find out soon enough. Better he go in prepared." she said before taking a deep breath and leaning against my side. "I heard Phil tell you, and I guess you got word over the phone, but oh God... Will it was Sue." she managed before starting to choke up and burying her face in the breast of my jacket. "I was just over the other side of the hill when I heard the shots. We were chasing after a few of the young. I thought I heard something and stopped to check to see if it was a pup and Sue kept running. They shot her again and again. I... ran and buried myself in some underbrush with the pups until I heard Brandon get there...by the time he got close they found Sue's body, shot her a few more times and left. I don't know what happened after that. If Brandon had their scent..."

"Stormy! Don't you say another word!" Patrick yelled. "Brandon knows the rules. He wouldn't kill anyone. He probably just scared them away to their vehicle to get a plate number or something." he said taking Stormy by the arm and pulling her back. "Now come on, Brandon is waiting for him and we have to keep the perimeter up. Phil can take him in from here."

It was strange to see the youngest person present take charge of things but it made sense among the wolves. I was an outsider, and while they would recognize some authority from me, this wasn't my territory in their eyes. To the pack, I was here to play hall monitor and take care of any human problems. Phil hadn't even been part of the pack for a year and Stormy was a born wolf who had only been in this pack for about five years. Patrick had been in the pack three times as long and now that he was old enough to exercise some measure of the authority, those years counted to all but the most elder of wolves in the pack. Needless to say, I nodded my consent to the wiry fifteen year old's orders and patted Stormy on the shoulder once as Phil and I walked by.

"He likes her you know. Not a good idea to let her hug on you like that." Phil said shaking his head. "And they told me you knew something about werewolves." He added with a chuckle.

"I've made myself clear to Stormy more than once." I countered to Phil. "One of my first assignments was taking care of an issue in her old pack and to get her here. She's been a bit... attached ever since."

"Don't dig girls with a bit of a wild side?" He questioned glancing back over his shoulder to undoubtedly take in the view of

Stormy's back pockets. "Cause I was just starting to think of it as an advantage." Phil chuckled.

"I've got no problem with lycanthropes." I said. "I've just known Stormy since she was sixteen and I was twenty five then." I chuckled. "I'm not going to say she isn't attractive, but she's too young and I don't date work."

"Wait....you were twenty five when she was sixteen. That means you're…"

"Yup the dreaded thirty." I answered as we finally broke through the tree line and into the large clearing that acted as the wolf pack's camp.

The clearing the pack uses as a campground amounts to about two acres of cleared forest in the middle of the reserve. Back when the land became protected by federal law a lot of the non-forested area had been set to be replanted, this little patch had been conveniently forgotten by the workers who had also been members of the pack at the time. A wide shallow fire pit had been dug out and bordered with stones for cold autumn mornings such as this and the rest of the ground was covered in a carpet of dull green winter grass. Except at one border where a spring cut through the corner of the clearing. It would have been a large open area had it not been currently filled with thirty or so tents set up about the clearing that turned it into something that looked like a small multicolored bazaar. Around the clearing, partly hidden by the shadows of the tall pine, were more pairs of young people all keeping a diligent eye on the forest. Most of the pack was gathered about the fire in a large circle talking amongst themselves, passing out what looked to be eggs and sausage for breakfast while watching the children play in a circle of their own near the fire. In the middle was the man I was looking for. Brandon, the pack leader stood partly bent over in a wide linebacker style stance as the children of the pack ran at him in either a wild attempt to tackle him or to make a grab for a red shop towel tucked into the large man's back pocket.

Brandon appeared to be a giant next to the children. Granted Brandon appeared to be a giant next to just about anyone. When fully upright he stood well over six and a half feet tall and was built like he was manufactured in a steel mill. Tanned olive skin and long black hair with a hint of gray in the temples revealed a strong Native American heritage. Alert pale brown eyes with hints of gold marked the large alpha male, a natural born wolf. Brandon had been a part of this world for over forty years and it showed in every movement as he jumped ducked and spun about dodging the attempts the young pack members made at their prize. In the circle about him a couple of the young would break out into short violent bouts among themselves. The winner would stand and wait for his moment to run after the towel tucked into Brandon's back pocket while those who lost tried to run interference.

On the surface, it looked to be a horribly violent game. But, when you considered the fact that these children had supernatural abilities to heal, the fights were on par with normal childish rough housing. In reality, both the fights and the grabs at the shop towel carried much more weight than that. The game, as it was explained to me by Sue, taught the young wolves several things. First, it taught them about the nature of the hunt. Secondly, it taught the value of strategy and cooperation in defense or when taking down large prey. And finally, it acted as the beginning of their life in the pack with each of the children learning that while thinking and teamwork was the path to life, leadership was won through dominance. Despite the fact that the children had to work together to take the prize from Brandon, the strongest and fastest wolf in the pack, only one of them could claim the prize. In case of a tie, matters are often settled with an especially bloody bout that can easily cross the line. Still even that part of the game was encouraged to a point. Already, at this young age, the next generation of the pack was forming up. This early in their lives they were establishing a pecking order that would influence their government later in life.

"Just wait here until Brandon's done with the kids then you can head in when he is ready for you." Phil said as he arrived at the outer edge of the circle.

"Don't think so, thanks for getting me inside Phil. I'll take things from here." I said patting my escort on the shoulder and pushing past him as I moved to step forward into the circle of pack members. Poor Phil reacted exactly as I had planned.

"What do you think you're doing..." he half shouted, as he grasped for my shoulders trying to stop me from advancing.

In the human world what I did doesn't make much sense, but you have to realize that the moment I stepped onto the campground I left the world of human psychology behind and in doing so got rid of most of my fancy degree. I had to fall back on what I had learned from documentaries, TV specials, and the fact was that this wasn't my first time around werewolves.

When you deal with one werewolf individually the rules of human society more or less apply. But when gathered up like this, as a pack, human rules like "Don't beat upon those weaker than you" don't always apply.

All of that in mind, I still felt bad for Phil when he grasped my shoulders as I stalked towards Brandon. I'd known this was coming from the time Patrick had ordered Phil to guide me down to the pack. To be escorted like this once I was inside the camp was saying that someone thought I wasn't strong enough, brave enough, or trustworthy enough to be left to act alone. If that was left unchanged I would never be able to speak to Brandon on equal footing.

I twisted to my left against Phil's grasp and brought up my left arm and let it crash into Phil's forearm before wrapping my left arm over both his arms trapping them in a headlock type movement before throwing two strong punches into his side. As I figured, it hadn't taken much effort at all for Phil's super human strength to break my hold over his arms and he came back with a hay-maker of a right cross.

Now before you get any ideas, I am not Bruce Lee or anything like that. That Hapkido technique is taught in first semester martial arts in several colleges or in self defense classes across the country. Phil was easily stronger and faster than me, but he had all the control and know-how of a seventeen year old. I stepped inside the wild punch and took hold of his right forearm with my left hand and pulled him towards me as I snapped my left wrist down and let the silver amulet fall to my hand as I drove the palm of my hand into the underside of Phil's chin using the momentum to lift him up a couple of inches before taking him to the ground.

Remember what I mentioned about the inherited silver being effective but not particularly powerful? Well, while Bethany and I don't get along now what matters with gifted silver is the emotions attached to the gift when it was given. Bethany had given me the pendant in question just over six years ago. We had been deeply in love and she had saved and skipped meals for months to afford the custom piece of jewelry. As the silver made contact with Phi's skin it exploded with white phosphorescence and gave off a sound like meat hitting a grill. Phil tried to scream, but the shock to his vocal chords was so great that he didn't produce much noise, just a powerful exhale and wheeze of pain as I followed him to the ground. I didn't let up the pressure until I was kneeling over Phil and delivered one more swift right hook to his ribs before standing up to turn and look toward Brandon.

As I suspected the large werewolf had called off the game at hand with the children and was glaring in a way that would make most people's mouths get all dry and make their knees start knocking together. I was no exception. I just knew I was dead if I let on.

"I ordered them to bring you down to me Codex." Brandon started as he moved to close the distance between the two of us. "That wasn't necessary." He said standing only a few feet away casting a shadow over me that brought to mind images of just how much smaller than Brandon I really was.

"I could find the camp on my own. I don't need a pup's help to make my way to you. Nor do you need to be sending them out with orders to kill trespassers." I countered while stepping toward him with the amulet gripped in my hand. I'd managed to make a declaration of strength. Now the hard part was going to be backing it up enough to stay on my feet without challenging Brandon and thusly getting into a fight I couldn't win.

The giant of a man was quiet for a long moment before he looked down toward poor Phil who was currently turning about on the ground in pain. Brandon grinned "He will heal, it's a valuable lesson learned anyway. Never underestimate an opponent before starting a fight." Brandon said looking back at the circle of young wolves. The vocal lesson was more for their benefit than for Phil. The young adult wolf would just have to reflect upon the morning and learn the lesson once he regained full control of his senses. "But be careful with that thing in your hand. A little silver trinket isn't going to get you out of here alive in a real fight." Brandon said as he looked back at me and rolled his shoulders like a animal waiting to be let out of a cage.

I managed not to anger him enough to start a fight, yet, but I was on thin ice. We both knew that much, but he had to say it out loud for the audience. "Nope it wouldn't Brandon. That is what I have the law for." I said refusing to back down but not quite letting my gaze meet his. I really didn't want to challenge the most powerful supernatural being for several miles while he was surrounded by all his friends. "And if the law isn't going to work anymore I have silver bullets that tell me I might not make it out alive, but you are going to be hurting in a bad way if it comes to that. Now, if you are done posturing perhaps we can talk about what happened to Sue."

Hindsight being what it is, my words had been a bit too strong, but I still hold to the fact that Brandon over reacted. As his form started to melt away his skin went flush and fur began to grow at a rapid rate. I reached behind me and pulled out my SIG.

Like I said earlier, I'm not a short guy, so when I grab a pistol and hold it straight out no wolf should be so big that he is looking said pistol down the barrel.

The hairs on the back of my neck started to stand on end as the tension in the air started to build to the proper level. It was taking most of what I had not to shake or to cough thanks to my suddenly very dry throat. If I made the slightest outward showing of fear I would be dead where I stood. I had managed to challenge one of the largest, strongest and most experienced werewolves in the country. Not the kind of fight where you bet on the underdog.

Truthfully, all I could think in the moment before my inevitable death was, I really should have stopped and enjoyed that second cup of coffee this morning.

Here are a couple more things that you should know if you ever find yourself in a situation where you need to know how to spot a werewolf. First, they look like wolves. They don't come in the two legged furry variety. The only time you see a werewolf on two legs is when they look just like you and me. Not that there aren't supernatural "nasties" in the world that are furry and stand on two legs, but if you see one it is not going to be a werewolf. Secondly, if a wolf has shifted recently and he shifts again he is still in control of his actions, for the most part. There are some significant psychological changes when a werewolf changes form. Most of them are sensory based, but when the change first occurs the wolf-like instincts of the lower brain can take over. How long the wolf's baser instincts are in charge mostly depends upon how much time has passed since he last shifted.

Right now that second fact was all I cared about. If I could keep Brandon calm long enough his human logic would eventually take over and we could talk this out. If not, it really wasn't going to matter if the beast I was standing across from was on two legs or four. Hell, it wouldn't matter if he was a werewolf or some strange furry evolutionary off-shoot. Brandon was going to kill me.

Before you say it, yes I know I have a gun. Trust me, in my line of work you learn pretty quickly how small of an advantage a firearm really is. I was standing within arm's reach of a nearly four hundred pound evolutionary throwback. If I ran, it would trigger his kill instincts and he would be on me before I could turn around. If I decided to pull the trigger, I would have to hope I could pull the trigger faster than he could jump at me or dodge the shot.

"Ok, Brandon we got off on the wrong foot. Tensions are running high. I've had no rest and I know after what happened to Sue, part of you is really.... under a lot of pressure to keep things together." I wanted to tell him it was okay to be hurt or weak in a situation like this, but saying something like that to a grieving werewolf in front of his pack would be asking to get mauled. As a rule, it really is hard to appeal to someone's softer side while not insulting their four hundred pound killer side. "Sue was vital to the pack and to you. I can't imagine what a loss like that feels like, but I know I'm going to miss her too. I've been doing this for what, five years? Two on my own? The first time I don't have her help not to put my foot in my mouth around you guys and look what I go and do."

Part of me sighed in relief as I heard a couple of voices around the circle of spectators chuckle at the last part of my statement, but the black and gray wolf with the all too human eyes hadn't moved a muscle except to curl up his lips and to expose his teeth. *My what big teeth you have,* repeated over and over again in my mind as I took a slow shallow breath making sure not to do so much as move a muscle.

"Okay Brandon, no one can help you find the guys that killed Sue if you kill me right now." *I hope the guys who killed Sue are still alive.* I couldn't help but to think as I glanced down my sights at the wolf. One should never have to look down the sights of a gun at a wolf that was near eye level with you when on four paws.

Standing that close to death makes your body start to do things. Your mouth gets dry. Your vision starts to brighten and get spotty as your pupils dilate. Your chest tightens up and your breath begins to quicken. This is all due to a small part of your brain called the amygdala. This is the part of your brain that defines emotions and remembers baser things like fear. After that, your hypothalamus triggers your fight or flight response. That is when your body starts to buck against silly upper brain functions like logic. Located in the frontal lobe of the brain however, is the rostral anterior cingulate cortex. This little guy regulates your fear response allowing you some degree of emotional control. In other words, just like I was having to wait for Brandon's brain to catch up with his killer instincts and slow him down I was having to wait for my own brain to catch up with me so I wouldn't try to run or pull the trigger. And here I thought that fancy degree wasn't going to do me much good with the werewolves.

Just as things where starting to slow down, I caught movement out of the corner of my eye. A quick flash of tawny fur cut in behind me and to my right. At the same moment Brandon dropped his shoulders and growled. Seeing the movement and Brandon re-posturing, I did what any sane person would do when being flanked by two large wolves. I got the hell out of dodge. Diving to my left, making sure my finger was off the trigger of my SIG, I hit the ground shoulder first rolling on my side once before coming up to a crouched firing position with the pistol gripped tightly in both of my hands pointing back in the direction I had come from. My amulet now hung from my left wrist by its bright silver chain.

Brandon, still a bulk of black hair and canine muscle, had shifted his position to where he could face both me and the intruder. Wolf number two stood across from him growling viciously, the hair along its back standing on end, muscles tense, and ready to attack. It wasn't until I saw the smaller wolf's pale blue eyes that I realized what had happened.

Hearing the commotion Stormy must have come running to my aid. Not nearly as abnormal as Brandon in the wolf department. Stormy in human form couldn't have weighed more than a hundred and thirty pounds. In truth she would have likely been upset at such an accusation. Thanks to the law of conservation of mass her wolf form made for an impressively large wolf, but one that still fell within normal range for the discovery channel. Her stance was incredibly low to the ground and tense. She was trying to play the submissive while still ready to launch an attack against the larger animal before her.

"Stormy, back up!" I yelled, catching both wolves by surprise, apparently interrupting a silent conversation of some form. Both sets of all too human eyes looked my direction as I slipped my gun to my back beneath my jacket making sure it clicked safe into its holster. "No one is going to fight for me!" I said loud enough declare my independence in my actions. "I don't need be rescued by anyone. Especially not you!" I declared while locking my gaze to the wolf Stormy as her head dropped and she let out a low wine. "So Brandon, you can either change back so we can get to work or you can attack an unarmed federal agent. No one but me knows my check in number and if I don't call in a couple of hours they are going to come looking." It was a bluff, but it was one I had made several times before. I did have a check in number but it would be several hours before anyone came looking. No one was nearby enough to back me up with any form of immediacy.

As I slipped my pendant back into my sleeve I felt the twinge of supernatural power gathering around the two canine forms. There is a kind of soft whisper of the paranormal at work that only the sensitive or the experienced can detect. I only pick those things up because I am starting to fall into the latter category. I could have sworn that, at the last moment, I saw the lithe tawny wolf wink at me before her form started to change.

When your life isn't flashing before your eyes, the transformation of a werewolf is, for lack of a better term a beautiful thing. Both of the wolves simply closed their eyes and stretched their shoulders and by the time their paws were out in front of them the change had started. First a five fingered paw then a hand gripping the dirt as the change rippled up their body as they relaxed their wolf shape and let it fall as if a wave of some invisible liquid washed the wolf away leaving a human being behind. By the time either of the figures were at a canine sitting pose most of the change had already happened. As they stood small details shifted back to normal to reveal fully human bodies.

Brandon, being the older wolf was the first to stand. His signature black hair was left loose over his shoulders the rubber band holding it lost in the change along with whatever else he had been wearing. If standing next to a monster of a wolf who had been intent on murder just a moment ago wasn't enough to point out how out gunned I was, the point got driven home when I saw what I had been standing against in human terms. Muscle ripped over the form of the giant man as he looked about the circle of on lookers. Brandon didn't have the type of muscle you see on body builders or guys who have nothing better to do than to live in a gym. His was the toned subtle but obvious muscle of a man who had spent his life doing hard work. As if that hadn't been intimidating enough Brandon was covered in scars from his legs to one that ran across his face that was already starting to become lined with age. I caught sight of the scar again running down his neck and across his shoulder. *Damn I need to start working out more often.* A fact that only got driven home all the more as Stormy stood.

Toned but hidden muscle rippled beneath the surface as the girl rolled her shoulders as if she was getting used to being in a human suit again. Long legs and hips lead up to the bare torso and modest, but all too distracting, breasts. I honestly tried not to look, but little Stormy really had grown up and I am only human. The only thing that some would see as a flaw in her lithe figure was a scar that ran from the back of one of her shoulders down her back and started over the flare of her backside. Even that one ivory line had been accented with tattoo ink so that it looked like a living vine of ivy wandering down her back.

By the reactions of the rest of the pack, that being just a few appreciative glances over either of the duo, one could come to the conclusion that werewolves where used to nudity. One would not be wrong. What I hoped wasn't too long of a moment later I managed to put on a professional face and give Brandon a quick nod as I slipped my dark gray sport jacket off my shoulders and handed it to Stormy.

"Don't like what you see, Codex?" Stormy chided as she looked at the coat and back to me, a sly grin crossing her face.

"No....it's cold." I said doing my very best to keep my professional face on.

"Oh?" She feigned asking as she looked down over her own naked form taking in all the prominent details. "I guess it is. Thanks Will." She said taking the jacket and throwing it over her shoulders and pulling it on, perhaps a bit more slowly than she really needed to.

"Codex!" Brandon's voice shouted breaking the silent tension and snapping back into the present as he grabbed a pair of jeans from one of the other pack members and slipped them on. "Work to be done." He shook his head.

I just nodded to Brandon before looking about at the rest of the pack. "Have you guys moved the...Have you moved Sue?" I asked keeping my tone soft not letting my eyes leave Brandon's as I spoke. Werewolves are big on eye contact and nonverbal communication. Actually if you've ever met someone who seems to always insist upon looking you in the eyes as they speak to you, you might not want to make plans with them on the full moon.

"No, I knew you would want to see things as they were. Thankfully it stays cool until much later in the day this time of year," he said. His tone was tight and professional as he motioned for me to follow him out of the camp as he headed for the edge of the forest and in the apparent direction of the site of his mate's murder. Sue hadn't been Brandon's only mate, monogamy as we think of it isn't exactly the order of the day with wolf instincts, but Sue had been his mate since shortly after she had been bitten fifteen years ago and she was held in higher regard than any other. When I first met this pack I asked Sue, in one of our meetings, how relationships worked. She hit on me in return. Five years later she would still occasionally half seriously mention the idea while claiming I was too attached to human ideas but as time passed it had changed into more of an inside joke.

Brandon and I walked down one of the horse trails that crisscross the forest heading south through the woods in near silence for over twenty minutes before turning east into the risen sun and heading off the beaten path into the forest. "Not long from here. Sue was teaching some of the young to hunt last night. She would have taken them up this game trail towards a few rabbit burrows she likes to reserve for that purpose. The young don't have to compete for game with the rest of the pack and Sue spends some time before hand clearing it out of anything large enough to be a threat." Brandon said breaking the silence.

"Then this is where we start looking." I said with a nod as I glanced about and started soaking up the details of the landscape. "So Brandon, level with me, I'm not out here looking for a couple of already buried bodies am I?" I asked as he knelt down to get a closer look at what was obviously a mess of wolf tracks that would have confused me in most cases but thanks to Brandon's description I knew to be Sue's and the pups'. I also spotted what I guessed were Stormy's tracks remembering her comment that she had been helping Sue that night. "If something bad happened and you tell me now I can lessen how hard the book falls."

The large man just looked at me judging the honesty in my words before shaking his head. "No, they are alive as far as I or anyone in the pack knows. It wasn't for lack of trying on my part. I chased them out of the woods, but they had motorcycles. By the time I got to this area of the forest, it was too much ground to make up. I made it to the parking area in time to see them leave." He looked over the forest around us, his own eyes higher up than mine, looking for threats instead of clues. "I'd even tried to chase the truck they had loaded the bikes into until I hit the main road."

The chuckle that came with that mental picture wasn't one I managed to suppress and as Brandon's glare caught me I just shook my head. "Has to be one of the few times that a dog chased a car and would have been able to do something if he'd caught it."

Brandon raised an eyebrow at me before a slow grin spread across his face, but disappeared an instant later. "Oh yes, I suppose it would have been." He said before the stern face slipped back on.

"She's just over this rise Codex, I can show you the dirt bike tracks as well.

"Sure thing. You get anything else during the chase? A license plate, descriptions maybe, one of them called the other by name?" I asked as he moved up the trail.

"No plates, no names and... the Chevy truck they drove could have been red... or green." He said shaking his head. Not all werewolves are color blind but the born wolves do tend to run a higher chance of it. They also claim to have better senses in the dark. Still if studies know very little about the senses of normal wolves, you can imagine how little is known about werewolf senses. "The bikes are both black Honda trail bikes, maybe 250cc engines. Pretty new models with a good bit of aftermarket work, improved suspension, and I think they had some kind of infrared headlights. They looked really strange in the dark. I doubt you would have seen them at all."

"You know a bit about bikes?" I asked as I looked up from the set of pup tracks Sue had followed into the clearing. I wasn't an expert on the subject of motorcycles, but I'd heard about set-ups like what Brandon was describing and it worried me. Trouble makers and guys making mistakes don't have bikes set up to be undetected at night. However I didn't want to tell him just yet that Sue had been taken out by poachers at best.

"I do some small engine work on the side from time to time when I don't have a lot of orders at the shop." he chuckled. "I wouldn't ride anything except for a Harley, but I have fixed more than my share of Honda motors. Part of the reason that I stick to real bikes. I'm working on restoring a ..."

I nodded my head as he spoke thinking I had finally gotten Brandon to relax, but that had been too much to hope for. His freshly started sentence died just as quickly as we stepped off the game trail and into a small glade that held Sue's body.

The clearing wasn't large maybe about ten feet across at any angle. This wasn't an established place like the pack's campground but simply a spot where nature hadn't taken hold as strongly as it had in the rest of the pine forest surrounding it. Merely a sparse carpet of green winter grass, a couple of struggling saplings and a couple of easily spotted burrows dug into the ground that had obviously been widened by large clawed paws. And of course just off the center of the clearing, laying on her side, was Sue.

I can't imagine how hard the sight caught Brandon who simply stopped at the edge of the clearing, refusing to go forward. I stopped for a moment as well, standing beside him at the edge of the forest before I could put my professional face back on and move forward. The figure lying on the ground wasn't Sue. She couldn't be Sue right now. She was just a human female. She was in her latter-thirties or early to mid-forties with curly auburn hair that was just starting to see touches of gray. She stood approximately five feet four inches, about a hundred and twenty pounds with an almost invisible tone of muscle beneath soft curves typical of werewolves and habitual runners. Just a touch a sun damage on paled freckled skin. From a distance she could have been sleeping except her right leg and left shoulder had been obliterated by high powered ammunition.

The latter hadn't been the kill shot. A couple more entrance wounds from a smaller weapon could be seen in her left leg and hip as well as another at the small of her back. Finally another small caliber round could barely be seen in the depths of her red hair. They'd filled her with enough bullet holes to slow her down then high powered rounds were used to disable her completely. After that they finished her off from a few paces with the round to the head. Didn't matter if they used silver or not. A well placed bullet to the head shuts down brain activity. End of story.

I slipped on a pair of latex gloves as I took the last couple of steps toward the body watching where I stepped to avoid any existing tracks. "Brandon, am I the first human to approach her?" I asked carefully as I knelt by her body.

"No one in the pack has come by while in human form. Stormy says that the shooters investigated the body before shooting her one more time and getting on the bikes and riding away. I arrived a few minutes later to find a couple more of the pack protecting Sue while Stormy and a few others gathered in the pups." He said from his place near the edge of the woods. "Once I arrived, I followed the scent and saw those head lights in the distance in the woods. By the time I caught them the bikes were loaded in the back of the truck and they were driving off and I made chase to the main road."

I nodded my head before I reached around for my cellphone, opened the camera application and started snapping photos of the scene making sure to get Sue's body from several angles. With a few minutes of searching I managed to snap a few shots each of a couple sets of boot prints before I turned my full attention toward the body.

Now here is the complicated thing about gunshot wounds and werewolves. The same law of conservation of mass that dictates that a guy Brandon's size turns into a wolf the size of a black bear means that the wounds a wolf takes don't change size as they revert back to human form upon death. However the location and shape of the body does change and that can do funny things to a gunshot wound. As skin, muscle and bone change shape the damaged parts and tissues move around. This means that the skin might break at one point and have damaged muscle tissue a few inches away. When dealing with werewolves turned back human broken bones they make absolutely no sense.

Lividity had gone into effect hours ago creating a dark purple bruise along the right side of her body that was facing the ground. Upon closer inspection her pale skin had started to gray and tighten over her frame as rigor took its grip only two to four hours ago. The story I'd been given so far was adding up. I would get a medical examiner to look over the pictures and give me more details than I could gather on the scene, but as far as the body was concerned it looked fairly straight forward. The larger wounds looked to be the result of a high powered rifle of some kind. Those rounds were going to be hard to find in the woods as a one man operation. I reached to the compact multi-tool at my side and flipped out the knife blade. After taking a deep breath I cut across the skin near one of the bullet holes in the upper leg. Human or wolf the meat up the upper leg is very similar so my best chance for finding a bullet was going to be from that wound. This wasn't exactly standard operating procedure for an investigator, but I'm a one man operation. Support staff in a central office on the east coast does most of my lab work. Long story short, this wasn't my first time to take a bullet out of a dead body.

"I'm going to do as much work as I can from here Brandon. I don't think we are going to have to gather any more forensics so you can take care of the body however you see fit, clean up the scene as much as would make your pack comfortable, but I'll have a crew of no questions black suits hit it in a day or two for a wipe. Just make sure no one uses the woods to change for the next few nights." I said as I reached my pliers into the newly expanded wound and started digging around. Thankfully it only took a minute or so to get a hold of the round.

Brandon grunted something in the affirmative from somewhere behind me but further to my side. "Fair enough, I have a friend who will take care of the body with no questions. They are in the know." Then he stepped back into my field of vision continuing his apparent search for the bike tracks.

A few moments later I liberated the round from Sue's leg and held it up to examine it. I dropped the bullet and damn near fell back from my legs to my butt once I realized what I saw. "Brandon, we need to clear the pack out of here now." I got my feet back under me and picked the bullet up from the ground. "We'll go to camp and then I'll help you move the body. This is a much bigger problem than I thought." I said as I stared at the nine millimeter steel jacketed hollow point with a bright silver core.

It had taken Brandon and I just over an hour to get back to the pack's camp and to get everyone to clear out. Normally those of the pack that don't have issues in the human world to attend the day after a run socialize into the evening of the day after. However when Brandon came back to the camp and started, for lack of a better term, barking orders they cleared out rather quickly. A few members of the pack grabbed the majority of Brandon's supplies on their way out to the forest trails. A redressed Stormy slipped by on her way out of the camp and handed me my jacket before hugging me again and slipping a piece of paper into my jacket's front pocket.

"Thanks Will." She whispered before stepping away and moving out of the camp ushering a few of the younger members forward with her as she left. Not all the children in the pack had parents who made the change. The care of those children normally fell on Sue, and I suppose that as Sue and Brandon's ward that duty now fell to Stormy.

"If you have any intention of laying claim to her Codex you should act fast. Talk has already begun around the pack." Apparently I had watched her leave a bit too carefully.

"You're the second one to mention that today." I said as I gathered some of Brandon's remaining supplies over my shoulder and started down the trail that would lead back up to Sue's body. I'd only taken one or two items from the remainder of Brandon's gear so I could make sure to leave my right hand open in case I had to go for my gun. "I'm not going to deny that I look," I started. "But, come the end of the day she is still that little girl I got out of that pack in Odessa and brought to you guys. Besides, I avoid dating work. It complicates things."

"Human sensibilities. I just don't understand them sometimes." He said as he started to follow me down the trail. "Hell Codex casual sex isn't even that uncommon in the human world anymore."

"Says the werewolf that was born during the free love movement." We continued down the trail. Apparently investigating a killing and conspiring to move a body without the knowledge of the local authorities does a lot to calm frayed nerves. "Besides, what if we did hit it off and then she went rogue?" I regretted saying it almost as soon as the words had slipped past my lips. Brandon had just lost his mate and now I'd just managed to threaten the closest thing he had to a daughter. Thankfully the giant of a man just nodded his head and kept moving down the trail in front of me.

It was another hour until we got back to the glade, gathered Sue's body, and moved her out to the parking area the wolves used. Brandon had insisted on carrying the body on his own leaving me to carry all his remaining gear out of the woods. Most of our hike out of the forest was in complete silence. I had too many things spinning in my mind and I was pretty sure Brandon was finally letting himself mourn now that the pack wasn't about for him to care for. I know I saw a tear well and fall across his face at one point, but there are just some things you don't point out to a man. I'd offered to take the body wherever he liked in my own truck. but he had insisted upon carrying the body to the man the pack worked with.

"Well, let me know if your guy mentions anything unusual and I'll keep you posted Brandon." Grabbing my own keys in one hand and reaching into my jacket pocket with the other I pulled out my card and held it out to Brandon. "My contact info in case anything comes up or you need to blow off some steam at someone." Prior to joining the agency I had been training to help people talk out their problems. I even kept a small office at home for talking to those that had issues to work out, but due to their nature they couldn't talk to just anyone. It wasn't part of my job description, but if I could help a grieving werewolf work out his issue on the big black leather couch before he exploded and went on a killing spree, my job would be a lot easier in the long run.

"I remember Gideon telling me once you'd been training to be a shrink when he found you." The alpha wolf chuckled as he looked at the card before taking a deep breath and looking back up. Brandon the human was all that existed in those eyes for a moment. "Thanks Codex. I'll keep in touch if something happens." he stated while taking the card and slipping it into his pocket. "But don't expect a call otherwise." Stepping into his large blue Dodge pickup, he spoke one more time. "Don't call me with any information either, unless you need help to bury the bastards when you find them." Brandon growled slamming his door shut, cranking the truck to life with a roar, and pulling out and driving toward the main road.

I shook my head and turned toward my own vehicle. My dark blue Chevy Colorado wasn't a monster truck or anything like that, but the small pickup was a lot more than met the eye actually. Given the nature of my work I'd opted for the crew cab, the small block V8 engine and the four wheel drive option. I liked the little badger of a pickup. In my job you learn not to get too attached to cars. I'd gone through four last year and if this one managed to survive till the end of the year I will have only destroyed two. So far this year I'd manage to run head long into a minotaur with an old Jeep Cherokee. I pissed off a gang of gremlins that did in the Jetta I had before that. At least I never have to worry about getting tired of a car. I turned out onto the highway and headed north to catch up on some long awaited sleep.

I had been on the road long enough to hit the city of Lufkin and grab a cup of drive thru coffee when my phone started to ring. "Hey, it's your mother calling. She's loved you your whole life and you really should pick up. She's a nice lady and she really wants to talk to you. I'm sure this isn't some silly question about the internet." The phone shouted at me before I picked it up to answer.

"Hey Mom. How are you guys doing?" I answered before taking a sip of my coffee. As I turned my truck back onto the main road. *Well, I needed something to do to pass the time.*

"Oh we're fine. I called you a few times this morning, but you didn't pick up. Late night?" She asked over the sounds of cooking food and a barking dog in the background.

"Good. Yeah I'm sorry about that I've been working and couldn't take a call. Haven't made it to bed yet. I was just about to head home actually."

"Another all-nighter for work?" I was sure I could hear the shake of her head over the phone. "Where did they have you this time."

"You know I can't say that. I can't see the house from here and I'm still in the country." *Oh I'm heading back from the Upland Island after checking on the werewolves and helping them move the body of a woman who was gunned down by supernatural hit men.*

"You would think I'd get used to the run around after all these years but you are worse than your father, William." She chided. "Are you by chance going to be nearby around dinner time?"

"You know what I do mom I work for the FBI...."

"....as a criminal profiler and negotiator. It isn't exactly a nine to five kind of job." She recited my normal line back to me. "I know William. It isn't as dangerous as your father's job when he was your age I guess. I just wish they would let you sleep."

"Well then I'm glad you understand mother." I said with what I was sure was too audible of a grin. *You see in all actuality I work for the Holzer Initiative. What is that you ask? It's a beyond top secret level branch of the Federal Bureau of Investigation dedicated to the protection of and the law enforcement of non-human intelligent entities that live within the United States.*

"Ha ha ha mister." I heard her say over the sound of a couple of pans clanging together. "What about dinner tonight?"

"I wasn't planning on being in your neck of the woods, but once I get home and get some sleep I'll head that way unless something comes up I guess." *Like another supernatural murder or something big like a zombie apocalypse. Though we aren't due for anything like that for a few more years,* I thought, snapping my phone into the hands free dock hooked to the dash of my truck. "Whats with the sudden invite?" Don't get me wrong I enjoy going home for the occasional home cooked meal just as much as the next guy, but my mom was right, the type of job I worked didn't lean itself to spur of the moment visits.

"Oh nothing." She quickly countered as she continued working. "Have you talked to any of your old friends recently?"

So your trying to get me to see one of my old friends. Well, Allen had been practically family for years, but we had been out for a couple of rounds just a couple of weeks ago. That left one person for her to talk about really. "Just Allen and Melody."

"So Melody is the one I need to talk to in order to find out anything about you." My mother, for all her good traits was a bit nosy. Not in a truly annoying fashion, just enough to keep her on the good side of the tolerable type of annoying. And she was right. If she wanted information about my personal life she would have to go to Melody. Allen wouldn't give anything away. Even if he was the type to pay attention to those types of things. It's good to have a best friend who doesn't notice the little social details when your job title is a few steps above top secret. Allen's wife Melody, however, would be all too happy to mention that the last couple of times I'd gone out with the pair I'd brought a friend along.

Hannelore was a sorceress who, despite lack of difficulty she would have blending in to humanity, suffered from severe agoraphobia and fairly mild OCD. We are not an item. We aren't even really dating. Still, unless someone wants to deal with an insane sorceress with no concern for human life in about forty years I am going to make sure that she got out at least once a month for desensitization therapy. Besides, there was really no better group of people to take her out to be around. Practitioners by their very nature are studious people. So even while having to hide her real academic pursuits she can keep up with Allen the mathematician and Melody the emergency room doctor better than I can most of the time. What can I say? I might have grown up a bit more blue collar than some. I also admit, I landed a really unusual job. But I've always been a nerd, birds of a feather and all that.

"Well if I can make it I'll be coming out alone so don't get your hopes up when you talk to Melody." I slipped across another couple of lanes of traffic and accelerated into the open road. My truck wasn't exactly easy on the gas, but I was willing to raise my gas bill at this point to get home and to bed sooner.

"Well I suppose if you aren't bringing a guest they aren't as nice as Bethany."

I laughed. "Let's not start this one mom. You and Beth are friends and I respect that, but you have got to let go of that idea."

"I don't see why I have to..." She started, but I honestly wasn't listening. Bethany and I had been an item through most of my college days. And yes, she had been the one to give me the amulet I carried when I had to deal with werewolves or anything with a problem with that type of magical energy. We had a really good thing going until her involvement with the paranormal reared its nasty head, pulled me into the supernatural world and almost ate me alive. Too long of a story for here, but let's call it "personality differences". That's what I told the folks when they found out that we had split and every time it has come up since.

Sorry Mom, I have no interest in dating the reincarnation of the Greek Goddess of Revenge who has tried to harm me and has likely befriended you to keep tabs on me or to make sure I know that she knows where you live. It was a sound train of thought but it was going to stay just that.

Even if I had wanted to say anything about it, which I didn't, my phone started to beep over with another call. "Hey mom, I got work on the other line. I'll call you when I get the chance. Maybe things will change, but don't plan on seeing me tonight. I plan to sleep like the dead."

"Awfully convenient. I'll talk to you later, William. Be safe."

"Yes ma'am. Tell Dad I said hi." Hanging up the line I picked up the other. There was a brief pause and two beeps as the line was scanned for traces or bugs before signaling the go ahead. "Norm!" I shouted as the line beeped clear.

"Damnit Codex" Norman Hayward, my handler, groaned. "You're too damn young to even understand that joke."

"It's called syndicated late night TV Norm." I laughed as I increased the volume of the phone a bit to allow the deep voice to carry more. "Besides I'm not that young. I remember when Cheers was on the air. You get those pictures I emailed your way earlier?"

"The computer kids check my email. They'll let me know if I got anything important or good looking to review. Probably forwarded it all to Medical." Norm had mastered the art of the telephone and thanks to a vast amount of field experience and good management skills, saw no need to learn anything beyond that in the field of technology.

"Well, read it over and get someone to look into groups with that kind of attack profile with some supernatural knowledge. She was full of silver slugs." I rolled my eyes. It was true. Norm was good and had built a whole team of people to make up for his weaknesses, but it isn't like email was hard to master. "What do you have for me to check out after I get some sleep?"

Norm just laughed. "You know what they say about this job. Coffee is for now..." "...Sleep is for the dead. Unless they decide to get up and start walking around." I sighed.

"I'll grab an energy drink in route. Please tell me this one is at least close to home Norm."

It'd taken just over two hours driving north of Lufkin, Texas on highway 69 until I got to my destination. It would have taken me less time to pull up to the gate sectioning off this particular little bit of east Texas farmland, but I'd stopped to grab an energy drink and to wash and shave in a gas station bathroom. I also might have made a detour so I didn't get within eye sight of the turn off to my house.

I own a house in Tyler, Texas. It isn't exactly the center of the known world, but it is more or less the geographic center of the area of the country left for me to watch out over. Granted I only actually stay in the house part time. I probably spend half of my time or more on the road living out of hotels. Not that I am complaining. I liked the house enough, but I'd never been the homesteading type.

As I pulled through the wide open cattle gate I reached over to the truck's center console and flipped it open, unclipped the SIGs, rig from my back and set it down in the console. In its place I pulled out the carefully wrapped under cover harness that held my normal service piece. Not a lot of people in law enforcement carried something like a Colt 1911. It was a bit of overkill in most cases, but not for me. The few times I'd ever used the gun it had never been against a human and half of those times I wish I'd had something bigger than the notoriously brutal forty-five caliber.

At the end of the day it just boiled down to personal choice. About six years ago I'd learned very quickly that the Colt felt natural in my hands. While I wasn't a crack shot at long range, when it came to medium and short range shooting I could put a round just about anywhere I wanted and do it pretty damn quickly. Checking my left side to make sure the gun was secure and my right to make sure the two clips were locked in place I reached over to the passenger side, grabbed my scarf, and slipped it on over my shoulders before I pulled my coat on and stepped out the door.

It wasn't all that unusual a piece of farm land for this area of the country. From the top of the hill I could see about twenty acres of smooth pasture covered with a carpet of light green winter grass outlined with encroaching pine forest on every side but the one facing the black top county road behind me. A small corral was set off to one side with feed and water troughs. Large round bales of hay were scattered across the field in various states of collapse. As a matter of fact the only thing that made this plot of land look different from any number of others was the half circle of law enforcement vehicles parked about twenty yards ahead of me and the buzz of activity about them.

I had just clipped my identification badge to the breast pocket of my coat as a uniformed officer noticed my approach and started heading my way flagging me down with a wave of his hand. "Going to have to see some identification before you get any closer sir. You don't happen to be the ...oh you're the Fed. Walters said we would be seeing one of you soon. Was hoping you were the land owner." He couldn't have been older that twenty four or five with close cut dark hair and pale skin turning red from time in the sun. He wore the khaki shirt and dark brown pants that mark almost all local county law enforcement in this area of the country. He was a bit shorter than me, but still had forty or fifty pounds on me. Most of it was good weight. As for the rest, you try riding in a car for most of a duty shift, living with a high stress job and staying in shape. It isn't as easy as TV cops make it look.

A lot of feds think they are somehow superior to uniform cops. I hate guys that think that. Police, sheriff's department, and highway patrol are as vital to our way of life as garbage men and mail carriers. Unfortunately it seems that a lot of people now days treat them about the same. Not me. When I get called in on something involving traditional law enforcement I make a point to show as much professional courtesy as possible. If for no other reason than the fact that I eventually go over their heads or lie to them. It was part of the nature of the job, and people take things like that better from someone they like.

More importantly my father has been wearing the uniform for thirty years and counting. You grow up watching your dad strap on a vest and go out every night wondering if it would be the night the bad guys got him and you start to respect the uniform and badge. The first night you have to go see him in the hospital instead of him coming home to see you, you start revering what those guys do.

"Yeah that's me. Sorry it took so long to get here I was a ways out when I got the call." I said stepping up to the deputy holding out a hand for him to shake. "William Codex, but that's just for the report. Call me Will... Finsen" I added as I glanced at the man's brass name plate. "Did you say Walter's was in charge?"

"Yeah" Finsen was already walking toward the half ring of cars and trucks. "He's been in charge of all this cattle mutilation crap for at least as long as I've been with the county. You know him?"

"In another life I'm afraid." I muttered as I walked upon the scene.

Now I don't know how many of you have ever had the opportunity to see cattle mutilation up close and personal, but for those of you that haven't, it's not as frightening as it is strange. Most reported cattle mutilations are surgical in nature. Anywhere from one to three cattle or other herd animal with no evidence of prior medical conditions are found dead with the skin and muscle cauterized off one leg, organs missing, drained of all their blood, or other strange symptoms.

More accurately they are cattle dissections, harvestings or vivisection as the case may be. I can tell you exactly what kind of supernatural activity, if any, is involved in each and every one depending on the injuries or nature of those wounds. It's part of the job. This however wasn't a case of cattle mutilation. No, the scene was missing two very important things to fall into that category.

First of all, the bodies strewn about in the field had been killed with nothing that resembles surgical precision. Limbs had been ripped from sockets or worse yet snapped at the bone and removed between joints. One body's neck was snapped and turned backwards and looked as though something had tried to tear its organs out from the back. Whatever had done it didn't bother avoiding ribs as it went. It had just punched through them. The other body was tossed about in such a careless fashion that I couldn't ascertain exactly how it had met its demise yet. To figure that one out someone was going to have to be a medical professional and a jigsaw puzzle enthusiast.

More importantly, and this is a key detail in cases of cattle mutilation, the bodies involved are cattle. As in they are not human. The young man with the snapped neck couldn't have been too far over eighteen. Dishwater blond hair streaked with blood and his one remaining eye looked over his back and to the sky. The other, would be much harder to get details on. As I scanned the site of the now human mutilations I saw the remains of a weather worn arm, or maybe a leg, about ten feet away.

Werewolf murder with a side of supernatural hit men for breakfast and a big double helping of human spaghetti o's for lunch. Yeah, it was going to be one of those days.

"Fensin! Dammit boy! Keep an eye on the perimeter means make sure no one comes walking up onto my scene without me knowing!" I looked up toward the booming voice and stomping steps moving in my direction from one of the cars near the perimeter. The man stalking over was quite possibly the perfect polar opposite of the young, somewhat soft and, polite Deputy Finsen. He looked every bit of fifty years and a handful more. The man's hair had been buzzed short leaving bars of silver and white on the sides of his head and ethereal traces of hair over the top. His skin had that kind of dark year round leathery tanned skin that only came with a lifetime of hot southern summers.

Despite all of that apparent age, if I ever had to pick between fighting young strapping Finsen or this old warhorse, I would take the friendly deputy to the ring any day of the week. Despite an obvious stiffness in his right knee the old man moved with a kind of barely controlled power that one normally only sees in nature, like in charging polar bears and avalanches. His teeth gritted and his dark twilight blue eyes narrowed as he closed on the two of us.

"Yeah I know Sargent, but this is..." Fensin started his voice faltering a bit as the man stopped only a few feet away.

"I don't really give a damn who it is! You didn't stop them and I didn't know they were coming!" yelled the man with the name plate reading 'Walters' on his chest. "I can see he is a Fed, Fensin. That makes it even worse. You already let one unauthorized person on the scene. Now you just let someone walk up and take control of the scene from us. Get your ass back to the line and I don't care if you have to shoot the next person that walks up. I don't want them over this way until I know they are coming!" The man yelled as the younger officer who started to talk back, but bit his lip and turned to walk back toward his post crestfallen.

"Looks like it is one of those days all around." I commented as I looked from Finsen back to Walters.

"Damn. Thought the kid was actually going to stand up to me that time." Walters shook his head. "He's got the makings of a good officer, but he needs to toughen up some." The old officer said before looking up. "Oh....yeah hell of a morning. Took you long enough to get here Fed. Hey wait a second. Will? Will Cunningham your daddy told me you went off to work for the feds, but he said you sat behind a desk doing that head shrinking thing..."

"Must be a mistake Sargent Walters, I'm special agent in charge William Codex." I said holding out my hand and shaking my head as my stomach tightened. My father always said that John Walters, his old partner, was a really sharp officer.

"Oh...well sorry about that, Codex, For a second there I thought you looked like an old buddy's kid." Walter's shook his head as he took a second look at me. "Good thing. I'd hate to tell Evan that I told his son where he could 'juris-his-dick-tion'."

Roger Walters acted just how I suspected he would at work. When he was sitting around a campfire or a grill on the weekend Walters was friendly, but once he got a head of steam there was no stopping him. By the way he told his war stories I always knew he would be a hard ass at work.

"How about we make our way to the doctor's van and talk over some of the details? Then you can sign off on a report or whatever you need to do to get out of my hair and let me get back to work. I'd at least like to get myself some coffee before you try to take my case." Walters said with plenty of emphasis on the word "try".

"That is the best idea I've heard all day, Walters. The part about the coffee not the case. I'm just here to investigate. You can keep the lead unless things get crazy or the voices from on high tell me to do otherwise. Let me do my job and you can do yours. I find it works out better that way." I said as I fell in step beside the man as we walked toward the large box truck marked as the medical examiner's.

"Ah. You're going to try 'good fed, bad admin' eh? You can teach an old dog new tricks, but you're going to have to get up pretty early to pull that one off." Yeah, John Walters knows me and I've known him and his dislike for federal agents for most of my life.

Well, technically he knows William Cunningham the son of Evan and Samantha Cunningham. You don't work on patrol with a guy for as long as Walters and my father had without getting to know one another's families. However, just then I was William Codex instead.

You see the idea that names hold power is almost as old as spoken language itself. When you know something's name it creates a bond. To most people this bond only takes the form of a mental impression. Someone capable of and trained in magic can do things with those impressions. They can find that named object no matter where it is. They can summon a being to themselves via its quickest way of travel. They can exercise a form of mental control over something. The list goes on and on but needless to say, names have power. And when you are in my line of work that isn't power you can afford to give away. Thankfully, for both the protection of my identity and to keep me safe from those that would use my name for ill, I have two.

I was born William Evan Cunningham. That is my name and with intimate enough knowledge of those words and what they mean to me someone, with the right power, can use that name to take partial control over me. Upon joining the Holzer Initiative, I was given a second name. A powerful practitioner... ok a wizard, who works for the department from time to time, gives each special agent a second name. As I mentioned, on the social level, a second name provides me with a buffer between my personal life and the department just like any other alias would. But, that is where the similarities between an alias and a second name end.

A second name works on a magical level as well. It actually creates a second impression for people to associate me with. Granted it is a false impression. That means they are going to have a hard time connecting William Codex to William Cunningham or rather they will have a hard time thinking that they should even attempt to. And, as is the case with Walters, if someone has associated me with the name William Cunningham and they hear my second name spoken they will re-associate me with the new name and it blurs the lines connecting the two. And, next time I see Walters at the folk's place all I have to do is say my real name and Codex is blurred and Cunningham is who he associates me with. It works better than Clark Kent's glasses, but that doesn't mean it is perfect.

If someone gains an intimate knowledge of both names and is put in circumstances where the truth is undeniable there is a chance they will see past the illusion of the second name.

By the time we arrived at the van I was confident that Walters connection to Codex and Cunningham was thoroughly blurred as he pulled out and filled two little foam cups with black coffee before handing me one of them and taking a sip of his own. I reached over and grabbed one of the packs of generic pink sweetener set to the side of the large steel coffee urn.

"You know that shit gives you cancer, Codex." The older man said taking another sip from his cup.

"Yeah almost as quickly as breathing does now days." I said pouring the torn package into the coffee and stirring it with a nearby tongue depressor set aside for the purpose by the urn. "So, what are we looking at Walters?"

"Two bodies…way more than two pieces." Walters said as he looked over the field before us. "Best the doc or I can figure they came running across the field from a third... someone. Must have caught them here. The younger body has some defensive wounds we can't tell much about the other yet. Male, old enough to have to use bifocals. Neither of them have identification on them and there isn't much left on the scene in the way of valuables. By the way they were dressed they looked to have been out hunting this morning. If they put up a fight it wasn't worth a damn. Preliminaries are showing that all the blood on the scene belongs to one of the two bodies. In the pasture about fifty yards away just past the top of the rise we found a rifle tossed in the grass. No signs of a hit however. We haven't checked to see if it had been fired yet, but being this time of year the round might have gotten used earlier today and dropped in the run or maybe they fired and missed the shot under pressure. No blood splatters to match up a gunshot wound."

Or whatever they shot wasn't hurt by something so trite as a high powered rifle round.

"Anyone follow the trail back into the forest yet?" I asked suppressing the thought. No need to bring up something like that with the locals.

"Nope, doctor has taken two of my four patrol guys and put them on body part finding duty, Finsen is keeping an eye on the road and my last one, Stewart, is interviewing the last person Finsen let walk up. Local girl claims she had a dream about the killings and drove out this way. Hell, she actually found the gun."

"You had a local come out and find a gun on the scene?" *Another piece of evidence to look into when no one else was looking too close.*

"Oh she doesn't walk up and tell us about it. She drives up, runs right past the line, passes Finsen, ignores the bodies, and right out to the gun before she passes smooth out. Fell back asleep on the spot. I've seen weird things Fed, but that competes for the weirdest. Well the weirdest to happen in broad daylight."

"Normally something like that ranks telling about Walters," I half laughed over my coffee. "Yeah normally you don't sip at coffee over a couple of corpses that are spread out over a couple of acres either. A local running up on the scene claiming to be a psychic or some shit just doesn't amount to much next to all this. Besides, aren't you boys all 'Just the facts ma'am.' when it comes to that kind of stuff."

"I suppose it doesn't. Still before you and I go off and look down that trail let Stewart know I want to talk to the girl before you let her go." *If an actual medium got a look at the crime I might get some information.* "Helps to interview a civilian who's seen things."

"You make a habit of talking to crazies, Codex?" Walters commented with a nod as he pushed off the side of the truck and walked around the scene toward a parked patrol car.

"As a matter of fact." I started with a laugh. "The special part of special agent is because of my psychology degree. Knowing how to talk to the crazies can get you some valuable information."

"Oh great. You're not just a fed special agent William Codex. You're a damn head shrinking fed." Walters said shaking his head as he took off from the van in that same barely controlled stride. "You're going to be a uniform's worst nightmare Codex. I can tell already." The old deputy said with a shake of his head. "See if you can manage to find that trail back to the woods while I go talk to Stewart."

As Walters made his way to the patrol car, I walked along the edge of the crime scene before veering off and heading across the field to the evidence marker where I gathered the rifle was found. The long arm was an older bolt action number composed of well-oiled steel and time polished wood. It was a hunting gun, really common in this part of the country especially during this time of the year. As I knelt down, I grabbed a pair of black leather gloves from my back pocket before picking up the firearm and checking the chamber. I watched as the brass jumped from the chamber and dove away into the grass before another round chambered. That spoke volumes. If the round had been fired while hunting any hunter worth his salt would have chambered another before moving out to find the kill. If the brass was still in the gun when it was dropped, it was probably fired in a hurry. It means the victim most likely fired the weapon while he was running from whatever chased them.

Pulling the butt of the rifle up to my shoulder I aimed down field away from the bodies and leaned into the gun's scope looking over the edge of the forest trying to find any signs of the chase. If you knew what you were looking for, the disturbed grass wasn't too hard to track back toward the edge of the forest. With any luck two people on the run and something chasing them big enough to tear them limb from limb wouldn't be too hard to follow. In most people's world an experienced hunter with a well maintained weapon with a scope couldn't miss a shot at something large enough to rip a person apart from any distance between here and the edge of the forest if he tried. In mine lots of things could take the damage, dodge the shot or in some cases, allow a bullet to pass through without doing them any harm. What concerned me more was the fact that other than two sets of human sized tracks in the grass there were no other tracks along the ground. That concerned me far more than the mystery of the bullet.

Taking care to set the rifle down, I got up and walked along the trail in the grass toward the forest keeping my eyes on the ground. Upon closer inspection the victim's blood trail wasn't exactly hard to follow. But, it was all blood from close combat wounds. No gunshot splatters that I could find along the path all the way back toward the forest.

"Weapon was fired?" Walters asked a moment after I heard his dragging right steps come up behindme as I neared where the blood trail crossed into the forest. "Seems like a hard shot to miss."

"I was thinking the same thing when I looked down the scope. But, not everyone is trained to fire at something trying to kill them." I nodded in agreement as I slipped my colt from my shoulder holster after we were a few steps into the woods. "No problems keeping the girl on hand?"

"Nope. We got you a date all set up at Stewart's car whenever you're ready Codex." The older man chuckled. "You planning on blowing down a wall with that hand cannon? I thought feds carried those little pea shooter Glocks." Walters grinned as he pulled his own thirty-eight service revolver.

"Yeah I don't like things getting back up after I shoot them." I said with a chuckle. It was a true enough statement. I put a smaller round in someone's undead minion once and it fell down and just kept coming on its hand and knees.

"Fair enough. Should we be expecting trouble?"

"Whatever did that didn't leave a trail heading to or away from the scene. Means it either was smart enough to take the same trail or to cover its tracks. I don't want to run into a bear that smart without my gun." I said before stepping back in before hovering my hand over the last piece of sign, another definitively human boot print, before heading along the trail and into the small patch of forest.

"Yeah, bear... sure." Walters quietly followed suit after that occasionally pointing out a bit of the trail as I started to hesitate in my own tracking. Ironically enough it was my father and Walters that taught me how to track through the forest. I had never taken strongly to the life of a hunter, but my outdoors education was never wanting while growing up. As the older man, who I knew was too prideful to wear his glasses, spotted another track in the forest before I did it really drove home the fact that I needed to brush up on this type of thing.

The next half hour was spent in near silence as we tracked the chase backwards as it crisscrossed through iconic East Texas pines. "I'll be damned." Walters muttered. "This thing is invisible before it starts chasing them, tons of prints here and at the kill site, but no tracks in between. Even then it's all broken limbs and pushed over grass no tracks until we get close" The five toed footprints were nearly twice as big as my own size twelves and sank over an inch into the dry earth. The fact that our only hint toward the identity of the killer was a print of a big foot in the ground wasn't lost on me. Still I only knew one Sasquatch in the area and I just couldn't picture him doing this. That didn't eliminate an out of towner however.

"That's the first thing you questioned today?" I couldn't help but ask as I looked at the most definitive of the large tracks we had seen since we started down the trail and the complete lack of tracks preceding it into the clearing or following it out after the two hunters' trail.

"Not the first time I've been on a scene with something strange and a Fed showed up to look things over. You guys really think you're fooling us?" Walters said as he pointed up toward a tree about ten feet away from the clearing we stood in. A game trail camera was strapped to the nearby oak. "Wonder if it stopped and smiled. I can call up the boys back at the site, we can have it warranted and down in by lunch."

I couldn't help but smile as I held up my FBI badge as I

walked toward the tree. "No time and no known representation. As the supervisory law enforcement officer I'm declaring it FBI evidence." I started pulling at the straps tying the camera to a tree.

"That is bullshit, Codex."

"It's freely shared FBI bullshit." I grinned as I cut down the camera and started working out the camera's locking mechanism. A few moments later I flipped open the game camera pulling out the camera's memory card.

"You just ruined some hunters month." Walters said shaking his head.

"I think something did that already this morning. Hopefully it's on this memory card." I slipped the card into a small evidence bag and slipped it into my breast pocket beside the folded piece of paper Stormy had slipped me that I hadn't checked yet. "I have a laptop in the truck that'll clone the card's data so we don't disrupt any evidence. I can set it to work on that while I talk to the girl."

"Damn, you kids and your toys are really starting to get on my nerves as they slip into my work Codex." Walters said shaking his head. To be honest I wasn't quite sure if he was shaking his head at me still or if he had somehow acquired a swivel neck. "And you probably got a digital camera in your pocket to take pictures with as we walk back along the trail. All you kids do right?"

I just grinned and held up my phone. "On my pho..."

"Shut the hell up and take the pictures, Fed." Walters spat as he started walking back through the woods. I was almost sure at that point that he was pretending to be mad, but with a guy like Walters, you never chanced it.

It wasn't long before we broke back out of the tree line and into the pasture now under the gaze of the high noon sun. The medical examiner's van was now gone as were one of the patrol cars leaving just two cars and my truck. Finsen nodded from the edge of his car. "Doc's got the bodies and is taking them into Tyler to use some of his equipment. No more drive ups, but the girl is getting really impatient."

"Did we ruin her schedule by holding her after she crossed a police line and found a weapon she shouldn't have known about. " Walters chuckled. "She's just going to be in for a bad day."

"Let's see what she actually knows before you take her in. It would be a waste of time and money if she doesn't know anything." I said as I walked toward the patrol car. Walters started to speak up, but I stopped him. "If she shows any signs of guilt I'll hand her over."

"Best of luck to you. She hasn't been much for talking just muttering about not knowing where she is." Said another officer. A tall thin dark haired man in yet another tan and brown uniform with Stewart carved into a name plate across his chest. "Cassi Ross. Longview resident. She isn't in any shape to drive. I was about to call in a tow when the medical examiner's assistant agreed to drive the car to a parking lot at their office. Walters said you could take her back to her car after you interview her before the two of you started into the woods."

"Oh....Thank you, Walters." I muttered looking back toward the older cop's large grin as he opened the door of his car as he waved.

"No trouble Codex, call me if you get anything. I put my card under your windshield wiper." I could hear his silent laughter as he slipped into his car and a moment later pulled away and out of the pasture.

"Well then I tell you what guys. How about I just do that interview on the way to the Medical Examiner's office?" I said with shrug of my shoulders. Neither of the two remaining officers seemed to object as I walked toward the open back seat of the patrol car and looked inside.

The woman in the back seat of the police car was the kind of pretty that never had to try at it. A rather doll like face and arms of porcelain skin escaped a slightly over sized navy blue shirt with "I may not be perfect but parts of me are pretty awesome" printed over the curve of a generous bosom. Her legs were covered by a tattered pair of jeans that had either been a favorite pair for a long time or had cost far too much at a designer store, a pair of low top casual canvas shoes printed in a red and yellow tartan pattern, and multicolored striped socks. Her face was partly masked by a cascade of dark auburn hair the rest of it was held back with a writing pen. It wasn't so much the exaggeration of one feature that called your attention to the woman, but more the fact that the sum of the whole was greater than those individual parts. Some people are born with a certain "je ne sais quoi", but very few of them could exhibit it without ever speaking or for that matter while snoring lightly in deep sleep.

"Cassi," I said as I knelt down so I wasn't standing above the car. "Cassi, I need you to get up and answer some questions." I said slightly shaking the woman's shoulder until her snoring stopped and she started to shake herself awake before sitting up and opening a pair of bright emerald green eyes.

"Hmmmm...wha...question?" She started as she looked over toward me and squinted her eyes. "FBI? What did I do exactly?" She said sitting up more and sliding away from the open door and deeper into the backseat of the car.

"No Cassi." I said trying to put on a friendly smile. "My name's Will. I'm just a specialist they brought in on the case. I would like to ask you some questions, but more importantly your car is in Tyler and I thought you might enjoy a ride in my truck more than a ride in the back of a police car." I said sitting on the backs of my own legs as I extended my hand to her.

"Oh. Well that would be nicer." She stated as she started to slip out of the car, reaching forward and grasping my hand. "You did check this guy out right Ronny?"

"Yeah, the Sarge had me check him out when they were out in the woods." said Stewart with a nod. "Besides, Finsen and I aren't going to get to head down into Tyler for a while yet."

"Ok." She said with a smile as she pulled against my hand and slid out of the car to stand no taller than five feet and a few inches. "Well Mr. …. Codex? Well, Will, let's get out of here. I'm only going to be awake long enough to answer questions if coffee is acquired." She said as she walked toward the truck further down the pasture.

I stopped and looked back toward the pair of officers and nodded. "You guys need anything else?" I said pulling off my overcoat and knocking off the twigs and dirt that remained after my trek through the forest.

"No, unless you want to trade places. The patrol car for the nice truck. Stewart for your new riding buddy." Finsen said with a chuckle. "Have a good one, Will."

I reached into one of my coat pockets and pulled out three white cards each with the FBI seal, my name, and my phone number. "Get one of those to Walters if you can and keep the others in case something comes up. Be safe guys." I said with a wave before turning about and walking to my pickup.

I used the remote on my key ring to unlock the door for Cassi as I neared the other side and opened my own door as she slipped into the passenger side. I reached around back and pulled out a small tablet computer, hitting the power switch. "It'll be just a moment. I've got to get this set up and we can hit the road."

"Fair enough. Coffee and my wallet was in my car." She said reaching over and finding her belt and pulling it over to buckle it in place. She stopped as she saw my shoulder harness. "Is that thing loaded?" She asked.

I looked down as I tossed my jacket to the backseat of the truck. The extra magazines for my colt were on the side facing her. "Yeah, don't worry it won't fire unless it's being held." I said as I started working on the small laptop and slipped in the memory card from the game camera into the computer. After that I plugged in the charger, partially closed the computer and slipped it up onto the dash of the truck before grabbing my phone and started to send a text.

"Just not used to seeing so many guns. Everyone I've spent my morning with has one. I'm starting to get jealous." She said with a chuckle. "Texting?"

"Yeah I'm letting my analyst know I have some data on the computer they need to clone over for me to look at." I said as I put my phone down, put the truck in gear and let it roll forward , started turning it about, and heading out of the pasture. "Can't tamper with the original copy of digital evidence."

"Just like the crime shows. Is your analyst a hot goth chick?" Cassi asked raising an eye brow as she started playing with the air conditioning settings.

"No, but last time I saw him he had a picture of one on his desk." I chuckled, turning out onto the road. "Kevin might be a bit wilder on the weekends, but the dress code is a bit more strictly enforced at the FBI."

"Ahhh... turn here." Cassi pointed to the left as we neared the intersection. "Coffee," she said emphasizing her point toward one of those ultra-tall interstate signs at almost every major interstate intersection across this country this one marking a Jack in the Box in the distance.

A few more moments driving and a trip around the drive-through later we had sausage biscuits and coffee as we turned back on the highway heading south into Tyler. "So,Cassi, while I was on the scene Walters mentioned some strange circumstances about your arrival. Mind going over things with me?"

Holding up a finger and taking a long drink of hot coffee before pulling the pen from her hair and re bundling the auburn locks. "Probably just like he told you, I dreamed about the murders. I don't remember getting in my car and driving out there, I've only been to the state park once or twice. First thing I remember after the dream was looking around over the gun, seeing the bodies and fainting. How messed up are you guys that you can look at that kind of stuff."

"Some say we develop a problem with desensitization. Kind of like some people like to claim violent video games cause. What exactly did you dream?" I asked.

"It's not very clear. I don't think it ever really was." Cassi said taking another drink of her coffee and a deep breath before starting again. "I was running with the two men but they didn't look the same, I mean as far as I could tell. I heard the older officer say something about one of them being older, but they were both young in my dream. I looked back behind them... behind us at one point and it was like they were running from a mass of black fire." She said taking another shaking breath, the memory of the dream obviously taking its toll. "More like dark green flames that cast shadow instead of light."

"This your first time to dream of anything like this? Where things actually happen." I said slowing the truck enough for me to look her direction as she answered. Her description of the dream hadn't exactly been what went hand in hand with prophecy or precognition, but the symbolism was too strong to be ignored and the details, however abstracted, were too accurate to be ignored.

"I've never had anything..." She started before she stopped and brought her bright green gaze to mine. She hesitated for a moment before taking a deep breath and nodding. "...I dreamed like that a few times before. Not every night or anything. Just three or four more times in my life. Last time was when my grandmother died three years back. It happened a couple of times when I was little, before they told me my mother died. It's never good things. I really wish I could dream up the lottery numbers or something." She finished with a weak tone. "So, are we still going to my car or are we going to drive to a different part of the hospital now?"

I shook my head and smiled before looking back toward the road. People who claim to have something like this tend to brag about having a "gift". They aren't afraid of it. "We're still going to your car. I might need to interview you again later."

"Just like that I walk up on a murder and admit to having premonitions and I get to walk?"

"You do this job long enough Cassi and you learn when to tell if someone is trying to pull one on you, and when someone is scared to say something. A lot of things in this world don't fit into a nice tight bundle either."

"Special Agent William Codex, are you telling me that 'the truth is out there'?" Cassi quoted with a grin. As she leaned back in her seat finally sitting down her coffee and taking a bite of the sausage biscuit on the dash in front of her. "I mean aren't you guys supposed to keep the aliens a secret?"

"I haven't said anything I'm not supposed to." I said checking the scribbled address for the medical examiner's office. "Besides my personal beliefs and the FBI's professional statements are different things. You just don't see some of the stuff I do year after year and believe everything you are told to believe." I hadn't meant to play things that open, but Cassi needed someone to believe her and I don't get to open up to anyone at all about my job normally. If it put her at ease I could at least play the role of 'Fox Mulder' for a little while. However I have pretty high clearance among government entities all things considered and while I might have read files upon files on werewolves, magic and cattle mutilations none of it was ever related to aliens. Either it was a clever cover up for my kind of work or those guys were in a higher pay grade. "So you didn't know either of the victims?"

"No." Cassi said with a sigh. "Though I didn't feel like that in the dream." She said finishing off the sausage biscuit. "I felt, connected to one of them."

"Could you tell which of the two at the scene you felt the bond with?" I asked tossing the paper remains of my own breakfast into the bag it had come from.

"They looked mostly the same in the dream. Well, I mean they looked young, dark hair similar face. From what I saw even the dark haired one at the scene wasn't all that recognizable." She said closing her eyes and shaking her head trying to push back the memory. "Damn, everything I remember at the end was just pain."

"Fair enough. I'll leave you a card if you think of anything else." I said as I turned on my blinker and turned into the parking lot for the building addressed on the back of the medical examiner's card. "You okay to drive?" I asked as I opened up the center console and pulled out another white business card and passed it to her.

"I have coffee now. I'll manage. Thanks Will." Cassi said before taking the card in one hand and grasping my hand in the other and shaking it. "Of all the times I've been in what is effectively a police car this has to have been the most comfortable. Front seat, coffee, and breakfast. What more could a girl ask for?" She chuckled before the light passing though my windshield bounced off something that caught her attention. The chain leading to the amulet around my wrist tucked beneath my sleeve.

51

"Oh what's that?" She asked reaching for the amulet pulling the edge of the cross out of my sleeve. As her fingers touched the silver memento I felt a stab of energy pierce my wrist and run up my arm. Cassi's grip about my wrist tightened along with the rest of her form as her body curled into the fetal position starting into a coughing fit before gasping in a deep breath and bringing her gaze up to match mine. Her pupils had expanded to the point that her bright green irises only existed as glowing emerald rings.

"Cassi!" I cried reaching forward and working to pry her hand from my wrist and the amulet. "Let go Cassi." I tried to coach her as I pulled her hand away as the pain started to spread up my arm and into my shoulder. Cassi's body started to lock tighter on itself while shaking with seizure.

Once her hand was free her body relaxed, but those glowing green eyes still stared blankly drawing all of ones focus away from her normally distracting features. "They.... they all died....each and every one of them....dead. You killed all of them." She muttered as her eyes relaxed and returned to normal for a moment as her body continued to spasm, in spite of her unconsciousness, before she collapsed back into her seat.

My eyes had drifted closed for only an instant before snapping open again to stare at the computer monitor in front of me. I hadn't slept in a very long time and I only had a couple of hours to get these reports typed up and turned in or I wouldn't hear the end of it. I took a long pull from my coffee cup trying to coax a bit more liquid from the empty vessel before cursing and turning my attention back to the reports. I heard the key turn in the lock and I honestly wanted to get up and get the door, but I didn't trust myself to return to my computer after I left. Besides three people had a key to my apartment and I trusted all of them.

I must have almost fallen asleep again because when her hands wrapped over my shoulder and warm lips kissed the side of my neck I found myself waking up. A soft moan escaped my lips as I reached up and took one of the hands in my own and pressed a kiss to the smooth knuckles before squeezing lightly and returning the hand to my chest. "Hey baby." I said before looking back to the screen and trying to get back to work.

"You're not getting any real work done at this point Will." Said a soft voice as the hands slipped down my arms and pulled them away from the keyboard and started correcting the underlined red words that littered the screen. "Come to bed love."

The needful tone in that voice and the scent of cinnamon with sweet undertones almost caused my legs to spontaneously stand and walk back to my bed. "Can't. I only have four hours to get these reports taken care of." I said pulling her hands away from the keyboard and starting back to task.

"I won't keep you busy for a full four hours. Just a few of them." Said the voice again with a chuckle as the hands started to rub at my shoulders.

"I wish I could Bethany. I really do." I said with a sigh as my shoulders started to melt under her touch. "I'm barely going to have time to get things done. What did you want to talk about?" I said tiredly as I gave up at the keyboard and turned about to face her.

Bethany, my girlfriend, was dressed in a black skirt that left more of her upper leg exposed than it hid with a light green top that brought her eyes out against her golden skin and accented her eloquent curves. "I have a favor to ask you Will. You're not going to like it, but you're the only person I knew to come to." She said her eyes already started to swell with the stress she had been trying to avoid.

I smiled and took one of her hands and pressed it over the silver cross laying against my chest. "Bethany, love, we're... I mean we haven't made it official, but we are going to spend our lives together. Your problems are my problems. What's the matter?"

"Well..."

"You want to go where people know, people are all the same! You want to go where everybody knows your name!" came the chorus of voices from my phone shocking me out of sleep and rocking me off the couch in my living room. Scrambling I reached for the phone on the end table and picked it up hitting the answer button. "Norm!" I mock cried into the phone through a yawn.

"Sleeping on the job Codex?" a familiar voice on the other end of the line questioned. "I don't mind helping you out and pointing you in the right direction kid, but I am not your alarm clock. Got it?"

"I know... I haven't slept in ...thirty two hours. Why are you calling?" I asked standing up and looking about the living room of my home.

"A Hannelore Meyer called me from your office and asked me to ring your phone. I told her to go down stairs and wake you herself, but she was rather insistent that she not 'invade William's space' and then she started instructing me on thresholds like I was kid. Not that she sounds much older than twelve. Mind cluing me in Codex?" Norman said his deep voice not sure rather it was going to get upset or start laughing.

"Well, you know that case you sent me on after the werewolves this morning?

"Yeah Smith county sheriff's department, double homicide I remember." He answered. "What have you got for us so far?"

"Most certainly falls into our department. Had to be a non-human perp. Supposed psychic witness on scene by the time I got there. Things got complicated after that." I said with a sigh.

"Well get me the details as soon as you can. Miss Meyer's said she needed you upstairs quickly"

I nodded my head to the voice on the other end of the line, realized how ineffective that was and spoke up. "Sure thing Norm.... I should have the results from some tech work done by Kevin. As soon as I check on the emergency I'll get a look at that and get back to you before I move."

"I don't miss field work Codex." The line clicked and Norman was gone. Grabbing the remnants of the Coke I'd apparently started before falling asleep I started heading toward my office.

Walking into the front door of my home one can either turn left through another door, which I often leave open, into my living room or walk up a flight of narrow walled stairs. At the top of the stairs you turn to the right and through a doorway into my office. I keep the space workable, but while most of the time it sees use as my personal study it also sees double duty as a meeting place for any of the more peaceful cases I encounter in my work. Hard wood floors and ivory colored walls lined with a couple of oak book shelves and a large matching desk into the corner of the room with an old fashioned black leather high back office chair. The rest of the office was dominated by a thick blue area rug with a soft golden ivy border and a single large window with matching drapes and a black leather chaise lounge resting below. My degrees hung on the wall behind the desk. All in all it looked like a traditional office for a psychologist except when you took a closer look.

First the degrees were wrong. I'd had a few ideas of going for a Doctorate at one point during school, but the offer to work with the initiative was too tempting. The schedule doesn't really open itself up for doing post graduate work however. Also most professionals don't have firearms certificates and FBI academy certificates hanging beside their degrees.

The moulding along the walls was marked in each corner by a bit of Celtic knot work serving as safety and privacy wards. The rug in the center of the office covered a brass circle about four feet across. One of the book shelves slid aside to reveal another shelf filled with more esoteric texts. All of that wasn't considering the more current additions to the room.

Cassi was laid on the lounge sound asleep and breathing evenly just as she had spent the last several moments of the trip back to my house except now she had a spiral of white paint over her forehead that turned down the left side of her nose and across her face to form an opposing spiral on her cheek. Individual delicate knot like patterns were carefully painted over the top of both of her hands which lay crossed over her chest.

Perhaps stranger still was the woman sitting vigil over her. Hannelore was one my best and most regular patients. Ghostly pale skin was almost completely hidden beneath a black garment somewhere between the style of a trench coat and a strait jacket beneath which she wore what looked to be multiple layers of black silk skirts the tips of black boots escaping from beneath. Her hair flowed over her shoulders and past the small of her back and was colored to match the white pallor of her skin. The features of her face almost seemed to disappear, washed away in a sea of ivory, except for the dark shading of makeup about her eyes and stark contrast of ruby red lipstick the only color in her entire ensemble. The flash of color was only disrupted by a silver ring through the left side of her bottom lip. Her jacket was closed to her high collar with matching silver buttons that ran up her front in rows of three and in single lines down her sleeves. Two rings traced over one of her eyebrows and her one ear not hidden by her hair revealed an array of bright silver jewelry.

Her appearance was enough to take most off guard given her perceived age. To most Hannelore didn't look to be a day over seventeen except for those that looked deeply at her pale ice blue eyes. To those that locked gazes with the woman she appeared infinitely older.

And she was floating. Sitting in the center of the room legs crossed in a meditative stance jacket and skirts hanging below her, hands sitting on her knees palms up, back straight, and eyes closed floating almost three feet off the ground bobbing up and down slowly with her breathing.

As I stepped forward her eyes snapped open and she looked my direction smiling and revealing perfectly white teeth. "William. Next time you speak with Mr. Norman could you tell him I apologize? I just couldn't. I mean it's your living room." She said her grin straining before she set her legs on the ground and stood to a total height of just over five feet in her high heeled boots.

"Not a problem. He sounds grumpy to everyone, but he isn't exactly my answering service. You're always wel..."

"No! First of all that is your space and I just... But, that is your threshold; you never invite anyone like me in. That can be dangerous." She chided before taking a deep breath. "Sorry, I understand the context and I will try harder next time." Hannelore said, her tone softening to its normal sugary note. "As long as I am not invited in."

"You're not invited. As long as you know you're welcome to try to come in anytime you like." I chuckled as I walked toward my chair and pulled it out for her before sitting on the corner of my desk.

Agoraphobia is an interesting psychosis especially Hannelore's expression of it. She regards her home as the sole safe location in a world she constantly sees threats in. She would have still perhaps developed the condition had she not discovered her magical talents, but it has only exaggerated things if it isn't the direct cause.

A threshold, or the barrier of magic that marks the beginning of one's personal space. In the case of Hannelore and those like her it is also the center of their power. In the outside world her magic is weakened somewhat, but inside another's threshold her gift is significantly difficult to utilize as well as weakened. The fact that she could hover in midair in my office spoke highly of her talents, but within her threshold a sorceress of Hannelore's power could stare daggers at someone and fill their lungs with salt or just manifest and make real the proverbial daggers she was staring. To invite one such as her into your home is to allow them to bypass the barriers that dampen her access to her powers. "So, what's the verdict?" I asked nodding my head toward Cassi still asleep in the chair.

"Very unique, very sad from all I've read about her ilk." Hannelore said shaking her head as she hesitated for a moment before sitting in the chair I offered her. "She's just stumbled into empathy."

"Empathy? Sensitivity to someone's emotions?"

"Yes and no. In the classic definition you are very empathic William and perhaps in other circumstances the same could have been said for Cassi here." Hannelore said as she reached up and brushed a bit of hair from Cassi's face. "Your poor darling here isn't empathic like you, William. She is an empath. Gifted with the psychic ability to tune into, sympathize with, and absorb emotional energy."

"My poor darling?" I questioned shaking my head. Before turning on the computer I had left up here when I put Cassi in Hannelore's care. "I just met her this morning and this is all work related." The chime on the computer pulled my gaze away, demanding I type a password. "Besides I thought psychic empathy wasn't a terribly uncommon ability."

"It was just a general endearment, William. I hadn't expected you to react so strongly." said the little woman with a giggle as she caused my office chair, which she had never taken offer of, to roll across the floor so I could join her near the lounge. She had only used the barest wave of her hand to do so. "She is a whole different breed than that. Lots of people, some could even go so far as to say most, have some small amount of supernatural empathy under the right circumstance: a husband and wife who eventually finish one another sentences, twins who know when the other is hurt, or people who develop deep bonds via one or two especially powerful platonic relationships. The potential for someone to develop a psychic bond is surprisingly common. The difference is that Cassi doesn't require such a bond to establish an even more powerful connection than most can manage. Her empathic ability is more like lightning. It reaches out and takes hold of anything close enough or charged with enough emotional energy. I hear when they are trained it can be a beautiful gift. Sadly, things never work out for empaths."

"What do you mean Hannelore?" I questioned as I turned away from my computer and my email to take her offered chair.

"They don't just read emotion; they harmonize and absorb the emotional energy about them. Every feeling they absorb, they become. Joy, depression, belief, doubt, love, rage, and anything else they happen to strike upon. Imagine dealing with all that emotion. Some go insane. A few especially poor souls end their lives. Training can help them concentrate on their power, learn to focus it, and protect themselves. Even then, they eventually strike something too powerful for them or their protections wear thin. You very rarely encounter or hear about an old empath. From what I can tell, your friend makes those empaths looks like ungifted mortals. I've never read, much less seen, someone with this much potential power for empathy." said the petite woman with a soft sigh as she bit her lip opposite her ring while she looked at Cassi again. "It's a shame really the two of you..."

"So why did touching my amulet set her off?" I said with a sigh as I pulled the pendant and the chain free from around my wrist.

"Your little supernatural tactical nuclear device?" The sorceress said with a grin as she looked back up and locked her eyes on the amulet. "You used it recently; the energy is close to the surface. Werewolf trouble?"

I nodded as I tried to scribble down some notes on empaths and remind myself to track down some tutelage for Cassi. "Just this morning. Nothing serious just had to prove a point."

"Lightning striking the tallest tree. You got that from an old girlfriend or something like that right. Did things end well?"

I couldn't help but laugh at that one. "Nope, we went down in flames. Literally."

"Then no I don't suspect it was a pleasant experience, but that might explain the bond I saw." Hannelore said not holding back her grin. "There's a good chance someone is going to wake up with a crush if she didn't have a taste for steely eyed, tall, dark haired men in nice suits already. It really is a shame she's probably going to die. You two would...."

"I know you just call things how you see them Hannelore, but that's just more than a little upsetting and a little presumptuous on both counts don't you think? Someone is going to fall for me, but they are going to die soon." I said shaking my head as I looked back at the computer screen looking for a change of subject. "Ah, my guy in the lab got back to me already." I said clicking the download link to get the information from the cloned drive. "Do you know anyone nearby that can help her?"

"I...yeah I think I can find someone. I'll need to make some phone calls, but all the information I need is at my home. I will get in touch in a couple of days." She said. "If it helps any I think she would have liked you anyway. Oh, I guess it doesn't help with the near certain death factor at all does it?"

"It's okay Hannelore. Near certain death doesn't mean the same thing in the world behind the veil. Besides, whatever side effect the amulet might have brought on she's part of a case. You know my rules." Hannelore could be brutal sometimes, but I'd discovered over the years that it was just a side effect of her agoraphobia. She really relaxed inside her home. It was just that her perception of the world about her tended to lean a bit more to absolutes when she felt uncomfortable. It wasn't that Cassi was cursed to an early death; just that statistically empaths died from unnatural causes related to their gifts. Or at least I hoped she wasn't cursed.

"And yet we go out for drinks with two of your mundane friends at least once a month. Melody texted me earlier today saying that she told your mother all about me. Granted she still thinks I'm a theoretical physicist." Hannelore said as a ruby grin turned up across her face.

"Hannelore, you know thats part of your treatment. Granted, not that I don't enjoy having you around, but we aren't... I mean we can't." I started. Remember that whole idea of being careful about what you say to someone who wields magical energy?

"I know that silly." Hannelore said with a laugh. Before placing her hands on my shoulders and giving me an honest open smile. "Besides, you're not really my type. Married to your work you are, William Codex." And with that she walked away and turned to walk down the stairs. "Besides, you have a thing for redheads."

I sighed after hearing the front door to my home open and close before I pulled my chair back around to my desk and took a seat so I could look down to the computer and back up to the beautiful girl laying on the couch in my office still sound asleep. I couldn't help but think that this was turning out to be a banner day as I opened the folder of pictures from the cameras memory card.

Looking at the image on the screen in front of me I had to stop, push my chair back a little bit, and bang my head violently against the desk once before resuming my previous position to stare at the picture. "Damn."

"Damn, what exactly?" came a sleepy voice from the lounge across my office.

"Ever had one of those existences?" I asked rubbing my forehead. "I just got some of the evidence from the scene this morning." I said with a shake of my head.

"Kevin, with the cute Goth girlfriend?" She asked standing up and walking toward the desk, stretching her arms over head creating a display of curves that took my eyes away from the picture on the screen for a moment.

"Yeah, but she can't hold a candle to the person I had come to make sure you were ok." I said with a chuckle. "She headed out to look into something for me just a few minutes ago."

"Are you saying that the mysterious FBI agent with fringe beliefs has a gothic girl friday?" Cassi said with a chuckle shaking her head. "Thats too much."

"She isn't my assistant." I replied with a chuckle.

"More than that?" she said leaning over the desk suddenly interested.

"Even less true. She's a contact that owes me a favor or two. I used one to get her to check you out after you passed out and another to get her to look into something else." I said leaving the computer behind to match her gaze.

"Fair enough." she said with a grin. "Two questions. You want to answer the easy one or the hard one first?"

"No such thing as an easy question when pretty women have ultimatums, but I'll take what you think is the easy one" I replied internally bracing myself.

"Can I see what's on the screen? I mean I'm pretty sure you are supposed to tell me it's classified or something, but hear me out." Cassi interrupted my reply with her hand. "You have your rules and regulations and I'm sure it's all in place to protect the public, but whether or not I'm a part of this, I can't forget that thing in my dream, Will. I can't just walk away from this." She said placing her hand upon mine. "Please, Will."

I started to speak, but I couldn't help but listen as she pleaded the rest of her case. She was right. It was all classified. I was supposed to tell her to go home and that the nightmares were going to stop and I would send someone her way to explain her issues and to help in a couple of days and if they couldn't help I could set up an appointment. I was only supposed to expose as much information to her that she was at risk of learning on her own. It was a simple cut and dry decision.

"If you look at this computer screen you won't be able to look away. We are talking about changing your entire world view. No, make that your entire life." I said taking her hand in mine and locking my eyes to her. "What you saw early this morning and later on, those are tip of the iceberg types of things. You won't be crossing a line. You're thinking about jumping off a cliff. You can't come back from this. No one paid me this courtesy before I jumped. Hell I was pushed off the ledge. Part of me wishes it never would have happened." I said before letting her hand go and pushing my chair away from the desk. "Just take another moment and think about it before you do anything."

Cassi stood there on one side of desk and watched as I walked toward the doorway out of my office. "Where are you going?" She asked the panic in her voice evident just below the surface.

"This is the type of thing you need to see on your own. The only classified material you'll be able to get to is the pictures I have pulled up. Take a moment and decide. If you look or not, that's up to you, bring the computer down and I'll have a couple of beers opened up." I said before looking back into the office one more time. "Down the stairs and take a left."

"That's it you're just going to let me decide if I am going to get involved in a world of mystery and danger?" Cassi shook her head and walked towards me as I stood in the door. "It can't be that easy."

"You picked up on this particular crime for a reason. I don't know why, but I doubt this was a random event." I said casually guarding the door way from her exit. "I don't like that you're getting to know this much. I'm probably going to get into trouble over it."

"Then why...?"

"Because I think it's the right thing to do. Now, take a minute, think it over carefully and come down when you make up your mind. If you don't mind bring the computer with you either way." I said before turning around and starting down stairs.

"How will you know if I looked?"

"Oh I'll be able to tell." With that I made my way to the kitchen, retrieved and opened two bottles of Shiner Bock from the cabinet, set them down on the living room table and waited. I spent several moments alone in the silence of the room until I heard the sound of steps walking down the stairs before I saw Cassi walk into the living room looking about, the laptop closed under her arm.

She looked at me her own gaze wide as she moved across the room and set the computer down in front of me grabbing the beer I left out for her, and taking a long pull of the dark beer before she asked the question I knew was coming. "Bigfoot?"

I nodded my head before taking a drink of my own. "Yup, Bigfoot. It at least looks kind of like him. Now what's the hard question?"

It had taken most of an hour for me to explain the idea of physic empathy to Cassi, what it would mean to her for the rest of her life, and to excuse myself to my first shower in what was now a day and a half. I had left out the part about the life being shortened for the time being, at least until I found more time to look into the issue myself. I wasn't going to give up on a fellow human being so quickly. After my shower I changed into the more practical version of a FBI uniform, a well maintained pair of black work boots, a dark blue pair of jeans and a white button up shirt tucked and belted into place and covered with a black sports coat. Almost anywhere else in the country someone doing my job would have to put on the full "man in black" getup to work after hours. Thankfully in this part of the country millionaires wore blue jeans and boots to work on a daily basis. Between blue collar dress code and the necessity to blend in at work I kept one black suit in the back of my closet for the rare occasions it was required.

I managed to type up and send an email to Norm about what I'd found and where I was going before I opened the coat closet and pulled out a backpack and tossed it into the chair with my closed lap top. "What's in the bag?" Cassie asked as I pulled open my counter and grabbed a six pack of beer and set it beside the pile of things I was starting to collect.

"The bag has some basic wilderness gear and a few extras you want to keep on hand when you are going to go walking among the things that go bump in the night." I said before I pointed to the beer. "And where I'm heading I might have to bribe a local or two. Sometimes it's easier to appease them than it is to go through the proper channels." I stopped, slipped off the jacket and pulled on the undercover harness for my colt, took out the weapon, checked it to make sure a round was in the chamber and ready to go, and put the weapon back in its holster before pulling my jacket back on.

"Did I just hear an FBI agent admit to bribing someone?" Cassi chuckled as she unzipped the backpack and started looking through its contents. "What extras do I want to start keeping around?"

"A few of the basics; enough salt to create a circle, iron shavings, a good knife, a bottle of spring water, a couple of old Roman coins, a can of air, a reliable lighter, and a jar of honey." I said with a grin before I held my empty arm out for the bag as she zipped it up and handed it up to me. "It'll take too much time to give you all the exact details before you ask. The basic rules will have to do for now." I nodded thanks for the bag before adjusting it over my shoulder. "One, keep your head down. Two, ignore it. Three, if it won't be ignored, don't promise anything, make any pacts or, invite anything into your home. Four, if all the previous rules fail, run. Five, as a last resort everything hates fire."

"Don't think I'm going to let you off the hook with just that. Now that you've brought me into this world aren't you obligated to teach and protect me or something?" Cassi replied picking up and looking at her purse. "I could carry most of that in here." She held up the minuscule bag.

"I don't see how. That second X-chromosome must give you some special space management powers." I said shaking my head and opening the door. "I can teach you everything you need to know eventually, but right now let's head out so I can lock up. Time for my night shift to start up."

"Some magical lock or super-secret government technology?" Cassi asked before heading out of the door. "Night shift, haven't you worked all day?"

"Nope, dead bolt and no signs on my door and yes I have but I cover mornings, days, evenings and, nights." I said with a grin turning the locks over before we walked around towards the parking area behind my house toward my truck. I clicked the locks open and took to the driver's side before Cassi jumped into the passenger side as I cranked the truck and pulled out to the street.

"Where are we going?" Cassi questioned as she pulled her seatbelt down and clicked it home before looking back toward me and playing with the air conditioning again.

"We are driving to the medical examiner's office then you are getting into your car and driving home. I am going to go talk to an informant." I shook my head to her predicted objection shutting it down before she could vocalize it. "I know it's a lot to take in, but you have to get home, get some sleep, and let things settle. I'll give you my direct cellphone number and as long as I'm not in a tight spot I'll pick up."

"I'm your only positive ID on this thing Will." she said not quite waiting for me to end my statement as she turned about in the seat and stared at me. "This thing is ruining my life. I ended up driving over an hour unconscious to pass out in the middle of a field and I don't even want to think about what I saw the second time I passed out today." I wasn't even sure if she knew how well that gaze stabbed into the side of my neck.

"Look Cassi it isn't like I don't want to help you or that you won't be able to help me later, it's just that where I am going I don't think you really want to..."

"Uh Will....I think we are being followed." Cassi's voice interrupted my train of thought causing my eyes to glance back into my rear view mirror. I didn't remember seeing any lights and after a study of the view provided by the mirror I realized why. The two black motorcycles rode back and to my sides mostly keeping to my mirror's blind spots. Beneath the sound of the oversized engine in my truck and the muffled sound of their motors the bikes couldn't be heard. They also seemed to have no visible lights. The only way you could see them was to see the lights of the night about them running and curving over the body of the bikes and the perfect matching black clothing of the riders. After a moment of study I could see that the bikes were both off road vehicles. Not the best kind of motorcycle for city streets, but the tough frames and long suspension made them perfect for riding through forest trails and escaping an enraged werewolf.

"Yeah, I think we are." I said as I watched what had to be the two bikes Brandon described as the pair he saw leaving the forest the night before. "This is going to get interesting. Lean back in your seat and let the belt go tight." I said while checking back behind me again. They must have noticed at that point, because the bikes started closing on Cassi and me.

"So, I take it we aren't going back to my car despite how much I would like to all of a sudden." Cassi said slouching down into her seat and sitting back as I put the gas down and started building up speed in the pickup. Most law enforcement vehicles don't exactly come with stock packages, and thankfully my truck was no exception. However, a larger motor, better transmission, and a few other add ons were not going to do me much good against two lighter and more nimble vehicles in the confines of a city. I could utilize the trucks size to push them around on a more open road, but on small city streets a few hours before they were completely empty of traffic I couldn't risk hitting a motorcycle and knocking him into another vehicle or pedestrian.

"Nope afraid not, at least not until we lose them." I said suddenly turning right onto a side street without a signal. I was answered by the squealing of two sets of tires and two loud sharp pings that could only have come from small arms fire hitting the tailgate or some other part of my truck. Cassi cried out and buried herself down into the seat before I glanced back again turning the wheel over slamming the weight of the truck to one side and sliding it onto another cross street before skipping the proverbial and putting literal pedal to literal metal as the two bikes fell in line behind me and started to accelerate. The chase was on.

We finally started moving in a straight line long enough for the truck to catch a couple of gears as we ran along one of the larger side streets running parallel to one of the local hospitals, but the bikes, thanks to their lighter weight, had me beat in the acceleration department. I faintly heard the sound of another round hitting the truck over the roar of the engine, and as if my heart wasn't beating fast enough, another set of rounds crashed into the rear windshield causing large spider webs to develop across the glass.

"Shit! Shit! Shit!" Cassi let out a muffled cry from the center console of the front seat. Thankfully the glass in the car had all been replaced with bullet resistant pieces, but despite popular terminology, there was no such thing as bullet proof glass. The guys firing at us were using small arms rounds otherwise the glass might not have worked at all and now enough rounds in the same general location would eventually weaken the windshield to the breaking point.

It took an extra second to get a clear picture, but when I looked behind me the two motorcycles each spread out to the left and right and started accelerating in order to ride up on either side of the truck. I tightened my grip on the wheel and kept on the gas giving the truck almost everything it had as we neared the crossing ahead.

The two lane street we were now on ran over a larger highway below. Keeping to the small two lane roads would give the bikes the advantage and kept us out of the public eye. As long as the chase stayed safe getting seen by the police would eventually work out to my advantage. The only problem was that I had to stay fast enough for the bikes not to catch me and unload on my windows, but maintaining this speed would make the upcoming turn suicide.

"Cassi, stay down and hold on tight." I said taking a deep breath and glancing to my speedometer. I was nearing a hundred miles per hour and the bikes were still eating up the road between me and them. Locking my eyes forward again, I waited. Another instant and the bikes both became visible in my side view mirrors as they started to run along either side of the truck. As the intersection neared I got ready to maneuver. This was going to be a battle of inches played out at triple digit speeds.

I reached up and flipped a toggle switch I'd installed below the dash of the truck and killed all of the trucks interior and exterior lights. I wasn't running no lights with a black vehicle like my pursuers, but my dark blue pickup suddenly devoid of all light had the desired effect. I tapped my accelerator once to start the process, then let off the gas. By the time the two bikes knew I was slowing down I was full into the brakes. Another half second later I was off the breaks, back on the gas, and pulling the wheel hard to the right.

The bike to the left of me shot forward, but the one to the right wasn't as lucky. As I cut across the road in front of him he was moving too quickly to stop and he clipped the front fender of the truck. Due to the compact size but heightened frame of my vehicle, it had the unfortunate side effect of stopping the bike cold but not the rider. The airborne rider and my truck kept pace for a moment as the truck continued to power slide into the turn before I managed traction and started moving forward.

It took several seconds to get the truck under control even after we were moving forward. It wasn't until we made it down the feeder and got onto the highway that I had the truck completely back under my command. I didn't hesitate to reapply the accelerator and start gaining speed. It was another couple of moments until I risked looking down and to my right to find Cassi still hanging on to the center console like her life depended on it. "Hey there, we're in the clear. Any luck and by the time the other one turns around we'll be out of sight." I said lightly patting her on the back before returning that hand to the wheel so the other could reach over and turn the trucks lights back on.

"I was ....He was so ...scared." Cassi said pulling herself up to sit back in the passenger seat. "When he hit the truck I.... could feel it. The fear, when he saw it coming it was... I thought my heart was going to explode." When I looked over she was digging though the drive thru bag from this morning to find a clean napkin to wipe the cold sweat from her face and neck. "I wasn't sure if it was him or me for a little bit. I mean I thought we were going to die anyway, but I felt it twice all at once." She managed to get out after her breathing started to slow down.

"You're still here." I offered as I pressed the gas a bit more before turning down a residential side street to see if anyone was following. "We'll make a trip through somewhere and get coffee and in a few, if we don't see any more signs of a tail, I'll get you to your car and..."

"Oh hell no!" Was the only reply I got. "Coffee, yes. Leaving me alone on the roads after that isn't going to happen." Cassi stated firmly sitting back in the seat as to reaffirm her location. "Who were those guys?"

I just shook my head. "Looks like they might be a pair of hit men I'm looking for in connection to another case." The fact that they had shown up this evening definitely meant that the guys who had gunned down Sue were professionals. Not only were they professionals, they were in the know about the government and the supernatural world.

When it came to mundane society William Codex didn't exist except for the occasional whispers of law enforcement officers and those who have encountered something in the domain of the strange. However, in the world of the supernatural, at least in my neck of the woods, I was a bit of a celebrity by way of exclusion. My little area of the world was the eastern half of Texas, most of Oklahoma, Louisiana and a good part of Arkansas and for the last three years I had been the sole full time officer in the area. The Holzer Initiative kept a couple of agents in reserve to go to the areas that needed help and everyone's first year is spent traveling to the different regions. If a couple of hit men were in the know about the supernatural world and wanting to make sure no one was on their trail after a high profile murder in this neck of the woods, they would gun for William Codex.

"Hey Will!" Cassi's voice interrupted my train of thought, shook me back into the current world as we passed the local junior college campus and turned onto another main road.. "I haven't seen any signs of them in the last mile. We are going to get the coffee?"

"Yeah. Coffee and then..." I started before letting out a sigh. "You and I will head out to the woods and talk to my contact. I can make a call and get someone to move your car. It'll be early tomorrow before we are back in the area." I said looking at the clock. It was already past eight. "We got about half an hour of drive time to get there, but we'll have a bit of a hike to my contact, and he doesn't get company too often so he might be a bit long winded. I can get you back to Longview after that. Might be early morning however."

"I doubt I'll be sleeping tonight." Cassi responded pointing to another fast food joint. "Coffee."

"You're worse than me." I said with a laugh as I turned toward the glowing sign. "I practically live on the stuff and you make me look like an amateur. What do you do for a living?"

"I waited tables till about two hours ago probably." Cassi said with a laugh. "I checked my voice mail while you were getting ready. I was fired while I was unconscious in your office."

"Fired over voice mail. That's a bit harsh." I said with a wince in my tone shaking my head.

"Well, it wasn't exactly the first time I missed work. Emergency aside, I probably had it coming, I'm not a very good waitress. I'll talk to the manager tomorrow evening, but I'm not expecting miracles. I was moving soon to start up classes here in Tyler."

"Starting up in the spring? What for?" I asked turning onto the highway that would take us to our destination.

Cassi sighed as she threw her head back against her headrest. "I was going wait till the fall but now that things are going the way they are, I'll try to get some core classes done and start selling my soul to student loans to pay the bills a bit early. In the fall I start taking the other classes for my English major. What about you? How much education does it take to be one of the men in black?"

I couldn't help but to laugh as I heard the question "They are actually more worried about life experience for this particular office, You still have to have the minimal bachelors, but I got my employers attention right before I finished my master's work and my second graduate degree. The big one is in Psychology and the second bachelor's is in criminal justice."

"What the hell did you want to become with a degree plan like that?"

"Hostage negotiation." I said with a grin.

"And you went and found something more off the wall than that. You live a charmed life William Codex." Cassi said with a chuckle.

"Oh yes. A life filled with dangerous monsters, beautiful damsels, flesh wounds, and a distinct lack of sleep." I laughed as we continued down the highway.

"I am not a damsel!" Cassi snapped back with a chuckle. "Damsel's are prissy girls and, psychic premonitions aside, no prissy girl would ever be seen dead with plaid shoes and striped socks." She said propping her feet up on the dashboard to illustrate her point. "So, where exactly are we going anyway?"

It was a bit over half an hour later when we turned down a county road away from the highway lights and signs of civilization and into the deep forest of East Texas. "Not too much longer. Open up the glove box and grab the key ring. There is one on there marked 'LSNWR'."

Cassi nodded and reached for the glove box and pulled out a large ring of keys that was nearly full with at least fifty keys. "Did they issue you the key ring to everything or something like that?"

"Not quite just the gate keys to a lot of parks and wild life reserves ...oh and my favorite bar." I said as she handed me the key and jumped out of her side of the truck as I jumped out of mine and we walked to the front to unlock and push the gate open. "This one is to the Little Sandy National Wildlife Refuge."

"That I can understand, I guess, but you're a key holder to your favorite bar?" Cassi questioned.

"Yeah, I don't exactly go during normal hours and my favorite bar tender has a problem with doors." I said as I jumped back into the truck.

"I don't want to know do I?" Cassi said as she signaled me to drive the truck through and manned the gate. I just shook my head. After I took the truck through the gate she jumped back in and nodded before I drove down a little traveled dirt road and switched the truck into four wheel drive. The road hadn't exactly called for it just yet, but with the recent rains I didn't want to not have it as I drove into the lowlands.

"Probably not quite ready for that one yet." I said in agreement as we made our way down the bumpy dirt road. It'd taken a few more moments before I slowed the truck to a stop. "OK, this is where we get out. Probably about a mile hike from here give or take a bit."

"Now that I am among the "abnormals" of the world, am I supposed to live in the middle of nowhere? Because this would make the commute to class horrible, and I would have to demand a gas stipend." Cassi said jumping out of the truck and heading down the trail with me.

"No." I said shaking head with a chuckle. "The initiative doesn't mandate where anyone lives, but some of the less discrete members of the supernatural community prefer to live out of the way. Some, like the man we are going to go see require it."

"Has to live in the middle of nowhere? Who exactly are we going to go visit, Will?"

Before I could answer, another voice spoke up from the forest to our right. The tone was so low that it almost could have been mistaken for a growl except for the lazy French accent that laced it. "Young William has, while not letting me know I had company coming, brought you to meet who some scientist have come to call Homo Gardarensis. However m'amie I have always preferred the name Gregorie despite my apparently popular nick name, Bigfoot."

"Oh hello, Gregorie. I'm Cassi." My pretty companion said politely holding out a hand. Gregorie, the Sasquatch, and I froze for a moment. Not that I was trying to pick on Cassi or anything, but I had honestly expected a different response to meeting the seven foot tall fur covered Frenchmen. I think old Greg had been taken a bit aback as well as he stared baffled at the auburn haired girl standing nearly two feet shorter than himself. It wasn't often he got to make a new acquaintance, and I was pretty sure he almost relished the idea of scaring the life out of them before proving that he was as refined a "monster" as he was.

Once he had worked his way past whatever thoughts that had halted him, Gregorie smiled and politely clasped Cassi's hand in his, nodding his head. "Charmed,Miss Cassi. Now don't mistake my curiosity for distaste, but what brings you to my forest with Mister Codex?"

"Oh. Well Will was helping me back to my car after what has to be the most interesting day of my life, and we were chased down by men on motorcycles. So, he deemed it safer to head out here than to leave me on my own. All in all it has been a rather enlightening series of events." Cassi chuckled.

Gregorie just laughed a loud basso roar of a laugh that shook nearby sleeping birds and small animals awake to run away. "OH! William, I like this girl! No running or screaming and talking about assassins as if they were bad weather." He winked. "I don't believe you reacted so well when I first met you."

"No I didn't. I'm more than a little impressed myself." I said with a grin toward Cassi. "Though I have to admit I was expecting a bit more of a reaction due to the circumstances of the visit."

"Oh...dear. This is where things get serious isn't it. I tell you what. If you have no objections in taking Miss Cassi on a moonlit stroll to my home. I shall take the short cut, clean a few things up and perhaps we could open those bottles you have on you while we discuss it." Greg said as he turned up a much less obvious trail through the forest. "Whatever your worries are I can assure you, nothing out of the ordinary is in my woods tonight William. You will be safe."

"Sure thing, Greg. See you in a few then." I said as the large human, make that humanoid, disappeared into the forest far more quickly for a creature his size should be able to. "Shall we?" I motioned to the trail leading off to our right guiding Cassi in the right direction before we started down the well cleared hiking trail. "So I take it by your reaction that Gregorie wasn't our perpetrator."

"No, certainly not. I mean. I'm no expert at this kind of thing and it would be stupid to pretend to be, but rather it looked like what I saw in my dream or not, I think I would recognize that thing and Gregorie is just about the exact opposite." Cassi said as she fell into pace beside me on the wooded trail. "I mean I can't put a finger on it but he feels at peace. I mean I didn't even expect Bigfoot to be able to talk much less have a preferred name or know his own scientific name for that matter."

"Yeah Gregorie knows a lot. He's had over three hundred years to study. Granted he was fairly hampered on resources until he got an internet connection"

"Wait....you're telling me that Bigfo.... I mean, Gregorie, has internet?" Cassi said, her surprise stopping her in her tracks.

"Oh yeah. Satellite link. He actually runs a pretty popular conspiracy website. Throwing out false trails about his own existence. Before that he was a bit of a T.V. nut. He even used some of his early government contacts to get himself a Nielsen box. Bigfoot is one of the few people in the country who decide the rating numbers for the TV networks.

"So there's a cave or something out here with a couple of satellites sticking out of the top of it?" Cassi laughed as she mimed looking about the forest.

I couldn't help joining her in the laugh, but I had to shake my head after a few moments.

"No, not quite, he has a house just off the nature reserve on a few acres of land. It has a heavy gate and a lot of 'No Trespassing' and 'Beware of Dog' signs." I said as I pointed to a small light in the distance that had just flipped on while we were laughing. "Not too much further now."

A few hundred yards and a bypassed barbed wire fence later we walked up the stairs leading to the small porch of a modest log cabin. The door was cracked open and the living breathing orange light of a fire danced about the entry way. "Greg?" I asked as I pushed the door open and stepped to the side to allow Cassi in as the giant sitting on the other side of kitchen table nodded us in.

Gregorie's home was, well it was a quaint little place. Interior walls of the same wood as the exterior, but in polished panels. The furniture was wooden and all looked to be made by the same hand as the cabin itself. In the back of the one room dwelling was a stone fireplace burning bright crackling fire so fresh it hadn't yet started to turn away the cool night air inside the cabin. Then there was the desk. A large flat screen TV and an only slightly smaller computer monitor were both currently black with a keyboard and mouse visible on the surface of the antique desk. Gregorie stood from his Bigfoot sized chair and nodded to the table. "Miss Cassi, William, have a seat."

I nodded and headed toward the table stopping to pull out a chair for Cassi before grabbing one for myself. The attempt at chivalry earned me a narrowed glance before I looked up to Greg who was still standing.

Cassi looked about for a moment catching my glance before looking toward Greg. "Oh! Sorry just not used this kind of thing. Doesn't happen all that often anymore." She said with a grin before taking a seat.

Greg and I followed taking our own chairs before I pulled the beer out and set it on the table. Gregg smiled before picking up a beer and quite literally pulling the top off the screw top bottle like a human would pluck the lid off a plastic ketchup bottle. He started to offer the bottle to Cassi before she shook her head, reached forward, grabbed her own, and with a ring that sat on her right hand pried the bottle cap off just as quickly as the hairy giant at the head of the table. "I appreciate the manners, but this is Texas not Paris." She said before turning up the bottle as I grabbed my own bottle. I started to open the bottle the proper way. When I saw Cassi and Gregorie trade smirks I stopped. I gave the pair an appraising look and set the bottle down on the table and started to reach for the pistol beneath by coat. By the time I pulled the colt and leveled it at the top of the cap Cassi reached out, popped the top of my beer, and slid it toward me.

I paused. "No hands." I grinned before picking up the beer and taking a drink.

After a moment when a round of laughs subsided Gregorie took it upon himself to place the proper air about the evening. "So, young Cassi mentioned that you've had an interesting evening, William. How can I help?"

I sighed as I pulled out my phone and with a few clicks brought up a picture that Kevin had spent to my phone. "This was taken less than thirty miles away from here this morning." I pushed the camera across the table toward the giant waiting hand.

Gregorie looked at the phone glancing down at the picture before picking it up to study the picture closer. "Oh...my, I realize the photo bares a strong resemblance, but that isn't me William." Gregorie said looking up toward me his eyes a bit wide. "I avoid going out during the day during this time of year specifically for this reason." He said before setting the phone down and sliding it back toward me.

"We know that Gregorie." Cassi started as she stepped into the conversation. "I don't think Will ever put it in so many words, but I think he wanted me to feel you out." She said looking toward me raising an eyebrow.

"It wasn't my original idea, but I was fairly certain it wasn't you and I had a feeling Cassi could confirm that for me. Confirmed and trusted physic premonition is good evidence in an Initiative case file." I said with a nod to Gregorie. "Any relatives in town? I know you aren't the only one that has drunk from one of the fountains.

"Not to my knowledge, but we don't exactly keep in touch. Not even the Initiative knows how many of us there are." Gregorie replied with a shake of his head. "I would have thought I would have heard word from other sources if another of my kin was in the area however.

"Relatives? Fountains? Sources?" Cassi replied looking back and forth between the two of us at the table. "There is more than one …. of you Gregorie?"

"Well, I suspect I have some human descendants left perhaps, but I've not had any children myself since the change. What William means by relatives is others who have drank from the fountains of youth. But, I keep a close eye upon my...."

"Wait.... the fountain of youth? You know where the fountain of youth is?"

"I have personally discovered one. My own research with the Initiative's help has led me to the locations of four others and multiple souls who have drank from them."

"There is more than one fountain of youth? How has this not gotten out?" Cassi asked wide eyed as she looked toward Gregorie. "How old are you?"

"First arrived with my family in the Americas in 1697 with one of the early French explorations of Newfoundland..... Louisiana. I was twenty-seven when I arrived so that makes me... three hundred and forty one years old."

"Ok so you were in your late twenties when you got here. Somewhere along the way you find the fountain of youth. Why didn't you ever tell anyone?" Cassi asked before she took in the evidence and filled in the blanks of the story herself. "Oh... the fountain..."

"Drinking from the fountain offers you life never ending under certain conditions, but it comes at a cost. Besides the obvious, I cannot live in what you would call civilization. The further I am away from the wild, the weaker I become. Eternal life, Eternal isolation." Gregorie said with a bit of a forlorn look. "Mine is as much a curse as it is a blessing."

"Isolation until the Initiative made contact and before satellite TV and internet." I added. "Yes the Initiative and its predecessors have been good to me. I have a small number of human friends as well as various others who visit me. Sonya, the woman who overlooks the wildlife reserve brings me almost anything I require from the world and yes, the electronic age has freed me significantly. But, at the time of my turning I could not simply go and tell my fellow settlers. I would have been received as a beast."

"Oh...." Was all Cassi could manage giving birth to a long moment of silence.

Feeling the need for a change of subject I spoke trying to steer things back toward business. "And you say that your sources in the wilds haven't noticed anything?"

"No, but that doesn't mean much. The perceptions of animals and of wild fae are different than our own. They would recognize a new predator, but they wouldn't necessarily be able to distinguish him or her from anyone else. That is if they take notice. This is hunting season, so those of the wild who will speak to me spend a great amount of time in hiding." Gregorie said with a shrug of his shoulders. "If you want to give me the coordinates I could check the site of the attacks tomorrow night and see if I can find a scent."

"It's a ways off, you might have to cross a few roads. You feel up to that?" I asked taking a sip of my beer and looking over to Cassi who had settled for an attentive gaze bounce back and forth between the two of us instead of asking questions. "Roads are a sign of civilization they carry a lot of life and thusly a lot of energy. As such Greg can have a hard time crossing them. It's not painful, but in the distance it takes to cross a paved two lane highway it will take a toll of his body like he had run a few miles. Crossing a five lane interstate could kill him." I explained to the woman. A psychic empath or not, her problem solving and perception skills were amazing for someone her age, but this was still a lot for anyone to take in. The fact that she accepted Gregg instead of blowing a fuse or breaking down spoke volumes for her.

Gregorie nodded his acceptance of the fact. "It will make for a long night, but I shall make do."

Another hour or so was spent in conversation, mostly satisfying some of Cassi's historical questions for Gregorie and explaining how dark beer was intended to be served at room temperature. Shortly after midnight I managed to excuse Cassi and I from the cabin getting us back to the truck heading to the interstate and driving toward Longview. By the time we arrived in the small city it was dark except for street and traffic lights. Cassi spent most of the trip from Gregorie's place to her apartment asking questions about the world she was now a part of. "So in case of werewolves, I need to have been gifted the silver if it is going to work. I need to be religious to make holy water work against a vampire and wooden stakes need to be fresh cut. Bigfoot can't cross the road and a witch or wizard isn't as powerful as normal inside of someone else's home. What about Dragons? Are they real?"

I couldn't help but to chuckle as I pulled into the parking spot Cassi had indicated. "You ever get wind of a dragon coming this way, you do the same thing Gideon taught me to do and get at least two states away if you can help it." I said as I looked toward her. "The last dragon to have anything to do with this part of the world was named Katrina by the media and destroyed New Orleans."

"You mean the hurricane?"

"You mean the storm the Dragon summoned to cover its attack?"

"Ok, I've officially had my mind blown." Cassi said setting her face in her hands. "You mean to tell me that a Dragon summoned a storm and attacked the gulf coast and no one was the wiser?"

"The whole reason the Initiative was started is because of how much of the population was extra-normal. If you count every person in the country with the potential to develop abilities beyond those of a standard member of homo sapien and other sentient beings they make up almost five percent of the population of this country." I said with a chuckle. "Odds are you know a few people who are like yourself to one degree or another and even more of them that have the potential to be, but nothing has ever happened to unlock it."

"Well after hearing that I am officially not walking past the door of the creepy old guy down stairs who is always undressing me with his eyes." Cassi said shaking her head before glancing toward my door. I nodded my head and pushed open the door and stepped out.

After we got out Cassi quickly walked across the parking lot toward her car and smiled before stopping and walking to the rear passenger side and reached under the wheel well to grab the keys and holding them heading back across the lot. "I just realized, I used to do that kind of thing all the time. Find peoples remotes and things like that. Think that has something to do with my gift?" She said as she pointed toward a building a little ways off in the distance.

We walked along the sidewalk for a few moments until we stepped up a couple of flights of stairs before we arrived at the door of the apartment. "Your locks work? Do you have a gun in the house?" I asked as I checked about for any signs of surveillance.

"Yes and no, but I have a sword an old boyfriend never got back a few years ago." She said with a grin as she worked the key in one of the locks. "I'll get all vorpral blade on any bad guys that come in the door." Cassi accented the statement with a vague approximation of a mimed sword swing.

"Stick to the five rules for now." I said with a shake of my head as she pulled open the door and stopped to look at me. For a moment I couldn't help but to think how pretty she looked. All but a vague hint of the color of her hair hidden in the dark and the moon light cast an opposing glow to her porcelain skin. I wasn't really sure how long I stood there, but I didn't think that my glance had turned into a leer before I coughed and looked away. I had definitely strayed into staring. "Get some rest Cassi. I'll call as soon as I get something lined up for lessons. Don't hesitate to call if anything comes up."

"Uh Will. I have your card, but did you get my number at some point?" She asked staring at me accusingly. "Sneaking through my phone while I was out of it?"

"No." I started thinking for a moment about reminding her that I was a federal agent and I could get anyone's number, but instead I just reached into my coat's interior pocket to grab a pen and a card. While I made the grab she'd apparently reached inside her apartment, picked up a marker, grasped my arm and started writing a number across the palm of my hand in large black marker numbers.

"Now you do." She said with a chuckle. "Goodnight, Will. Be safe." she said before stopping and shaking the hand she had been holding in her own and disappearing past her apartment door.

It took me a few moments after the door closed to get moving. I spent the first couple of them telling myself I was keeping an ear out for trouble as Cassi got settled. The next few I spent reminding myself about the rules I have about relationships and work. I wasn't quite sure what I convinced myself of in the end, but I eventually made my way down the stairs to my truck. I hadn't really slept in two days, and with the way things were starting to shape up, it didn't look like there would be a real opportunity to get rest for a while. So, I figured that my best plan at this point would be to go home and get while the getting was good. I made a stop for an energy drink and one of those health bars that resemble none of healthy foods they are said to contain. Hopefully that would be enough to get me home before I passed out behind the wheel.

It was another hour before I was walking up the steps to the back of my house, unlocking the door and stepping into my home. It wasn't the largest or grandest home ever, but for a bachelor like me, it was more than enough actually. My kitchen was what you could expect from a single male. My only real appliances were a microwave and a high end coffee maker. Between those, a fridge and an almost purely decorative oven the kitchen had just enough room for a table to be pushed against one wall and allow you to walk through to the living room.

Most of my furniture was new, but that was only thanks to the fact that I had finally replaced all of my old used college furniture when the back literally fell off my old favorite couch. Truth be told the pricey black leather number wasn't nearly as comfortable as the old floral one, but it did strike a sharp figure just like the gorgeous furniture saleswoman said it would. On the opposite wall from the couch was a large TV and a collection of game systems that I had always wanted when I was a broke college student. They were, for the most part, gathering dust now days. The Initiative paid me well for my work, but it was a sad truth of economics that if you work hard enough to make enough money to enjoy it, you have no time to enjoy it in. My coffee table was a more realistic picture of my life. A few open books from research and a half eaten sandwich left from earlier today. Or was it from the day before. I glanced up from the couch and back down the hall to my bedroom and shook my head reaching for the remote.

Another side effect of my job is the fact that I live off late night syndicated television. It was how my handler, Norm, got his nickname. "Cheers" was a constant favorite when I could make it home in time. Sadly more often than not I would turn to my favorite late night channel and see they were already an hour into old Golden Girls reruns. Tonight was a Golden Girls night. Not a bad show when you are sleep deprived, but when someone is expecting bar humor and not crazy antics it can be a bit of a letdown. It really didn't matter tonight I guess. I was asleep before the first commercial break.

When I dreamed it was all mixed images of the previous day. Exploring the site of Sue's killing with Brandon. Getting the call and driving north to find the two mutilated bodies. Glancing over Cassi asleep in the back seat of a police car. Her touch against my amulet. The chase across town on the way to see Greg. The time I almost tripped in the woods in one of Greg's tracks as we walked through the forest.

One of Greg's tracks? One of Greg's tracks! Greg always left tracks when he walked. He could move quietly and unseen if he wanted, but he still had to obey physics. Something as big as Greg was going to leave tracks in the earth. I saw tracks at the attack site in the forest and in the field near the bodies, but between the two points nothing was seen. Whatever had killed those two men and was strong enough to rip their bodies asunder didn't leave foot prints. The list of creatures that could rip a human being apart was morbidly long, but the list of them that would move with no tracks and tear someone apart that had to be significantly shorter.

Pushing myself off my couch, I looked about in the early morning hours getting my bearings before cussing a blue streak at myself for having an idea in the middle of perfectly good sleep. I walked toward the kitchen to set up the coffee maker and throw breakfast into the microwave. A hot cup of coffee and two of those little microwavable sausage biscuits in hand I walked back through my living room. After one longing look at my couch I passed through the door way that lead to the stairs that would take me up to my office. Once inside the room I walked toward the book shelf in the back of the room.

I have two shelves of books. One in the front and one in the back behind my desk. The one in the front was full of various books written on a layman's level about various psychosis and disorders. The second was filled with medical journals, textbooks and more or less the type of books most people avoid at all cost because they require a twenty page guide on how to read them in the front. While the journals and such still had use, even in my unique field of study, they hid resources much more valuable. Pressing my hand against the side of the shelf I shifted a wooden panel out, pressed my thumb into the scanner concealed within, and with a series of clicks the locks opened and the coasters freed up allowing me to push the shelf to the side revealing the room's third bookshelf built into the wall behind the second.

The array of books hidden in this third shelf were of a much more unique nature. The bulk of the collection had been gifted to me by Gideon, my predecessor in the Initiative, and a few more I had picked up over the last few years. Gideon had been doing my job since before the internet era. He claimed, even late in his career, that the amount of misinformation about the supernatural found on-line overshadowed the real information so greatly that it wasn't worth using as a source. He was right for the most part; misinformation in my field could very easily get you into trouble if not get you killed. I mean some people on-line thought silver hurt vampires or that you could think a ghost out of a home with positive thoughts. I had to admit the old man had a point.

None the less, I'd fallen victim to the same curse that most people my age or younger shared, a complete lack of patience when it came to looking for information without a search engine. I even had electronic copies of most of the journals on the shelf stored on an e-reader in my desk and most of them were more up to date. I kept the books school had required of me for both nostalgia and the fact that people expected the guy behind the desk to have a couch and a mountain of books. It helped set the mood for the counselor end of my trade.

Spending hours combing through old leather tomes that required special care hadn't been the way I wanted to spend a savagely early morning. Carefully scanning indexes and hand written catalogs for something that linked to my subject and then finding the proper location in the correct tome was just the beginning. I was, in general, considered an intelligent person. Still, looking over antique books, reading two or three different languages in the span of twenty minutes most of them pertaining to subjects not found in most common translation dictionaries would be a bit of a tax on anyone's brain. As a result, three hours later as the sun was starting to fully rise into the eastward facing window at my back, I nearly missed the fleeting reference in a copy of a journal from a priest during the crusades. The original text would be nearly a thousand years old. My copy was thankfully hand copied a mere two and a half centuries ago by a long passed researcher in the early modern occult.

One of the biggest paranormal threats encountered by European soldiers and knights during the first crusade, at least according to this journal, was that in the twilight hours of mornings and evenings, small units of men would be attacked, savaged and left dead and dismembered. No tracks, of man or beast, were ever found leading to or from the site of such an attack and all of the victims were stripped of all valuables. The transcriber of the ancient document also commented about hearing several Native American myths along the same lines. Neither of the men at the site of the murder still had identification. That means no wallets. The killer had torn the victim's limb from limb. The killer had not left any tracks. The killer had pilfered the pockets of the victims. Several different things fit each of those categories, but something that fit each of those that would narrow the field considerably.

Turning about and making myself slow down enough to carefully put up each of the tomes in their proper place before reaching for my most treasured tome, Gideon's journal. Where he had found the tome I have no idea. It was one of the many stories he would never tell me. Gideon would tell me several articles to read from the massive crimson leather tome, but whenever I went back into lexicon to find new information I would only ever find articles I had already read. Granted it served as a great reminder. Still the book would only ever present you with new pages and chapters when you had some idea what you were looking for.

"Seria. Teach me about it who will tear limb from limb, rend away life and possession and leave no trace of it." The tome Seria, which Gideon called the book even though he treated it like it was alive held a wealth of knowledge far beyond that held within a book of numbered pages. But, to reveal what one needed from Seria they had to think about nothing else. You didn't need to talk as if you were trying out to work at a renaissance faire. Simply put, the level of concentration required was easier achieved with heavy words. So, as I worked to clear my thoughts, I repeated the phrase again and again as I put aside my earthly concerns. My lack of sleep, the bodies, Sue, lying to an old friend, the sight of Hannelore hovering over my office floor, and even Cassi all eventually faded from my mind before I placed my hand on the book and opened it one more time.

Closing my eyes, I ran my hand across the leather tome. Inhaling deeply I grasped the edge of the cover and an undetermined number of pages before pulling the book open. After that I felt the edges of countless pages open and move beneath my touch. I thought about nothing more than the specifics of the knowledge I desired before I opened the book. Then and only then did I finally open my eyes and look down at the opened pages.

The left hand page was blank, but a faint image was beginning to form on the right. A horribly disfigured face covered in untamed fur. It had wide black eyes and a fanged maul that I could almost smell decay wafting from as the picture formed. It was a bust shot, but the wide furry body of the creatures was obvious. Above the horrible image now fully formed on the page black calligraphic text started to weave across like an ebony ribbon laid across sand.

"Wendigo".

I muttered the word to myself shaking my head in disbelief as I looked over the picture. I didn't know much about the creature and as I flipped the page I sighed. It appeared that Seria didn't know much about the beast in question either. None the less, I waited as a few paragraphs of curvy script curled out over the page.

All Wendigo were at one time human beings. A series of things had to happen to cause the transformation. A person had to be greedy. Taking the last slice of pie greedy wasn't what the book meant either. You had to be truly filled with 'throw your loved ones under the bus for a better deal kind of greed. Emotion on that level, of any kind, was rare and true greed was less common than others.

Secondly, that person had to desire and partake of human flesh with no other reason than to sate a lust. Just to make it clear, I didn't mean partake in the abstract since. They had to eat someone. They could not be starving, angry or curious. They had to take life from another being and devour the flesh of that person for no other reason than to satisfy a petty want. Needless to say that was rare. Even if someone fulfilled those requirements, the proper spiritual entities had to be present at the time of consumption. The power of the Wendigo was a spirit. Not a ghost or demon but a spirit of a realm beyond our own. Planar cosmetology wasn't an important issue at the moment however. If a greedy person ate human flesh to sate that greed and the right nasties were about, that person would be taken and changed by the spirit.

A horrible mutated mixture of physical changes gave them incredible strength and physical stamina. Their senses were also greatly enhanced along with a power to detect those things they lusted for beyond the limits of the physical world. Whatever form the greed of the Wendigo took, he could hunt it down like a hound on a trail after prey no matter petty things like wind directions, distance, or time. One report even mentioned that the Wendigo could move on the wind.

No tracks would be left in a Wendigo's wake then. The passage didn't include any details about how to kill the creature. Seria was a vast well of knowledge, but the book wasn't bottomless. Whoever had created the tome had heard tale of the creature but had never known how to kill one. That meant I didn't know either.

A Wendigo, from what little else I knew, wasn't going to be easy to kill. I didn't know where it fell in the field of supernatural toughness but I was willing to bet it was on the unfortunate side of werewolf tough. Unfortunate for anyone trying to kill it that is. Normally I don't even think about killing something this early in the game. The Holzer Initiative wasn't started to go forth and take out all things that went bump in the night. Well at least the modern incarnations weren't. We are peace keepers. Sworn to serve and protect the people of the United States of America. Granted we protected those people by monitoring a very small percentage of the population and enforcing a modified version of the law of the land, that in some cases we had to enforce with extreme prejudice. However, a creature like this could not be sated. A Wendigo, if left unchecked, would do nothing but continue to kill for no other reason than to satisfy its greed for the taste of human flesh.

And so I closed the book and carefully placed it back in its place before leaning back and sighing. The Wendigo, if I was even right about what the creature was, wouldn't be an easy issue to address, and that was still only half my problem. I still had to track down Sue's killers, before they tracked me down, again. I suppose, depending on the results of the car chase, I could only be tracking down Sue's killer in the singular. I'd seen footage of lesser wrecks with lethal context. On the other hand I'd seen people walk away from much worse. I guess I actually couldn't discount the assassin I'd hit with my truck. To be perfectly frank, the only place you could find more miraculous recoveries than the supernatural law enforcement world was a comic book.

I was rubbing my fingers against my temples and cursing myself as I realized the only rest I was going to get for the next couple of days had just likely been interrupted to read some books when the harbinger of doom wailed out across my office. Granted that was a bit dramatic of a way to describe my phone ringing, but I let out a sigh as I saw a picture of a smiling man a few years younger than me in a black polo style shirt and a pristine white lab coat flashed across my phone with the words 'Kevin the Great!' across the bottom of the screen. I lurched forward and grabbed the phone and answered the call. "Hey Kevin, do you realize how early it is where you are?"

"Yeah it's 9am." The smooth middle toned voice on the other end answered back. "Is this where you tell me how early it makes things in your time zone?" He said with a laugh.

"Something like that. What's the matter" I asked.

"Well, I sent the processed photos to the local uniforms. To that, Walters, fellow. Just like you, asked and..."

"I hate it when you use conjunctions, Kevin." I said with a sigh as I leaned back in a chair.

"Apparently he's a bit like our Norm. Gets a lackey to check his email and print out anything important to him. "The photo hit your local news stations website about 10 minutes ago."

"Are you trying to tell me that a picture of a Wendigo has hit the internet? Why don't we just disrupt it like we would anything else? You can kill a picture or two or at least discredit it."

"It hit hard Will. At least a few thousand people in the area have seen the picture and various online sources are talking about organizing hunts." Kevin said with a sigh. "I'm working on discrediting the pictures now and writing a virus to seek and destroy the file over the web but that's nearly as effective as you see on TV. Something like that is trying to shoot an ant hill with a shot gun. Lots of disorientation and some destruction but you're not going to get rid of the ants like that." Then what I said a moment before hit him. "A Wendigo? You sure about that? I mean tall, dark fur, and bulky less than twenty miles away from a sasquatch den..."

"Do what you can about the picture Kevin, don't worry. I've already interviewed the local suspect, he's clear. Have you contacted Gregorie or his handler about the forming hunt?" I asked already standing up, grabbing up my black leather shoulder rig and coat before walking away from my office and down the stairs of my house.

"I called them first. Being a little bit closer to ground zero I figured they needed to make sure Gregorie stays locked down and out of sight." Kevin said with a sigh. "Do you think he will actually try to stay clear of the torches and pitch forks?" He said.

"It isn't so much the ignorant masses I'm worried about. Greg and his type have been avoiding Bigfoot hunters for well, for forever. A skilled hunter with proof in his hands tracking down what he thinks killed two people. That could cause problems. I'll need to find a way to go and see him before the day,s out." I said as I looked at the grey t-shirt and jeans I had on before shrugging and pulling on the shoulder rig and tossing on my sports coat from yesterday. "Anything else interesting?"

"I called you as soon as I spotted the picture. Give me a second to see what else the normal search programs pulled up today." I waited while I grabbed a cup of coffee and headed out to my truck while listening to Kevin conduct the clicking of his keyboard as if he was a maestro leading a symphony, or perhaps a bit more like he was currently firing an automatic rifle or two until he spoke up. "I don't see any big hits on the radar. A couple of scams that might be physic in nature, an apparent crop circle in Louisiana, but those are always fakes in your part of the world. Oh a girl hit a prowler with a sword in Longview, Texas. Probably just came up because of the word sword. Other than that everything else is accounted for."

I stopped. "A girl hit a burglar, with a sword" I sighed before starting to walk again heading directly for my truck now with a funny feeling as to where I was going. "Is she in custody?"

"Doesn't look like it. Apparently the perp fled the scene. She was questioned and released. That castle law you guys have is pretty awesome."

I laughed. "Hell, she was in her rights to kill him if he was in her apartment. I know the answer, but give me her name."

"Give me a second. Yeah. Cassi. Cassi Ross." I banged my head against my steering wheel as Kevin spoke.

Thankfully my truck seemed to remember the path along the highway between my place and Longview because I was in no shape to drive. I clung to the wheel with one hand and my third cup of coffee for the day was in the other. The coffee was cold and down to the last sip by the time I started to see signs of urban traffic. Tossing the empty cup into the back seat, I turned down the Aerosmith on the radio, shook the cobwebs from my head, and started trying to get my head into the game.

I dialed my phone yet again, waited for four rings and sighed as it went right to voice mail just like it had for the previous three phone calls. Shaking my head I waited for the sweet recorded voice on the other end of the line to finish asking me to leave a message. "Sonja. This is William Codex, again. Kevin called you earlier, but I need to keep in touch and Greg needs to stay inside until we can get this whole thing to blow over. I have another fire to put out, but I'll be that direction as soon as I can. Until then, no matter what, don't let him get outside. Also stay with him, inside that is. There are some big hitters in the area and one of them might be looking for Greg." With that I hung up before the caffeine started making me repeat myself.

For the most part Gregorie was smart about keeping to himself. On top of that, he had centuries of experience in staying hidden, but when the pressure started building up his old world sense of honor would sometimes kick in and after that he would not easily abide trespassers, harassment or a threat to Sonja. He'd never been overt in his actions, he was smarter than that, but he had never been above scaring off poachers on the wildlife reserve. Now that people were looking, that might be enough to get him caught or killed.

Gregorie, despite his special permission, rarely hunted on the protected land himself. It wasn't that the ancient immortal took issue with hunting, he had lived off what he hunted himself for the most part. When he had come to this country he had come as a huntsmen and fur trapper. However it was that same pride with the hunt that, just like his mortal human counterparts, caused him to despise those that held no respect for the balance of nature. He saw the reserve as sacred ground. And frankly for someone who had to have untamed wild land to live healthy, that wasn't too far from the truth.

However, in the end, Gregorie had been a part of this world much longer than myself and knew how to handle himself. Cassi on the other hand, either had horrible luck, or she had been followed home. In the case of the latter that would mean our tail last night might not have been trying to take me out. That would mean the professionals that had taken Sue were going to try to make a name for themselves in the area, or something about a newly discovered physic warranted killing in someone's book. What would Sue's killers want with Cassi? How the hell could I have not thought of something like that? I had stopped and waited outside her apartment door for some reason last night. I should have listened to my gut but then again, I rarely did.

Listening to my instincts had gotten me into trouble more than once before in my life. Gideon had taught me to look past things like temper and prejudice and to examine any given situation for what it was and nothing more. When the pressure was on, the sharpened mind couldn't just react. Details had to be examined. Granted they had to be examined quickly and with ruthless efficiency, but decisions still had to be measured. Going on instinct alone was as good as deciding who lived and died by flipping a coin in my world. I just hadn't put the pieces together quick enough last night. Thankfully I'd gotten lucky, or Cassi had rather. I'd been clumsy.

I pulled into her apartment's parking lot a moment later with enough speed to cause my tires to sing on the pavement as I entered the drive right beside the sign that read Parkway Apartments. I'd almost forgotten to pull my sports coat back on before I got out of the truck which would have not only left me exposed to the cool winter air, but it would have left my shoulder rig and the gun it held in open view. With my temper the way it was at the moment the cold wasn't a problem, but I didn't need to attract the attention that a .45 caliber pistol would get me in a not exactly top notch apartment complex.

I managed to put away most of the self-loathing by the time I walked from the truck and to the stairs that led to Cassi's apartment. The remnants of yellow police tape marked the top of the stairs. As I started up the stairwell an elderly man on the first floor looked out the door briefly, before catching my eye and stepping back behind his door after I narrowed my gaze and nodded toward him. I guess I wasn't the type of person he wanted to get an eye-full of. After a few more slow steps I walked up toward the door, took a deep breath, knocked twice and waited.

After several minutes I heard the sound of a chair or something heavy moving, a chain lock sliding open, the click of a door knob lock, and finally the sliding sound of a deadbolt before the door slowly opened into to the apartment to reveal a very tired looking Cassi who gripped an honest to goodness Scottish basket hilt broadsword in one hand. The blade of the sword was just a bit shy of three feet in length and a hair under two inches wide at the base and tapered to less than an inch at the end of the blade before coming to an abrupt but still sharp tip. Where the base of the blade met the cross guard, Cassi's hand disappeared beneath the elaborate polished steel guard that wrapped about her whole hand. The appendage was further protected by the red felt under wrap between Cassi's hand and the steel cage about her fist. When she had told me she owned a sword she'd taken from an ex-boyfriend, I'd been expecting a cheap katana in a plastic sheath or something that was meant to look pretty against the wall not a polished and sharpened steel blade of visible quality that bore more than a few signs of real wear. Note to self, don't trifle with the ex.

"That is a real sword, Cassi." I said letting my stare fall from the blade to the girl standing behind the threshold. Even tired and stressed that effortless beauty she held was apparent. She now wore a less tattered pair of jeans and a black knit sweater that made an impressive effort to envelop her completely but still didn't manage to completely hide her form. The black sleeves were too long and covered half of the hand that held on to the steel sheath of the sword so tightly her knuckles were white.

"Hello Will." She said carefully looking me up and down before stepping back from the door a couple of steps and turning to walk away out of sight of the little entry way to the apartment.

"Ummm, mind if I come in?" I asked leaning into the doorway trying to keep my eyes on her as she walked into her living room.

"I don't know. Can you?" she asked turning to face me as she tightened her grip on her sword and stared me down from the edge of her living room.

I nodded my head and stepped over her apartment's threshold. After that I held my hands up for her to see before reaching over, unbuttoning my jacket pulling up the sleeve to reveal the black ink number still written across my arm before holding my hand out for her to examine. "Good idea all things considered. Anything else you would like to do to confirm me?"

Cassi sighed and shook her head as she positioned herself in a corner of her living room that gave her balcony access and kept the whole of the room in her field of vision. "Not yet. I'm going to save my other idea for a rainy day. I figured if you were something changing how you looked it would be hard to keep it up after the threshold."

"A sound theory. Not a lot of things holding a different form can keep that shape if they cross over a threshold uninvited. It isn't a universal rule however." I lightly warned as I took a look around the apartment proper. It wasn't the largest space ever. The living area was only slightly larger than my undersized kitchen but had that economy of space that only came with practiced apartment living. A large amount of shelves held a fair sized library's worth of books, a set of red and white splatter paintings covered the bare spaces on the walls with the same jagged signature painted in the bottom corner. The obviously mismatched furniture was all wrapped snugly in matching black covers and a red rug in the center of the room held up a little black table with a laptop computer resting upon it. "Nice place."

"Thanks." she said motioning me toward the couch in the living room before she backed into the kitchen still holding the sword in her hand never letting her eyes leave mine "I suppose someone got word to you about what happened last night?" Cassi said with a grin as I heard the sound of the sword being sheathed. She returned a moment later with two almost comically large cups of coffee, handing one to me before quickly retreating back to her corner.

I nodded to her questions before gathering my hands together and bowing lightly in thanks before taking the coffee from her hands and taking a sip and raising my eye brows. "Blueberry?" I asked with a quirked eyebrow.

Cassi nodded. "Blueberry vanilla, I flavor it myself." she responded before she took a sip of her own cup after she sat in the chair opposite the couch making sure that the sword was propped on the side of her chair in arms reach.

"So what exactly happened?" I asked setting the cup down only after taking another sip of the surprisingly tasty blend and looking toward her.

Cassi took another long drink of her coffee before setting the cup down herself and matching her gaze to mine. "Honestly it's a bit of a blur. About two hours after you left I'd just gotten out of the shower and gotten dressed to try to go to bed." she'd started with a shake of her head. "Like that was going to happen. Anyway, someone pounded on the door a couple of times. I got up and checked the door thinking it might be a friend who had had a few drinks too many. It wouldn't have been the first time, and they tend to have a horrible sense of timing." she said with a chuckle as part of her mind started to escape into another memory entirely for an instant before she caught herself, took another nervous drink, and started up again. "I didn't recognize the man on the other side of the door through the peephole. More like I couldn't really see him. Knit beanie pulled down over his brow and his head was looking down, away from the peep hole. I tried to tell him that he had the wrong place. I tried a couple of the normal excuses. That he was going to wake up my fictitious boyfriend or one of my incredibly concerned neighbors." she added with a laugh. "By the time I tried that I looked out again just in time to see him put his shoulder into the door. I ran back from the door and went for the sword while he tried to knock down the door. I dialed 911, but by the time I got a hold of someone the door came open as the guy stumbled in and came in after me."

I nodded my head as I listened to the tale while I took a silent drink of coffee. "So you dropped the phone and went with the sword?" I questioned.

"Yeah but not before he caught me and pushed at me once. He tried to get me with a sword of his own, but he missed." Cassi said as she pointed towards a spot with a long diagonal cut through the dry wall. "I couldn't believe it when I saw that he had one but it just spurred me on to get mine while the emergency operator tried to talk to me. I was just going to try to back away, but the guy ran at me, so I threw my phone at him, picked up the sword, and I guess I took a run at him. I didn't even remember the sword being so close at hand. I came up, took a swing and I cut off his arm." She said with a shiver and a shake of her head before continuing.

"He shouted out something I didn't understand, turned, and ran away. I chased him out the door, but by the time I got outside he was driving away on a bike a lot like those we saw earlier and my neighbors were waking up. The police showed up a few minutes later and there was no sign of him. I don't know what happened I was pacing around the apartment while the police looked around outside and I couldn't find the arm. The detective they sent kept me up most of the night asking me the same questions over and over. He eventually decided that I must have not cut the attacker as badly as I imagined and I was under a lot of stress or something like that." she said rolling her eyes. "There was still a lot of blood and the police took samples, dusted the door for prints and measured the cut in the wall. But, the guys that did that think it was my cut that tore the wall." Cassi finally stopped to take a drink of her coffee and sighed.

"In the end they still left me with the rest of the blood to clean up." She sighed. "I managed to get all of that done by the time maintenance put the new door on near four or five in the morning. I've been up ever since." She said taking another drink of coffee and looking up to me waiting for my opinion.

I rolled over the details of the story in my head as I looked from Cassi to the sword while I thought over a few different scenarios. "Could have been a mystical construct of some sort or a creature not native to this plane of existence."

"I don't even want to know, do I?" Cassi said with a shake of her head hiding her eyes. She stopped an instant later and looked back up as her eyes darkened. "Correction. I am going to know, Will. I'm starting to think it might be too much too fast." she said with a sigh. "Too late for complaining I guess. Jumping off the cliff and all that." she said patting the sword's handle as she let out a forced chuckle while her eyes started to brighten despite the beginnings of tears forming in her emerald orbs. "So yeah, constructs and extra planar beings?"

"Long story short, a construct is a magically assembled creature of almost any substance given some semblance of life magically. A powerful enough person can make them look alive and they aren't very easily stopped unless they cross a threshold." I said before taking a drink of coffee. "Extra planar creatures, if you can make this kind of thing short, are beings from a different plane of reality within our universe." I started before biting my lip and trying to think how to explain the rest of it. "When something like that dies it returns back to its home plane of existence, sometimes dead, sometimes alive. If you cut off a limb, that limb may or may not disappear when it dies on its own. Enough for now?" I offered. "The particulars take more time than we have right now."

Cassi sighed and buried her hands in her face and tried to hold it back with a few deep breaths but a moment later her sobs started to break through her controlled breaths.

I sighed as I stood up from my place on the couch and walked across to her before kneeling beside her and her chair wrapping my arm about her shoulder. "Sorry, Cassi. It's a lot to take in and life doesn't give you much of a chance to catch up when the floodgates open." I said with a sigh.

"We'll get you through this. I promise, Cassi." I said as I patted her back lightly. "And when it is done we'll get all your questions answered. For now you just need to keep being strong."

Cassi turned and locked her gaze to mine, green eyes wide and starting to fill with tears. We were caught like that for a moment, neither of us willing to pull away for several breaths. Have you ever looked someone in the eye? Really looked them in the eye and waited for that connection that happens a split second after such a stare becomes uncomfortable. Most people are instinctively afraid of that connection, of revealing that much of themselves to another. I heard it said once that those with magical gifts can receive more than a strong intuition in that moment but one way or another, it is true when they say that the eyes are the windows to the soul. It was right there, in that moment of clarity, that I felt Cassi shift her weight to face me and press her lips to mine.

It wasn't a passionate kiss as far as kisses go. Not that it was bad. Not that it was bad at all, but the embrace was far too hungry to pay heed to any emotion but the raw need of it. Need that promised to grow exponentially long before my brain would allow logic to remind me of my personal or professional policies. Warm soft lips moved against mine before taking in a sharp breath stealing my own breath away from me. Before I knew what had happened my arms were wrapped about Cassi's surprisingly taunt waist as she started to guide me to the floor leaving the chair. My back hit the floor and I was distracted by all types of sensation against my body as soft curves slid over me. Somewhere in the process Cassi and I both stopped to breath and the real world crashed down upon me as I finally got oxygen of my own and it manged to get to my brain.

"Cassi." I pleaded softly turning my head to the side avoiding her renewed approach . Apparently my neck was starting to think logically first since my hands still gripped her sides pulling her against me. "We can't do this now. There's too much going on, and you're in no condition." That start earned me a dire glare. "Oh no you're definitely in nice... very nice condition. But you've experienced a lot in the last day and I don't want to take advantage of that." I finally managed to say despite the mental images of what could be happening now if I would just shut up.

Cassi stopped and stared at me, her legs still straddling mine and her hands resting on either side of my head affording an excellent view of her startling green eyes and the pale skin of her neck leading more than just a little way past the top of her sweater. After a long moment her stone still lust filled gaze broke into a light blush and she chuckled before she rolled away to lay on the floor beside me. "Well, I wasn't exactly planning on that." She said with a forced laugh before I felt her look in my direction and sit up. "Didn't mean to put you on the spot. I mean, not a lot of guys would have stopped me, or at least I don't think they would." She said turning her back to me.

No good deed goes unpunished. I thought with a sigh before pushing myself up off the floor. "I don't know if I would have when I was younger. I wasn't as prone to personal masochism then." I added with chuckle.

"That might be part of the reason that I have always had the hots for older men." Cassi said with an exasperated sigh causing me to turn my head about to face her only to get an elbow in the ribs before she stood up. "Let's get moving, Will. If what I saw on my Facebook this morning is true, you have a long day ahead of you." She said with a chuckle. "We need to talk to Gregorie. Pass me your coat I'll iron it out if you make coffee for the road." Cassi added reaching for the coat as I slipped it from my shoulders and handed it to her.

"Sure I need to call the big guys handler or see if I can get him on twitter." I said before standing up, adjusting my shoulder rig, grabbing my phone and looking toward the kitchen.

"Gregorie has a Twitter account?" Cassi asked before disappearing down the hall.

"Yeah, you'll have to ask him what it is though "Big_Foot_Hunter" or something like that." I said with a laugh as I watched her go down the hall before turning my attention to the desperately undersized kitchen. Once I was sure Cassi was out I sight I leaned back against the counter and sighed. Personal rules and such aside that had been one hell of a kiss.

I managed to get my head on straight and get a couple travel cups of coffee ready to go a few minutes before Cassi walked out with my coat in her arms and quite literally dressed to kill. That auburn hair that I hadn't ever realized the true length of was pulled back into a single braid pulling it away from her face. Snug jeans and black leather low heeled boots that came up to her knees with one belt holding her pants and another holding a leather pouch with an elaborate silver clasp and her sword to her left side. A new dark green sweater that hugged her form a bit more and left less material to get caught up in her movement than the black one covered her upper body along with a leather jacket that flowed open half way down her thighs. Whoa! Cassi had been noticeable even in worn out jeans and an old t-shirt. Once she was, for lack of a better phase, dressed for battle I really regretted breaking off that kiss.

All in all the more intimidating part of the whole ensemble was the fact that despite the dark coat, high boots and sword on her hip Cassi's eyes were still filled with mirth. "So Will, who's Stormy?" She asked trying to hold back her laughter as she handed me my coat and a folded piece of pink paper.

"A contact in the werewolves. Why?" I asked as I took my coat and then looked to the piece of paper in Cassi's hand. The note Stromy had slipped into my pocket yesterday morning. Taking a deep breath I pulled open the piece of paper and read it over.

Hey Will,
Looks like you owe me one next time.
XOXOXO,
Stormy

"Well shit." I said. This couldn't be good.

By the time Cassi and I were closing in on the nature reserve, I had managed to explain the note from Stormy and how I rescued the girl from her former pack and brought her to the area to be cared for by Brandon and the now deceased Sue. I told myself I didn't know why I made sure to emphasize how "cute" and "ineffective" her plays for more attention had been. Making sure to drive home the fact that Stormy was and would likely always be a "kid" to me.

Cassi chuckled. "Sounds like a stripper name. Bambi, Candi and, Stormi." Her chuckle broke into a laugh for a long moment as I turned the truck down a county road. "She was what sixteen when you saved her?" I nodded. "That means she's what, twenty one, twenty two?"

"Twenty one. Like I said, a kid" I shook my head with a chuckle.

"Will, I'm twenty two." Cassi said with a renewed bout of laughter lasting almost as long as her previous one. The whole thing made me feel a little bit older than I actually was, but I managed to pay special attention to the road ahead of me instead of showing any signs of embarrassment.

"So, what exactly are we out to do?" Cassi asked after she had managed to catch her breath. "First we are heading back out to Greg's to check on him and make sure he is keeping his head down. After that we are going to talk to a friend about what might have come at you last night and beyond that, it'll depend on how everything else goes." I answered as we drove down the blacktop road.

"And I can't use the sword again 'til your friend checks it out?" Cassi asked obviously more than a little disappointed at the prospect.

"If you want it to work you can't have cut anyone else. It'll mess up the trace evidence." I said as I started looking for the turn-off we needed to take to get to the backside of the reserve. "As long as there is some trace blood left, and most cleaning techniques leave something, Hannelore should be able to dig up something on the guy who attacked you." My voice died out at the end of that statement to the point that the last words where barely a whisper as I looked at what was in front of me.

A small army of trucks and trailers had gathered on either side of the road leading to Gregories's and a fair sized crowd of people milled about near the gate up ahead. Of course, it was the gate that led up the dirt road to Gregories's cabin. More concerning, as I got closer, was the ground force of that army standing near the gate of the property a few of them shouting over the gate. "Ok, this isn't good." I said as I pulled the truck over to the side of the road into an open spot past the drive. "Stay in the truck. Keep the doors locked." I said as I started to get out. I glanced up at the sound of the passenger side door opening but with a quick glare I heard Cassi grumble and watched her close herself into the pickup before leaving the keys on the dash for her.

I adjusted my jacket and clipped on my FBI Identification card before walking down the blacktop road toward the small crowd at the gate. When I was about twenty feet away one of the stragglers, a young man in blue jeans and a dark camouflage jacket, stopped and looked at me as he adjusted a rifle over his shoulder. He looked me over like I didn't belong, which I suppose I looked like I didn't with my pressed shirt and sports coat among a crowd of people dressed, with one degree of professionalism or another, for the hunt. The moment his eyes moved over my ID they widened and he hesitated like he wasn't quite sure where to go. I pointed back towards the direction he appeared to have come from and he turned and started walking back across the road toward one of the various trucks. I hadn't considered how much attention someone moving against the flow of traffic would have caused. He pointed over his shoulder once and by the time I was standing at the edge of the driveway leading to the gate that barred the path to Gregories's land, I had churned up a wake of onlookers. It was about that point that I realized I was one federal agent, with no nearby back up, standing across the figurative line in the sand from thirty or more grown men with guns all of who, if voting trends were any sign, weren't really happy with anything on the federal level of the government in this day and age. This was going to be a delicate situation to say the least, and delicate had not been the word of the week.

Before anyone could speak up, I waved my hand over my head to make sure I had the floor. "Gentlemen, I don't mean to impose, seeing as how I can't see any law you've broken, but what seems to be the problem?"

Eight or nine of them started to speak up each shouting complaints about protecting their land, livestock, and families. At least that is what I thought the complaints were about. None of that I could complain about, but even in Texas the castle law ends at your property line. Most of the context was lost in a jumble of competing sounds anyway. This crowd was angry and angry people in large groups are never a good thing.

A few seconds after they stopped a singular voice shouted out from among the crowd. "We haven't done anything wrong! We're politely asking permission to hunt on private land. No one has trespassed or harassed anyone. We are just waiting for this land owner to return to discuss the issue with his wife; she didn't feel too inclined to speak with us." Drawled the voice as its source stepped out of the crowd. Knowing Sonja, that probably meant that she walked out with a shotgun and stared blankly at the men for a few moments before walking back into the cabin to give Gregorie the particulars of what was happening.

The speaker was about my height and perhaps at one time about my build, but that was twenty or thirty years of indulgence ago. His salt and pepper beard had been left to grow for a few days and his dark brown eyes were half revealed behind squinted lids. His skin was bright red from exposure to the elements and more than a bit of raised blood pressure. The rifle on his back was intimidating but not nearly as easy to reach as the .38 revolver strapped to his side.

"Never said you were in the wrong Mr..." I started
"Marshall."
"Mr. Marshall" I completed "However I can't help but wonder why so many of you are looking at trying to hunt on a four acre plot of mostly cleared land. However, it does butt right up to the back of thirty five hundred acres of national wildlife reserve." I said looking around at the man with a dull grin. "You've got to realize how suspicious that looks from here, Mr. Marshall."

I could tell by Marshall's expression that he had honestly not thought I would know about what he and his fellows were trying to do. None the less he walked through the crowed to stand no less than three feet away from me. "Look here...officer....oh... special agent in charge, William Codex." Marshall said with a chuckle as he read over the ID card clipped to my breast pocket. "Your being out here only proves something is going on, and we have a right to defend our land and families. We all saw that thing on the news. The most recent sightings are of that thing crossing the roads back here heading in this direction. Best we figure, it knows hunters can't come out this way, and is trying to get sanctuary."

Gregorie must have been spotted on his way back home after checking out the site for me. "So, the plan is to go and defend yourselves from theoretical wildlife all over an actual wildlife reserve?" I couldn't help but ask. "You realize that if this thing existed, and that is a strong if, it would be wildlife? You can't go hunting wildlife on a wildlife reserve." I responded shaking my head. "I understand your issues gentlemen, but your right to protect your land isn't a right to form a mob. The game wardens are surely searching the area, and they don't want you guys in the crossfire. Besides, no one here wants to go to jail for disrupting a federal investigation, do they?" I asked looking around the group of men shaking my head in response for them.

For the most part, the gathered crowd started to mummer as I explained that someone was already in the area and that prison would be an option if they overstepped their bounds. It had been what I was hoping for. Clearing the rest of the crowd wouldn't be that easy but it would show me the real threats in the situation and those that were just caught up in the action.

It's an easier effect to cause than it sounds. Most people don't feel strongly about much of anything much less feel strongly enough about it to stand against social absolutes like crime and punishment. Those rare souls who are willing to stand up to the establishment do have a strange power to pull up those with lesser feelings and bring them in their wake as they drive toward their cause. Not every German in the nineteen forties was a Nazi, but most of them fell in step with the party when World War II started up. However, that wake of power is like a wake in the water. If it hits a stronger wave it can be knocked off course.

By the time my not so subtle threat of jail time filtered back through the crowd, the majority of those gathered started to move back away from their gathering point and back to the twin rows of gathered trucks. I only afforded the exodus behind me a single glance leaving the majority of my attention on Marshall and his more resolute companions. The group that stayed numbered about a dozen counting Marshall.

Now don't misunderstand me when I say what I am about to tell you. This is coming from the mouth of a man who grew up in the pine forest laughing around deer lease campfires and, despite the fact that I had never been taken by the love of hunting, spent long hours throughout the year maintaining and improving woodland habitats ensuring the survival of the vast wild population of the land.

Yes, within the scope of the law, when the proper time came some of those creatures were harvested in a responsible manner to provide food for families. But that was a controlled version of a practice older than human history. To be honest, most hunters who cared for the land they partook of spent more time, effort, and money throughout a single year supporting the environment than they would reap in blood in a lifetime of the hunt. By the numbers, the most respectful and helpful wildlife conservation groups in the world were mostly comprised of hunters.

While I wasn't an expert, like those dedicated to their craft, I had learned to track and move through the forest with the respect of a guest visiting the home of another. I had been taught how to look out into a field and not only pick a target that could be assured a quick and painless death, but choose a creature who's loss would not negatively affect the environment. In short, a real hunter wouldn't have shot Bambi's mom. These men before me weren't hunters at all.

Sorry, I know I have a bit of a repressed soapbox when it comes to the narrow minded idea of the "evil hunter". But, the only thing that upsets me more than those who believe that all outdoorsmen are like these poachers are those that back up the stereotype. In other words I really hated guys like Marshall and his cronies.

The worst part is that it is really hard to tell the difference between the good guys and the bad guys. Especially this time of year. Dedicated responsible hunters, law abiding citizens, and scum with no respect for the law have all left the busy world behind for long weekends spent in the woods. Camouflage, flannel, and denim along with three day beards are standard uniform across the board. There are some slight differences in mannerisms and postures, like the fact that most real hunters carry a gun like it is a tool or an old friend, while in the case of their lesser counterparts you can see the ego boost generated by the fact that they have a gun strapped to them. Come the end of the day telling the character of a hunter is like finding the character of any other person, you can't judge a book by its cover. You have to stand across from them, look them in the eye, and hear them speak.

"Well, doesn't look like we're going to be over hunting that area now special agent." said Marshall as the crowd cleared out enough that his voice could be easily heard. "Thank you for your concern." he said with a grin spreading across his face as two of his cronies chuckled.

"Well at this point if you guys want to over hunt it isn't for me to stop you from having long boring weekends." I said with a sigh. "But I'm afraid you'll need to get off the land owners property until you have permission to be here."

"Last time I checked we were on the legal side of the fence." said Marshall as he leaned back against the gate leading to Gregorie's land.

"Actually the gate is set back behind the fence line and past the first two no trespassing signs." I said pointing back to the line of fence that ran just a few feet away from the road.

"Does the FBI have nothing better to do?" one of the men in the back of the crowd of would be poachers shouted inciting a round of grumbles.

"Yes, lots of things. Unfortunately I have to stop all those important things to instruct grown men on the law." I said with a shrug of my shoulders making sure to expose the black leather rig holding my colt. "Now, are you guys going to clear out and let me get back to work or are we going to keep at this long enough for the Sheriff's department to get here and help me sort this out? We can confiscate everyone's weapons, run serial checks on them to see if they link to any local crimes, and make sure they are registered. Then my boys with Smith County can run everyone here for warrants."

Marshall started to chuckle and shake his head, but whatever he was going to say in response never left his lips. In the moment he took to formulate the response the wind picked up and started blowing from over the group of poachers' backs and across my face and died. Then another cold blast of winter air struck across my face and grew faster. Faster and colder.

In a couple of seconds the wind blowing against me was fast enough to pick up the edges of my jacket and send them flying back behind me. In another instant I had to shift my weight into the gale to keep my footing. Marshall and his crew were turning about, most of their thoughts of me abandoned, and were looking into the wind themselves.

Two tree limbs broke from a nearby pine and hurtled across the field toward the gate. The two men who were standing in the back of the crowd from my point of view didn't even have time to think to dive out of the way. One was bludgeoned across the head with a limb knocking him off balance and into the wind to send him tumbling across the road. The other man wasn't so lucky. The broken edge of the limb entered just right of his sternum and punched out his back sending a crimson splatter over those standing in the new back ranks of the poachers. His now lifeless body was caught in the ever growing wind and blown backwards knocking three more men over like so many bowling pins. I dropped to a knee to give the hurricane power winds as little of a target as possible to do the same to me. By the time the gust rolled over the crowd the rest of them, except Marshall and one other who had dived for the ditch, were sent flying through the air.

I pulled my colt free from its holster and kept it down to low ready so that none of the coming bodies were in a possible line of fire as they flew toward me. A low stance and quick reactions will do a lot to keep you on your feet in any number of situations, but in a sudden burst of hurricane winds your center of gravity would need to be about three feet below the ground to keep you on your feet. I was no exception, but as the full brunt of the wind hit me, I fell backward instead of getting picked up in the wind that carried the collection of flailing bodies above me. The men caught in the storm looked to still be alive with the exception of the man who had the pine limb stuck through his chest and another who flipped silently through the air his head pointing the wrong direction.

The wind had broken his neck?

Then I saw it, for just an instant in the air above the men. A form coalesced out of the air as the gust started to die. It was nearly seven feet tall with a broad fur covered chest and shoulders, thick muscled arms and legs that were covered in dark fur as well, but below its chest and above its hips the creature was an emaciated collection of sallow skin covered bones. Its mouth and eyes were too large even for its giant form and within the gaping maul lay multiple rows of large needle like teeth. The large glassy eyes looked like opaque gems reflecting the creature's perception back at me. Two tiny images of me pointing a gun back at myself made me realize how little of a threat I appeared to the creature.

As the wind died, most of the men slammed into the sides of trucks on the side of the road. More than a few of them hitting hard enough to cause the sickening crack of bone and some of the more liquid sounds occasionally associated with sudden deceleration. One of the men fell short as the Wendigo rode him to the ground like a surf board. The full bulk of the creature upon the small of the man's back caused him to react more like a dropped piano than a surfboard when he hit the ground. It was about then that I realized that I was still lying on my back looking upside down behind me at the creature. With no small amount of haste I rolled over and up to my knee, pulled the gun up, let the sights settle upon the creature and fired.

Then I fired again.

And once more, for good measure, I squeezed the trigger a third time.

If you've never fired a forty five caliber pistol before, trust me, it is very loud. The flashes of fire and crack of mock thunder roared from my gun as fast as the action of the piece allowed me to fire. The first hit the creature in the concave of its belly, the second in the lower part of the rib cage and the third round hit the center of the Wendigo's chest. The first two rounds bit into the creature but the third bounced off a rib.

Let me reiterate to those of you that don't know much about firearms. The almost half inch in diameter bullet traveling at over eight hundred feet per second, over two thirds the speed of sound, hitting with well over three hundred foot-pounds of force bounced off the thing's rib. To make matters worse, by the time I had moved up and to my feet to get mobile I saw the wound of the first bullet finish closing back in upon itself stopping the pitiful flow of midnight black blood it had caused in the first place. The beast looked at me and actually smiled at me for an instant before opening its mouth and yelling.

No one had apparently taken the time to tell the Wendigo about dental hygiene or lung capacity.

I reeled back from the creature as fast as my two feet could carry me. By the time I could level the colt for another shot the Wendigo had ripped the leg from the body below it and threw it at me with the speed of a major league fastball. From less than twenty feet away I didn't have much in the way of options when it came to avoiding something like that. I curled up into a vague approximation of a boxers block to protect my head and neck keeping the colt in one hand.

The leg struck me across the side of my ribs and the glancing blow carried enough force to send me falling back into the pipe gate at the entrance to Gregorie's place. My head rocked back and cracked against the metal gate as I fell to the ground. The entire world was silent for a split second except for the ringing of the metal gate in response to the hit. Or it could have been all just ringing in my ears. Honestly, it could have been much worse. Had it not been for the minimal energy disbursement of the leg I am sure I would have broken several ribs from the hit alone. Not to mention what knowing how to take a fall had done for me. Oh my head hurt and it was going to for a long time, but I would be alive to feel the swelling and the bruises I would have by tomorrow. That being said on the assumption the Wendigo, or something else, didn't get lucky and manage to kill me prior to tomorrow.

The creature roared again and this time the wind about it picked up before it leapt into the air motioning to summon a greater gust of debris at me as the creature blurred back into the wind heading my direction. I tried to level the Colt fighting the wind as well as more than a bit of pain and dizziness that comes with getting thrown back into a collection of steel pipes. Even then I only had a vague impression of the creature to aim at, and if the two rounds I fired connected it showed no signs of injury. The Colt carried seven rounds in the magazine and I keep another in the chamber. I had three rounds left and if I was going to make them count I was going to have to wait till this thing was on top of me, literally.

I picked the line I would follow if I was going to jump across a road and onto someone's head. I let the barrel of the gun follow it and waited for the brunt of the wind that marked the creature's arrival. The breath that followed felt like it was long and shallow, but it was more than likely just a quick deep gasp entering my lungs as my fire line started to move over my head. In all reality it was very likely that I was going to be the next person today to do an impression of a fallen piano.

The moment the creature started to gather out of the wind above me it let out another roar that I almost answered with a gunpowder cry of my own when a sound that made my Colt and the Wendigo's roar seem like sad little cries rolled over the earth with enough force to shake the very ground. Just then a dark brown blur came over the fence striking against the Wendigo like a linebacker.

Gregorie landed on top the Wendigo. His ear shattering roar continuing as he rained down punches on the creature cracking supernaturally tough bones with each hit before grasping the creature by each slightly elongated ear and holding the creature's head up to level a head-butt against the bridge of its noise.

It had happened so quickly that the Wendigo never had the chance to cry out before the last vicious blow caused the creature to fall back to the ground unconscious. Gregorie stood up and uttered a few choice French curses beneath his breath and turned about to face me. "Is this where you are going to tell me that I should stay in my cabin, William?" said the giant with a grin as he held out his large hand to help me up.

I accepted the gesture with a nod. "All things considered I was going to go with 'What took you so long?' first." I laughed before stopping and feeling the side of my undercover vest. It had helped some but it wasn't designed to stop impact bruises. I was going to be nursing some bruised, maybe cracked, ribs for a while. "That was pretty impressive."

"Yes, well I might have left France long before savate got its official start but even in the late seventeenth century France wasn't a very friendly place, at least not where I grew up." Gregorie said with a chuckle as he patted me on the shoulder. "Come, it looks like a mess out here with all the bodies. I'll need to clear out before local law enforcement shows up, and you'll need to figure out what happened."

"I'll get Cassi to bring my computer and we can figure it out in a few. I'll get a cleanup crew over this way and we can hide the bodies till then." I said with a nod. "Bloody mess." I said looking around. Marshall looked to have been the only survivor of the encounter but he was curled up in the ditch muttering to himself looking blankly away. I doubt he had seen much after the Wendigo's first appearance.

The Sasquatch looked back toward the truck and grinned. "Oh, Miss Ross has returned? More trouble or..." I could have guessed at the rest of Gregorie's statement but I never had the chance to as the wind started to swirl and gather about us. One long fingered hand gripped Gregorie's shoulder. The large Sasquatch had blocked my view of the creature's assent and it had masked any sound it made with the cold wind gathering about it.

"Au revoir" The Wendigo said its speaking voice coming forth as a carefully modulated perpetual growl. Gregorie tried to jerk away from the hold but by the time he was over that instant of shock the wind about us howled and the creature grabbed hold of him and jumped backwards, over the road.

Now the small blacktop roads weren't going to kill Gregorie with their energy of civilization, but with all the recent traffic over them from the would have been mob of poachers crossing the back road would be harder on Gregorie than normal. Blue green sparks flickered from Gregorie's form as he fell back over the road stunned as the Wendigo tore him from the air and slammed him into the opposite ditch.

I emptied the last three rounds of my clip into the creatures shoulder and ribs managing to hit without ricochet this time but it still slowed the creature for only a moment before he grabbed Gregorie up in his uninjured arm and jumped back over the road pulling the friendly giant back with him in another shower of aqua sparks. Gregorie tried to punch the creature after he landed at the end of that flight but the wide hook was slow and clumsy compared to his earlier assault.

The Wendigo prepared to throw Gregorie again as I slammed a new clip home in the colt and brought the gun up an instant before the door to my truck swung open and Cassi stepped out from the driver side onto the black top road her sword in hand.

The Wendigo looked up once the door opened, and dropping Gregorie to the ground, wheeled about to face Cassi. "Found you." The half growl voice said before standing up to stalk toward her letting a windy roar loose along the way.

The wind and odor made Cassi jump back into the truck with a yelp. It hadn't been the most thought out plan but it had gotten the creature off Gregorie. It had after all said it had found her as if Cassi was what the creature was looking for. That would have to be filed away for later. Right now I chambered a new round in the colt and leveled it. I had to pull the creatures attention again so I shot it in the head. Granted it had the result I predicted as each bullet impacted the creature's thick skull and bounced away, but even though all the creature's bones were bullet proof my gamble had paid off. All the little delicate vibration sensitive parts that make up the inner ear didn't like powerful blows against the side of its head. The creature stumbled back with the shots before turning to face me.

I'd sent three of the seven new rounds at the creature before it turned away from the truck, gathered its wits, and landed its gaze on me. "Mortal man, give up, and I'll not kill you before I take the girl." the Wendigo growled before shaking its head.

"Can't do it tall, shaggy, and ugly." I said giving the trigger on the colt a half squeeze. "Put your hands behind your head and give up and I'll grant you the right to an investigation, if you can give up enough information you might get to go free." I said looking down my gun sights at the creature. "Right now you got enough against you for me to put you down where you stand if you want to play it that way." Sometimes it was really hard to remember that I wasn't just a monster hunter. The law had to be followed and I had to offer a peaceful alternative if the culprit had stopped to talk.

"I fear my lords more than I do your law human. Besides, I cannot give up a hunt like this. I'll enjoy eating your friend too much." It said with a chuckle, right before a chunk of its right shoulder disappeared in a fine pink and black mist.

The cry the creature let out was more on par for volume with Gregorie's battle cry than its previous ones. A low rumble mixed with high pitched wails before the creature turned to run into the forest as its ribs broke with the bark of another round and another spray of black blood. I pulled up my pistol as the creature turned back to the cab of the truck where the shot came from and roared letting a torrent of fowl air fill the cabin. I let three more round go and crash into the side of the creatures head throwing it off balance before another two muffled cracks of gunfire came from the cab of the truck both leaving gaping holes in the back of the Wendigo's body.

The monster cried out again before tuning and running as a couple of more stray rounds flew after it from where Cassi was held up inside the truck. Acting on reflex I raised my gun and fired another round into, well into its ass, before it disappeared into the forest.

I stumbled across the blacktop road and to the truck keeping my pistol at low ready in one hand before waving to Cassi with the other. The last thing I needed was a by proxy fear induced case of lead poisoning. *Or silver poisoning as the case may be.* I thought as I looked into the cab of the truck.

Cassi was still pressed against the back window of the truck holding my Sig in her hands. She'd been lucky that the wendigo was so large and so close. Her hands were shaking like a leaf making the barrel of the gun jump erratically.

A loud groan pulled my attention to the side and caused me to bring my gun up. Gregorie had sat back up on the side of the road nearest his property. He looked like death warmed over. His eyes were dull and half shut, his fur was without its normal shine and the remainder of vomit clung to his hair covered face and chest. I started toward him but the giant put his hand up and shook his head as he pushed himself up and turned toward his cabin.

"Sleep." he muttered as he finished working his feet under him after his first failed steps. "Hunt that beast down and destroy it before more humans try to invade my land hunting something that looks anything like me."

He didn't have to tell me what he would do to anyone or anything invading his space. I had never seen Gregorie forced to violence and I made it a note then and there after that display never to encourage such a behavior in him. With any luck no one else would come and try this again, but if they did... After a long pause I couldn't help but notice the new degree of complication this added to things. The last thing I needed was a fake Bigfoot ripping people apart, people hunting the wrong target and causing the real Bigfoot to do much worse.

It took me the better part of an hour to snap pictures of the scene and manage to move all of the body parts under a tarp and out of sight along the side of the road. Thankfully no one else drove down the road during the whole macabre process.

Marshall was starting to come to by the time I finished and while he was still in enough of a state of shock to go along with guided motions. I led him to his truck, sat him down, grabbed a syringe I kept in my clean up kit in the back of my truck and stuck Marshall in the thigh before pushing the plunger down. Methohexital injected intramuscular would take a few minutes to get to work, but it would keep Marshall asleep until the cleanup crew got here. He would most likely wake up at the hospital with a police officer waiting to ask him about the wild animal attack he had witnessed.

I stepped into the truck and looked to Cassi who was still holding the SIG in her lap. "You doing ok?" I asked as I closed the door behind me and leaned back in the seat. With Gregorie going to sleep I couldn't leave the scene unguarded until I saw the Initiative's clean up guys drive up.

"Yeah. Just coming to terms with the fact that I've decided to place my bets with a guy that carries body tarps, knock out drugs and magic bullets." She said with a long sigh leading into a pretty chuckle that was becoming a habit.

"They aren't magic, just silver, for werewolves." I answered.

"Silver vested with the energy of sacrifice. Sounds magical to me." She replied looking at the weapon in her lap over. "I didn't even think I knew how to turn off the safety."

"You knew how to do a bit more than that." I said as I watched in my rear view mirror as an unmarked panel van pulled up.

I grabbed the small LED flashlight from the compartment on the door of the truck and put it out the window before clicking it on and off twice before looking back to the van. A gloved hand stuck out the driver side window and I watch as a bright green dot appeared on the mirror flashing twice in return. "Well, that's the black suits. Time to head out." I said before starting up the truck and pulling out onto the road.

Cassi turned and looked about as we started down the road trying to catch site of the vehicle behind us. "No one's getting out."

"They won't until we are out of sight." I said. "It really isn't anything special just the guys in the black suits cleaning up the mess. They arrange the cover up and get the survivors to the hospital." I said.

"You mean the guys in the dark suits with the glasses that everyone talks about are..." "Cleanup crew. For me and the rest of the agency."

"Top secret Janitors?" Cassi finished shaking her head.

"Don't let them hear that or you might wake up with no credit history, bank accounts or valid ID" I said with a chuckle as I made a turn

"Wipe my credit history? Promise?" she said with a laugh leaning back into the seat finally picking up the SIG from her lap and putting it back in the center console. "And now we are off to see the wizard or whoever is going to find out who attacked me?" Cassi said after checking through the various satellite internet radio stations I had saved and finding nothing she liked.

"Off to see the sorceress technically." I said with a nod. "With any luck Hannelore should be able to tell us something with a bit of divination.

"Hannelore? Divination? I think I know what one of those are, but what's a Hannelore?"

I laughed. "Hannelore is the name of the person we are going to see. She is a very talented sorceress. The one that helped you yesterday after the incident here in the truck. Divination is a school of magic centered on the location of objects or the gathering of information."

"If that wasn't a textbook answer I've never heard one." Cassi replied with a chuckle as she leaned back in her seat and closed her eyes. "No issues with me getting shut eye along the way?"

"Of course not, I'll grab some coffee when we get close." I said with a chuckle before turning on a radio station and settling in to drive back toward Tyler.

It was a little bit over half an hour later when I pulled into the drive way of Hannelore's house. An old Victorian style castle of a home. It wasn't really a large house but the asymmetrical assembly of rooms, gables, balconies, and one actual tower on the front left corner all made of gray painted siding trimmed in white gave the home a particular majesty. The willow tree in the front yard was ancient standing nearly as tall as the two story home. Other than the tree, a row of trimmed hedges about the house and green grass over the yard no other vegetation existed. Honest to goodness gas lights flickered weakly in the early afternoon light on either side of the door.

I picked up the extra cup of coffee from its holder and waved it below Cassi's nose. She bolted up and tore the cup from my hand without her eyes even opening. I chuckled and opened the door, grabbed my own cup and slipped out of the truck. By the time I closed the truck door on my side, Cassi was sliding out of her own side while taking a deep drink of the coffee, as she stepped away and closed the door with her foot not willing to remove either hand from the cup. It was then that she got a full look at the house. "Wow it even looks like a witch's house."

"Sorceress." I corrected. "Witches and Warlocks work in covens to gather power from one another or third parties while Sorceresses and Wizards have the option to work alone and still command some considerable power." I replied to the unasked question as we walked up the steps. "But Hannelore does do the stereotype a great service." We walked down the drive and up the steps of the front porch. I reached up to make use of the old brass knocker. The door opened before us without ever giving me the chance to knock.

"No kidding." Cassi said with a nod of her head as she walked into the house. Dark stained hardwood floors gave way to a large living room framed by pristine white walls. Most of the decor matched the alabaster walls. White canvases painted in a variety of textures hung from the walls and an elaborate chandelier hung from the ceiling in a shower of crystals. Most of the furniture was white as well. But it was all accented with touches of bright pure black in the throw pillows on the couch, the ties holding back the drapes, and the massive rug under the coffee table and before the fireplace. "It's beautiful." Cassi breathed looking about the room.

Then as if her words had broken the serenity of the world that had fallen over us as we walked in the door, all silence was shattered by the sounds of clawed feet thundering down the dark wooden stairs. A pair of dark forms barreled toward us. Cassi yelped as she turned and I couldn't help but laugh as the two dogs started to slide in front of me, both of them falling to a shoulder and rolling over to stop with their bellies exposed, tongues out and eyes wide.

Ajax and Achilles were Hannelore's two great danes. I had long ago endeared the two of them to me, and the only down side to was that when I sat down anywhere in the house one or both of the nearly two hundred pound slobber machines tried to sit in my lap.

"What happened to black cats?" Cassi asked kneeling down to scratch both the giant dogs' chests. I had seen the two animals run down anything they perceived as would be aggressors, once going so far as knocking down the front door to get at a vacuum sales man who kept insisting to be invited in. But around those they knew or those their senses said to trust they melted into oversized furry black puddles and Cassi had apparently made the list.

"It is much harder to violate the laws of physics and turn ones ex-boyfriends into something as small as a cat." came the familiar ethereal voice of Hannelore as she walked into the room. Her white hair was pulled back in pig tails and her clothing was a dark skirted version of a school girl outfit with an open white button down shirt and a black tee shirt depicting a cartoon bunny holding a knife. "Or I don't like litter boxes. Take your pick?"

Cassi stopped and looked toward the sorceress and back down to the dogs before looking to me. I couldn't help but to grin. "Hannelore has had these two since they were puppies. Human transmutation is prohibited."

"Perhaps, but I was going to go with the fact that if a man had the right temperament to be a good dog she wouldn't have broken up with them." Cassi chuckled as she stood up from the two beasts and waved. "But if it is possible to do I would love a few pointers."

Hannelore laughed and shook her head. "If by tips you mean about nine or ten years of constant study, yeah we could teach you what you need to know to change a former lover into a dog."

"So, I guess that it's more than a few words and hand gestures then?"

"In the way that calculus is more than addition and subtraction." Hannelore responded leaving Cassi a bit dumbfounded.

"All math is addition and subtraction at its very core. We just expand upon those." I added as Hannelore motioned to follow her out of the black and white sitting room and into a surprisingly cheery kitchen full of blue plaid and ducks. "In the same manner magic is hand gestures and words but without proper knowledge, application, and the proper medium they are just tools with no purpose."

"Yeah I hate to fit the typical female stereotype, but math was never my strong suit. I was always more for English and art."

"Someone has to." Hannelore said without looking back. "But the sword goes a long way toward making a knit sweater look tough."

"Coming from the girl who's making knee socks and Mary Janes look as intimidating as they are cute, I'll take that as a compliment." Cassi added with a chuckle as she patted on the basket hilt of the sword while Hannelore opened what looked to be a closet but turned out to be a basement entrance. She held up a hand to stop us as Achilles and Ajax ran by and loped down the stairs ahead of us.

"So yeah, car chases and monsters and guns and cool guy stuff." I joked having nothing to talk about related to sweaters or little patent leather shoes that I hated myself for actually knowing the name of.

"You're just jealous that my weapon is bigger." Cassi said with a grin and a wink before heading down the stairs with Hannelore whose laugh would have given any evil witch or mad scientist a run for their money. A sinking feeling hit my stomach as I followed the pair down into the basement. A little voice in my head told me that I had just brought together two forces in my personal universe that were going to give my sense of humor and my pride a great deal of punishment. It also told me to stop staring at their asses as we walked down the stairs. About the time I realized that the little voice wasn't my own but another speaking to me mentally from the outside Hannelore started into another round of hysterical chuckles.

Funny thing about Hannelore's or anyone else's agoraphobia. When they are home or anywhere they feel truly safe people with that particular mental affliction are closer to being their true selves. In most cases, such as Hannelore's, it wasn't an incredible change. They just seemed more comfortable with the world about them and were a little bit more outspoken. Here Hannelore was master of her domain and had no need to fear anyone. The only difference between her and other agoraphobics was that in Hannelore's world she was right.

Hannelore's basement looked like a cross between an old library, an apothecary, a chemistry lab and an antique store. The whole room was lit by a collection of oil lamps that burned with different intensities and colors of light. Each lamp provided a unique brightness to the room that seemed to coalesce with the others to provide surprisingly steady white light throughout the space. Stacks and stacks of books over filled and caused oak book shelves to sag under the great weight. A couple of shelves were so completely and tightly packed with wooden and metal boxes of varying sizes that had long ago started to resemble abstracted card catalogs. A few marks of Hannelore's trade were left unboxed to lay about the room. A set of five silver candle sticks, each equipped with partly burned down candles of different lengths, marked each point of a pink chalk pentagram on an old round oak kitchen table. A dimly glowing liquid was left to bubble through a maze of glass tubes and drip into a stone chalice. A bronze knife, polished to a reflective shine, leaned back into a metal brace that had very obviously never been cleaned or dusted leaving it with several strings of cobwebs that led to the polished oak desk below and a couple of smudges of what could only be blood. The knife was guarded by a large blue plush dragon with green wings and a happy smile. The only touches of modern convenience, other than the stuffed animal, visible in the room was an Apple laptop and a series of those little hydroponic herb garden sets each growing its own variety of greenery. Some were spotted with colorful flowers. I was pretty sure that not all the things that Hannelore grew down here where necessarily legal. But down here, Hannelore's word surpassed most laws, and I always forgot to call her out on it for some reason. That was probably her doing as well.

The central eye grabber in the room was on the floor in the center of the most open space and far from any other decor. A brightly polished ring of silver about an inch wide and about four feet across was inlaid among the ceramic tiles that made up the basement floor.

The two dogs had already laid down on a pair of nearly twin sized doggie beds in the back corner having declared the lab safe for entry. Once Ajax and Achilles gave the room their approval Hannelore stopped at the entrance of the lab and turned about to face us. She stopped Cassi and I in our tracks before she spoke. This time that airy ethereal feeling to her voice was gone. It was still soft and the tone was still high but each breath thrummed with power and every syllable seemed to echo about the room.

"William Codex, friend, counselor and protector. Welcome back to my sanctum, my seat of power and my true home. You may enter in good will and peace of mind and safe from bodily harm as long as you grant the same." When Hannelore finished speaking I nodded humbly and stepped forward. Cassi stepped beside me and was stopped at the threshold to the basement as if she had walked into a stone wall. The wall dispersed the energy with waves of orange and red light as Cassi fell back to the stairs.

"Cassi, new friend and stranger, stand and look into my eyes." Hannelore commanded in that soft tone with no less authority than if she had yelled at the other woman.

Cassi replied by standing up and shaking off the pain and ignoring the blood that came from her nose. Hannelore stared blankly at her waiting for their eyes to make contact. Cassi looked forward obviously confused and with more than passing anger mixing with the tears in her eyes but none the less, they met Hannelore's and an instant later the two women were locked in a gaze that appeared to be nothing more than simple eye contact.

I knew from experience how much more it was. When we mere mortals make eye contact we can get a glimpse into the soul of another. Most of us don't even recognize it as such, but that doesn't change the nature of a thing. Especially one this powerful. When a practitioner of the art looks into another person's eyes, they can actively explore. I couldn't imagine what such experience was like for someone like Cassi who naturally could perceive, explore, and tune herself to the emotions of another. That instant stretched out for what felt like several moments before I felt what might have been a pulse of magical energy flutter over the room changing it in a way I couldn't quite perceive but could still feel. Then Hannelore spoke her voice piercing the silence like fire into darkness.

"Cassi Delores Ross, sister found, trusted companion to one of my dearest friends and kindred soul. Welcome to my sanctum, my seat of power and, my true home. You may enter in good will and peace of mind and safe from bodily harm as long as you grant the same."

What had been a confused, tear filled, and angry cast in Cassi's gaze melted to reveal a look of calm acceptance graced by slow falling tears. All doubt in her mind gone, Cassi stepped over the threshold of Hannelore's sanctum. "Wow" she muttered as she wiped at her eyes before allowing her gaze to catch mine. "That was intense. I mean there is looking someone in the eye and then..."

"It seemed almost as intense as an experience you had earlier today." Hannelore said a grin crossing her face. Perception wasn't

Hannelore's strongest gift but any practitioner of her level can pull up recent powerful memories during extended eye contact.

"You saw....you felt?" Cassi turned bright pink and buried her face in her hands.

"I think we are even, all things considered." Hannelore said with an actual sly grin across her face. That was a rare and dangerous sight from the sorceress and I had only ever seen it appear down here in her laboratory, her safe place, her real home.

The pair laughed again. I just walked back into the corner and scratched the pair of large dogs behind the ears. "So is it just human females, or are they all a little crazy fellas?"

Ajax, leaned into the scratching a little bit more than the stoic Achilles and exhaled sharply in a low "ruff" before putting his head down. I could only assume that the dogs knew the universal "one for yes two for no" code.

By the time I had finished paying the guards off for allowing me to pass into the basement, I stood up and walked back toward the other side of the room making sure to avoid the circle in the center of the room. Cassi had the sword drawn depicting the events of the previous evening as Hannelore gathered material from a few of the boxes on one of the shelves. I leaned against the counter and watched the swordplay demo. "So Hannelore, what's the order of the day?"

"Better yet, you tell me William." Hannelore said with a grin as he motioned to the materials on the desk I was leaning on. A chalk line of the type that normally saw use on construction sites, five small white tea candles and a larger candle sectioned off into thirds one blue one red and one yellow. As I considered the components in play Hannelore started to pull out a variety of crystals and a couple of old camera lenses.

"If I had to guess I would say that we could use the chalk and the small candles to build a circle using your silver one in the middle of the room as a base," I started, "But we could use that large circle compass you have if you prefer not to use that one. We then would use those crystals to power the lines of the circle with whatever power you have vested into them channel it all through a few lenses and into the blade of the sword. From there we bounce that line off the blade into the flame of the large candle using a few more lenses to ensure the entire reflection passes through that flame and another lens or two and with the right concentration, we should see an image come out the other side." I said with a nod more to encourage myself than to say I was right.

Hannelore nodded, "Very good, William, but can you tell me what you missed?" She added with a smile as she set a small unmarked dark wood box down on the table with a grin.

I considered all the pieces and focuses in front of me for a moment before leaning over and looking toward Cassi and her sword trying to think if any special circumstances would require all the regalia of the spell Hannelore was prepping. "Well you have a lot of extra foci out for what I thought would be a simple spell for you in your seat of power. I mean if I were going to cast the spell I would need a set up like this and some kind of battery but...." I stopped. "I'm casting the spell aren't I, Hannelore?" I said with a groan. "I don't have time for the set up required. I have to figure out if these attacks are related or not."

"The only way you are going to learn how to formulate a spell under pressure is to do it, William," the sorceress said. "I'll keep an eye out to make sure you don't make any mistakes and offer advice if you get stumped for too long, but I really do think you're ready for a working of this magnitude."

Cassi's sword stopped in the middle of what had become a surprisingly graceful series of movements of the blade. "Wait a second. Will is casting the spell?" She asked as I grabbed a broom and began to start to sweep the circle area clean of any signs of dust before returning to the table.

"Well more like throwing it in the air and hoping it comes down right. No working that I touch is graceful enough to be called casting." I said as I grabbed the chalk line and walked toward the silver circle in the middle of the floor. Cassi didn't look as though she was magically any less confused. "Hannelore, you want to handle this one?" I said before setting the chalk line's clip to one edge of the circle before pulling out a length of chalk coated line and considering my angle before setting to work.

"The fact that you are a warlock?" Hannelore asked before looking toward Cassi and with a very flat tone spoke. "William is a warlock."

"I am not a warlock." I said with a sigh as I clipped the chalk line's clip to another indention around the inside edge of the circle and walked out the second line of the spell form I would need. Thankfully Hannelore had brought down her blue chalk line for me to use. Maybe I'm old fashioned but it was hard to summon up all the inner strength of my male aura amongst a collection of pretty pink lines.

"William doesn't think he is a warlock." Hannelore said with the same flat tone but now with an almost audible roll of her eyes.

"I don't have the energy needed to use a spell. I have to use third party power. No power. No title." I said as I continued the task on hand.

"You have to have some spark of power yourself to set a spell in motion. Even if you don't have much of it, you have the gift." Hannelore said, her tone developing a chiding edge. This was not the first time we had this debate.

"I have no gift that can be detected by any test scientific or supernatural." I said as the spell form I'd chosen started to take shape.

Hannelore just shook her head as she stepped up to look over my work before looking back to Cassi who just stared blankly at the two of us. "William has an incredible talent for all the things one must know in order to perform a magical working. He believes in the power of the art. He has a well ordered mind capable of deep meditation. He also has a knack for the process and procedure needed to build a spell in energy, but enough of an artistic eye to see the abstractions between the physical and metaphysical. However, he doesn't have much of the actual power vested in those who work magic traditionally."

Looking up at the working I'd designed, I walked up to the table and grabbed the five small tea candles and reached into a nearby drawer to take three more. "Think of it like trying to paint a Picasso and do college calculus at the same time." I said as I walked back and set one of the small candles at each point of the eight pointed star I had drawn out in the stark white chalk as the main piece of my spell form. Each little flame would serve as an anchor point for the energy of the spell against the bounds of the circle and help the energy I set loose in the pattern stay on path through the foci I used for the spell. It was more than I technically needed, most practitioners used five points and the gifted sometimes used the circle alone, but with as little energy as I could bring to bare and with the rest being borrowed, I was more than a little paranoid about wasting it.

"His situation is actually perhaps the exact opposite of yours Cassi." Hannelore said as I gathered up all the foci for the spell and set about arranging them inside the circle along the line and inner points of the star making sure to leave room for the sword behind the large candle in the center of the circle. "You have great potential for the gift, but your mind is not that of a practitioner."

"I'm not smart enough?" Cassi asked quickly her tone rising almost causing me to break my concentration and laugh as I walked back to the table taking a moment to take my amulet off from about my wrist and set it on the table. My phone, my badge, my gun and my silver ring from my right hand followed suit. Each was laid on the table with care and order before I took up a collection of small crystals that Hannelore had vested with energy for the purposes of my lessons before returning to the circle.

"It has more to do with the type of intelligence. William is as left brained as he is right. You Cassi are emotional and artistic with an empathic magical ability that tends to random strikes of power. Constrained and controlled magic is perhaps not beyond you, but it will never be your strength." Hannelore said, her tone remaining that of the instructor avoiding any sign that she took offense to Cassi's change in tone.

"So you find a spell, set up all the ritual and then it is on with the precise magic words?" Cassi said as she glanced from Hannelore to me and back again before shaking her head. "You're not explaining everything."

"Your empathy is stronger than I thought." Hannelore said with a grin. "I didn't mean to conceal anything from you. It's just that the science behind what is normally called magic is really on the far fringes of quantum mechanics. Increased alpha and beta wave activity of gifted individuals or, as is the case for William and those like him, manipulation of a power source to change the world about them on a quantum level. In this case William is using the crystals as a type of battery to...."

"Yeah, English major. I couldn't make it through high school chemistry without cheating." Cassi said rolling her eyes. "Maybe when we have a bit more time for you to slow down the explanation some." Hannelore chuckled and nodded her agreement before whispering something into Cassi's ear that I couldn't hear.

During Hannelore's explanation I managed to set the crystals along the lines of the spell and settled in to get to work. Then I realized I'd forgotten the sword. Shaking my head I started to get up, but by the time I turned and before I could get up Cassi stood nearby holding the sword out with the steel basket hilt held out toward me over the edge of the circle, careful not to cross the edge of the working herself.

I took the sword with a smile and a nod before setting the blade in the center of the spell form propping it on its edge and connecting it to the spell form with two crystals. The form finally built, I touched the crystals one at a time letting my own will leak into them breaking the magical seals holding their energy back and releasing it into the form. As the seals broke, the energy started to flow through the form lighting the candles as it went. My mind dedicated a portion of itself to the spell each time a new crystal was opened. A dozen crystals were laid out in the spell form and each had to be monitored and controlled separately. I vaguely remembered hearing Hannelore explaining the process to Cassi. Telling her how I had to block out the world about me one sense at a time. After touch, sight, smell and taste I heard her describe how I was going to block out sound or at least my perception of it, but the world went silent a moment before she was done.

Nothing existed but the form of the spell and flows of power that traveled down that form passing into the candles at the edge of the circle each casting light through the lenses set up at the spell's interior intersections gathering that energy into one beam aimed to bounce against the blade of the sword. All that energy was being used to manipulate the residual DNA left on the blade as it reflected the light to achieve my goal. Honestly, I barely grasped the scientific part of what I was doing. Just another reason that a person like me would never be something like Hannelore.

I felt the life energy and traces of the blood of Cassi's attacker concentrating the spell's energy on that remnant before allowing the light to bounce off the blade, through a final lens and into the flame of the multicolored candle. Its own flame began to flicker from yellow to blue to red cycling though the primary colors casting light through another lens and out of the spell.

I opened my eyes to a form hanging in the air in full but dulled color like old daytime television. The figure spun slowly before me and I worked as quickly as I could to commit the details to memory before the spell collapsed upon me. Standing a few inches over six feet, the figure was thin but still well formed with muscle that spoke of a runner or a swimmer. A long face with eyes only a hair too large to be human with a bit of an upward slant and a nose that most people only saw after a trip to a plastic surgeon. Wavy black hair fell down to shoulder length and the only mark over the form other than those of rippling muscle was a black tattoo over the left side of the form's chest. A single downward facing black blade surrounded by an outline of a left hand facing palm outward toward the viewer. The mark wasn't known to me but the figures features meant it could only be one thing.

"Damn it's an elf." I muttered under my breath.

"Wait. You mean an elf. Like Legolas elf?" Cassi asked as she stepped closer to Hannelore, both of them taking in the conjured form. Her eyes were wide as she took in the hanging form of light that had appeared about six feet away from the center of the circle.

"Depends. Have you read the books?" I asked closing my eyes regaining my concentration.

"I have hold of the spell, William. You can relax and leave the circle." Hannelore said. "Good work. I will have to make you conjure up images of beautiful naked men in my basement more often." She said with a chuckle as I stepped out of the circle.

"The book." She said, obviously holding her hand out to the form as if it was obvious. "That is not like any actor that played one in the film." She said glancing back to the form. "The movie watered it down, like everything else, apparently."

"They stand over six feet, are dedicated to particular crafts and have an immortal life to hone their skills. Most of them lean to a light touch and incredible speed. Lots of archers and very few linebackers among the elves," I said. "They see better in the dark than us, don't have to sleep for days, and are more or less the superior version of humans and for the most part, they know it," I sighed.

"So, they are extra planar, not constructs?" Cassi asked before looking back and grinning toward Hannelore's light applause at her recognition.

"Yeah, they belong in the fairy realms, but like most fae, our laws limit how long they can stay. If they have a half human child they can get resident status in the United States, but that is one of the few exceptions." I leaned back against the table trying to place that tattoo. "So when his arm was separated from his life force it went back to its home plane."

"You mean if you kill one, they don't leave evidence?" Cassi asked. "Well, no body. There was blood all over the place."

"Not enough life energy in a single drop of blood to open a path." I said, grabbing my phone off the table and making a few notes on the elf's appearance. "The bone, blood and flesh in the arm would have been enough to let the limb pass back to its home realm. The blood will show up as more or less human, but the police forensics people will probably notice a few genetic quirks if they look close enough."

"Well, at least they won't think I went crazy and threw pigs blood around my apartment or something." Cassi sighed deeply as she settled down to pet who I thought was Ajax. "What's with disarming before the spell?"

"I can't take anything into an active spell that has strong personal or metaphysical importance. Or anything that runs on electricity." I put my phone away before grabbing the rest of my things.

"Will's own power is so slight that objects of metaphysical weight could pull on the power like gravity controls the tides making it hard to control and unpredictable. Electronic devices could easily overpower his own magical spark and obfuscate the power he is trying to use to set off the batteries placed in the spell form." Hannelore added. "It isn't a requirement for all practitioners, but Will has so little energy that he needs to take every advantage he can. I keep trying to get him to work skyclad...." Hannelore smirked with that wicked chuckle that only occurred when she was safe in the seat of her power and her agoraphobia was completely sated.

"Skyclad?" Cassi asked.

"Naked." I was already shaking my head as I gathered up everything but my Colt. I always saved the gun for last.

Cassi started to say something. I could see the spark of a joke forming behind her eyes, but it was like she couldn't decide which one to settle on and instead looked over the collection of items before looking up at me quirking an eyebrow. "The gun?"

I grinned as I picked up the black metal pistol. Its oak wood grips had worn and darkened over the last several years to conform exactly to my hand. "This is my gun." I started. "There are many like it but this one is mine." With the variation of the Marine creed I put my weapon back into its holster under my left arm. "I'm not a big gun nut or anything, but this thing has saved my life more than once." I said as I slipped the two clips back into the holder on my right side. "Inanimate or not, you come to respect things like that." Walking over and taking the sword up from the rest of the spell pattern, before wiping the blade down and turning it about - handing it back to Cassi handle first. "Funny how that happens doesn't it?"

Cassi grinned as she took her sword, and only after checking the blade over for damage, put it back in the scabbard at her hip. "I'm thinking of calling him Wilson." She said her cheeks taking on a light pink shade. "Where do we go from here?"

"You know that sentence shouldn't include we." I said looking her over. Cassi had been through a lot in the last day and she had already suffered one break. She would be good for now, but no one could take this kind of stuff for too long at first. Hell, I'd been baptized by fire into this world six years ago, and I still had a moment every few months that I had to stop and breathe to make sure I didn't go crazy, and that didn't stop the nightmares all of the time. "You should stay here with Hannelore for a while and get some rest."

"Well, the way I see it, I have to help you anyway. I can or go home, hole up in my apartment, and wonder when the next boogie man is going to knock down my door. Staying here might keep me safer, but for how long, Will?" Cassi said as she leaned back against the table beside me. Hannelore took to cleaning and reordering her equipment. She preferred to do the task herself. I was apparently not orderly enough for her lab. I had the mind to cast spells but not to put crystals in a box and put that box in a drawer. "I'll be good and stay in the car when I need to, but this problem is chasing me now. I'm safer near you even if you are running into the fire. I'd rather run to it than let it catch me."

"Good but there is the legality of it. You're not even cleared to know as much as you do already." I said with a sigh. "The mountain of paperwork I'm facing is already astronomical."

"I'll help with that. I mean as much as I can. I know I can't know any super-secret stuff but I can write." She said with a grin. "English major."

"With how much you love reports, William. It sounds like a match made in Heaven." Hannelore said with a giggle. "Besides, you will want to hurry if you are to catch the contact you are thinking about. If you wait until the sun goes down you won't be able to get valuable information from them."

"How do you know who I am thinking about? I don't even want to know." I asked the sorceress before realizing that I did know where to go next. That set me to wondering whether or not she had actually read my mind, put the thought in place, or if she had just known the conclusion I was going to come to. But as Hannelore said, we didn't have much time.

By the time we left Hannelore's and drove across Tyler to an old house in what was known as the Azalea Trail district, the afternoon sun was starting to fall from the sky. It was a fair sized but squat two story house composed of red brown iron ore stone that sat across the street from a city park. Like all the other houses on the street, the yard was well maintained and bore the off season signs of a home with elaborate landscaping and gardening. By late March it would be alive with the colors and scents of that flower that was the namesake of this area of the city. It was where the leprechauns lived.

This particular small group of the supernatural immortal mischief makers had taken up residence in Tyler nearly thirty years ago shortly after the Holzer Initiative was formed. Seeking shelter from an elder fae creature of some form or another, they came to this country and the Initiative had placed them in Tyler. My mentor hadn't been happy about that decision. They had been a constant source of harassment for Gideon most of that time. Incredibly intelligent and easily bored, leprechauns have a nasty habit of "playing games" with mortals. They often claim it is a cultural activity used to keep their skills sharp so they can ably defend their treasures, but the fae and humans often have a different opinion about what is acceptable risk for a joke. We mere mortals don't often see cut brake lines or assault and battery as good natured pranks.

Over all, I normally didn't like using them as a source. Immortal beings in general are hard to deal with and rarely kept up with current culture. The great tree spirits from places like the Black Forest in Germany or in the Redwood forest of the American northwest were incredibly hard to deal with due to the language barrier alone. If something that old spoke a human language, most of them spoke a dead one or something akin to old English. On the other side of the "problems about immortality" fence you have creatures like the leprechauns. Who cling to the wrong parts of modern culture and do so with such unreasonable ferocity that they border on insanity.

For instance, I had created a monster when I introduced them to violent video games. Granted they didn't spend as much time attacking humans when they could steal cars, run from the police, and kill hookers all in the comfort of their own home. Even more so, they had bought into the first person shooter genre on a whole different higher level. Have you ever played such a game online and come across another player who sounds like he is twelve or thirteen and still cursed like a sailor? Odds are you just got fragged by a leprechaun.

You throw in the violent video game habit and the fact that Gideon had long ago established a beer for information trade with the little fellows and they could quickly become expensive informants. But, like so many beings that lived for so long, they had a tendency to grow predictable. I gave Cassi the once over before knocking on the door and grinned. "Just remember we are going to be dealing with very ancient very powerful beings no matter how they appear or act." I waited to watch her nod her head before reaching up and taking up the large brass knocker ring on the door and bringing it down in a predetermined pattern. Bum bu bum bum....Bum bu bum bum, Bum! Yes it was the old Dragnet theme. It probably said a lot about what this lot thought of the initiative, but as long as they followed the rules I didn't really care about their opinion.

A few moments later quick footsteps moved to the door and two locks snapped open before the door pulled open. Standing on the other side was what looked at first glance to be a little person with a shockingly disordered mop of red hair. A second glance would reveal that while he was certainly short of statue the creature looked to be built more like a skinny youth of nearly fourteen or fifteen despite his height. Young in the face with skinny arms and shoulders barely showing signs of masculine muscle. He was wearing denim pants that had likely been designed for a toddler and a bright green Ireland soccer jersey. His bright red hair was kept short and stuck out in every direction and his face looked too smooth to have ever seen a razor up close. "Oi Willy boy. What's...." The low standing man stopped as he looked toward Cassi and grinned. "We'l be takin' two. Y'can leave this on here and bring the other on the morrow wit' more beer, we're almost out." Said the leprechaun I knew as Tristan. He stepped back to allow Cassi in with a flourished bow and blocked me from entry all in the same movement. Granted I could step over him but that would have just been impolite.

Cassi smirked knelt down to Tristan placing one hand on the handle of her sword and with a honey sweet voice spoke. "Is minic a gheibhean beal oscailt diog dunta." I couldn't help but chuckle. My Gaelic was horrible without a dictionary but I was able to catch the intention behind the phrase. Watch it buddy I'm not to be messed with.

"Oh Good Fatha, Son and Holy Motha Willie. She speaks th' tongue. Where did ye find this angel?" Tristan asked. I wasn't even sure if he was aware of the fact that his accent got stronger for the statement but knowing the silver tongued fae, he most likely did.

"He found me all nice and wrapped up in a police car just the morning before this." Cassi said with a grin before finally accepting the leprechaun's invitation in. I sidestepped Tristan and walked in after her.

"Cassi's helping me out on a few leads. Need you to go and get Conroy." I said with a greeting to a passerby as I stepped into the house. What I could see of the house so far told me that it was caught in its normal wave of activity.

The entry way and the main room were the only "big rooms" in the entire house. The prior often saw use as a kind of open market between the little men and several of their lesser fae kin. Small tables set up against the wall full of various wares both found and purchased in the outside world. One of them even had a variety of electronic essentials shrunk down to various tiny sizes suited for the leprechauns and the other fae folk of slight stature. It was quite a sight to see the little shadow nixie dance around on the table trying out a small mp3 player the very image of the popular silhouette advertisements.

The living room was set up like some kind of grand meeting hall. A few full sized metal fold out chairs were propped against the wall in either room for company that all the small size furniture wouldn't accommodate. Right now the meeting hall was set up for casual business meaning most of the furniture was against the wall except for a long couch a few feet in front of a large television screen depicting four first person perspectives of a man running about with a gun.

"Aye well, 'e's in the middle of... deliberations wit' a foreign entity but if ye would be willin ta wait a bit, I can see tha' the big boss is notified. Feel free to have a sit while ya do. I'll have someone bring a couple o' drinks by." Tristan gave a little bow as he motioned his head to the living room before moving away though a reduced sized hall on the other end of the room.

"Deliberations with a foreign entity?" Cassi asked.

"Means his girlfriend, the fairy, is in from Ireland" I said with a grin. "He won't be long or Tristan will send us out." I pulled out one of the metal chairs and unfolded it for Cassi before getting one of my own. Imagine waiting in the waiting room of a financial office of an incredibly successful group of stock traders if they were teenage boys. Three large TVs all sported video games the separate sound effects blending into some sort of disjointed techno beat that softly shook the floor beneath our feet. About a dozen of the leprechaun's were playing games from on top of small couches and that many more were moving about in the living area chatting back and forth, playing cards, wrestling, listening to music, or trying to impress one of various female fairy creatures also visiting the house. All in all thirty or so creatures of the fae type were milling about the room.

"How many of these guys actually live here?" Cassi asked looking about the room at all the various sights. "I mean this has got to be what... a three bedroom?"

"And one of them could be yours baby!" One of the card players shouted before ducking beneath the table as Cassi cast a glare his direction.

The other card players and myself couldn't help chuckling but, I eventually managed an answer. "Outside of the entry way and this room all the rooms have been split down into much smaller rooms. Counting the basement it is a twenty two bedroom five bath with one master suite set aside for Conroy, the eldest. I'm pretty sure they have a couple of kitchens and a weight room somewhere in there too.

"You know after the last couple of days, I was expecting a more complicated answer. Something like the house is bigger on the inside than it is on the outside.

"Like my pants!" a voice near one of the couches shouted back our direction.

Cassi sighed and looked back toward me. "And everything has better hearing than a human apparently."

"Just about. It seems supernatural really does mean "super natural" in that case I guess." It was about that moment that Conroy walked into the living room from a well hidden door in the far wall of the room a man who looked to be about eighteen or nineteen years old with the uniform red hair of the house's residents. He was dressed in black army boots and a dark gray kilt with his tiny muscled chest left bare. With the red hair combed and glued up into a fohawk style he looked like two and a half feet of celtic punk.

"Hey ya, Willie" Conroy said with a grin as he walked across the room toward us."Somethin' get so bad that you are actually willin' to put up with these scoundrels?" He laughed as he motioned to the occupants of the room.

"Yeah looks like it, Con." I said before reaching over and offering my fist toward the man. Handshakes are just awkward with someone less than half your size so, the fist bump had become my default greeting for all manner of little folk that kept up with modern society. "I've got elf problems."

"Ta' fair folk eh?" The leprechaun asked nodding his head. "Always good at somethin' ner good for anythin'. They bringing your trouble or causing it?"

"One of them crashed in a door and tried to take a shot at my friend Cassi here." I said as I pointed toward Cassi.

"Ahh, Cassi is the name of t'is angel young Tristan has already fallen so hard for. I'm Conroy leader o' tis rabble and it tis my honor, despite your company, to welcome you inta our home Miss...." Conroy asked placing his hand across his chest with a polite bow.

"Ro...." Cassi started to speak her last name in a polite tone apparently taken aback by the unique behavior of the gentlemen leprechaun. She didn't stop speaking until I reached up and placed my hand over her lips and shook my head. Cassi was bright and adapting to this world quickly too, but there were moments that it was obvious that she still had a lot to learn.

"Miss Cassi, friend of the local Initiative agent." I said looking to Conroy and shaking my head. "And my charge to protect under the old courtesies." It was nothing against Conroy personally. He most likely wasn't trying to trick Cassi out of her full name from her lips, but if he was struck with the want to commit mischief he would gladly use anything at his disposal.

"William Codex!" Conroy half shouted in offense as he stepped back a disappointed look growing across his face. "I had no intention o' using tha name agains' Miss Cassi. T'was nothin' more that an flailin' attempt at manners to bring a smile to tha pretty ladies face. Ya 'ave me word."

"And the word of every being in this room? Will you stake your honor and freedom on the behavior of this whole lot?" I asked looking at Cassi to catch her glance. She nodded and sent a mild glare back my way before digging in her purse and producing a small notepad. 'Things William better tell me about!' labeled the top of the page. I hadn't seen the notebook until now, but judging by the size of the list it had been started after she got home last night. I was going to be busy for a while once this whole matter was taken care of and we had time to address it. "What can you tell me about elf tattoos?" I asked turning my attention back to Conroy.

"Well 'hey aren't exactly enthusiasts." The little man said sitting back into an appropriately sized chair. "Not many of we immortal fae ar' really. I mean when one of ya mortals pick a tattoo that ya have ta live wit for life tha' means a sixty or seventy years commitment by tha time you get it. T'one tattoo I have is a mistake I've lived wit' it for twelve hundred years. But, a few sects or casts in elven culture use them as markers bu', even t'ose that don't see a bit of ink as mutilation, are very serious about it. Rights o' passage, outcast o', ascension of some form. Each in tha most extreme o' cases."

"Well what about an outward facing left palm with a dagger running over it?" I asked holding up my left hand to face Conroy and drawing a line down the center of my palm to indicate the placement of the blade.

"A pretender t' th' Order o' tha Open Palm." Conroy answered off hand as he looked at my palm and nodded his head in agreement with himself.

"How do you know it was pretender?" I asked. "And for that matter, who is the Order of the Open Palm?"

"T'are tha most feared group of independent assassins in all o' tha fair realms. T'kill without prejudice, care, o' remorse and they are all very good at it." Conroy answered. "Assassins o' tha order are tha stuff o' nightmares in the fair lands. Lords o' tha hunt and Fae royals are among tha ranks o' those they've killed. None of them have e're been caught. If it had not been a pretender, your friend would be dead o' Miss Cassi is a master swordswoman tha likes o' which no mortal has e're been."

Cassi's eyes widened as Conroy and I looked toward her and the sword hanging on her hip. It was then that I noticed several details about the girl. The second belt that held the sword was a thick hand tooled leather affair that looked to have been precisely measured to ensure that the blade hung perfectly at her side. It even had a matching pouch and delicate little elven silver clasp. She'd managed to carry a sword on her belt all day long. That doesn't seem like much of a feat, but for someone who has never done it, hauling around a five pound sword in a three pound metal scabbard over one hip can be a tiresome task, or at the very least, leave them bumping the tip of the sword into things as they walked by. Cassi hadn't accidently bumped the sword into anything all day. She'd been wearing the blade with proper gear and as if she was used to the weapons weight and size.

Cassi's hand gripped the blade of the sword an instant before I actually reached for the inside of my coat. Thankfully I did have a smaller weapon and the Colt cleared its holster before the sword had rung free.

Hopefully you never will find yourself in a room full of rowdy leprechauns; it normally doesn't go as smoothly as this visit had. However, if you do find yourself in such a situation one day, I can tell you an excellent way to shut them all up really quick.

Cassi's face was wide with shock as she looked toward the gun as her sword hung in the air at the ready. Her stance was perfect. The angle of the blade relative to my body was perfect. For all intensive reasons the coming strike should have been perfect and I had very little chance to block or get out of the way, but Cassi hesitated before the sword fell.

Stepping to the side away from the blade, I managed to buy myself enough time to bring up the Colt and block the edge of her blade with the bottom side of the barrel. Thankfully my favorite gun was one of the forged steel frames and not one of the newer aluminum ones or the blade might of chopped into the trigger housing or at least crushed the guard over my digit. Instead the clashing weapons let out a loud ring of steel on steel. My left hand flew up out of instinct and gripped Cassi's sword arm by the wrist digging my fingers into the tendons of her wrist and pressing against the back of her hand with my thumb. From there it was matter of leverage to press the blade down onto the neck of the person I had until now thought was Cassi.

"Where is she?" I shouted as I pushed the Cassi pretender against the wall bringing the sword closer to her neck. "What the hell have you done with Cassi!" Another press of my hand brought the blade ever closer and set the barrel of my gun into her shoulder at the joint.

Cassi, or whatever had taken her shape, looked up toward me, her eyes welling with tears. "Will. What are you talking about? It's me." She started trying to push the back of her head through the wall behind her to get further away from the blade. "Oh God. Oh God. Oh God. I'm me Will I swear." She was trying to hold back sobs.

"How do I know that? Where did you get that sword? How did you know what to do at Hannelore's threshold? Where did you learn to speak Gaelic?"

"I heard Hannelore in my head when she looked at my eyes!" Cassi sobbed "I don't know how to speak Gaelic! I got the sword ....I got the swo..." She paused and looked at the blade resting at her neck before looking back up to me her eyes red and her cheeks streaked with tears. "Oh God Will I don't know where I got that sword. It isn't the sword from my apartment. I swear!"

It's funny how adrenaline affects your brain. My body had reacted faster than I had known it was capable of. Stranger still however was that in that next infinite second a thousand different thoughts bounced about in my head. How many ways could this situation play out? Could I parry a second blow from that sword with my gun? What if I had just put a sword to the neck and a gun into the arm of the girl that a moment ago I was reminiscing about kissing, and I had done it for no reason?

"Ok. Here's how we are playing this out." I said doing everything I could to keep my tone level as I let a bit of pressure off the sword. "I'm going to step away, but until I'm out of sword reach the gun is staying pointed right at your shoulder. It won't kill you, but it will hurt. I hope this is me being paranoid, Cassi, I really do, but if you bring that blade to bare, my finger is going to move without me even giving it permission." I said as I let loose of the sword, took a single step back, and paused before starting to talk again. That never happened.

Have you ever been hit across the face with brass knuckles? Well, just in case you were curious, the massive steel hand guard of a basket hilt feels about the same. It wasn't a precise punch and I doubted that under normal circumstances that it would have been all that powerful. However, the angry redhead stepped forward and brought the strike up with everything she had body and soul. I managed to hold on to the fact that no one had ever taken me down in a single punch. However, I was forced back several steps, shaking the stars from my head, and trying to get my vision to widen back as I leaned back against one of the leprechaun sized couches. The sound of tiny sized screams broke the silence as its occupants retreated while I fell over the furniture and I went to the floor taking the fall on my shoulder I had slammed into the gate at Gregorie's, sending a shock of pain across my back and my arm. That couldn't be healthy.

"New deal, William Codex." Cassi started her own tone quiet and level as she stalked across the room toward me and stopped at the edge of the couch. "You are going to tell me everything." She said as she tossed the little notebook onto my chest. "I don't know what the hell is happening to me and you're leaving me in the dark half the time isn't helping. I know what the hell a threshold is. I can fight with a damn sword. A sword that until a moment ago I thought was my ex's stupid cheap katana. And for some reason every time I manage to put together what the hell happened to me when I touched that amulet I don't know rather I want to kiss you again or kill you for what I think you did!" She spat. "Start talking now and don't think about moving from right there until you tell me what the hell is happening to me!"

"Well..." I managed to start causing a laugh to break out across the room.

"Oi, Willie." called Tristan. "Lik'em wit a little fire doncha boyo!" Said the leperchaun with a laugh as he walked in having aparently just arrived after the confrontation to see Cassi standing over me with the sword. "I'd be explainin' yourself right quick lad."

"It's empathy. Granted, I've never heard of a case quite this powerful, but it's still technically empathy I guess." I started looking toward Cassi from the floor while propped up on my elbows. The sword wasn't at the ready. Still, with the speed she had moved, I was pretty sure that if she wanted it wouldn't be too hard to lay into me with the blade before I could get to my gun that now rested just a few inches outside my reach. "It just looks like you take back more than purely emotional impressions. Memories, knowledge, training. If it wasn't for the fact that you actually hadn't wanted to hit me with the sword I wouldn't have been able to block that attack."

"But the sword. I don't even remember it until I saw it up close." Cassi said motioning with the sword. "My ex's sword is in a bright blue plastic sheath with a dragon painted on it. I don't really see how I got the two mixed up."

I closed my eyes in thought trying to go back over what of the situation I knew. "Wait, you said you chopped off the guys arm?" I asked.

"Yeah, at least that is how I remember it." Cassi said with a sigh, but her stance stayed just as firm as it had been a moment ago. I would have rather been toe to toe with Brandon the werewolf again than in this kind of a spot.

"Stress hormones dumped into your brain along with adrenaline during the time of the attack would have heightened your reflexes and attention to detail to help you survive, but an overdose of those hormones can lead to short term memory loss. They will also grant you incredible focus in the present. Kind of like it'll help you remember brain chemistry formulas you haven't studied in six and a half years." I started. "Your brain would then try to put together the details of things you experienced with things you know. For instance, you cut off the elf's arm but you didn't know about the sword you did it with because it was brought into your world while you were in a state of incredible stress. When your mind put it back together it replaced it in memory with one you knew about. It's the same reason why witnesses to a crime or participants in a bar fight can never remember exactly what happened or more often than not have different stories." I said, taking a breath. "A wall hanger katana wouldn't have been capable of taking off someone's arm."

"That doesn't explain why I picked it up and strapped it to my hip." She said waving the sword in front of her in a complicated salute before returning it to the sheath at her side. "Or how I could do that!"

"Well, you could have at some point in the struggle made physical contact with your attacker and with his training with the sword being at the front of his mind as he came at you, you happened to take part of it back with you. That could have in return given you the reflexive knowledge you needed to disarm him and hit him with his own blade. One that I bet could lob off a limb." I sat up a little bit more while I thought over the rest of the situation. "Then when you realized after...." I stopped and looked about to the leprechauns and little fae gathered about the room listening to the fight in their living room with rapt attention. "...after our conversation, that you were going to be part of this case, your mind went for the most powerful weapon available to you by instinct." Cassi started to interrupt me again, but I stopped her with a hand. "Your imprint of the attackers skills causing you to pick up your trusted companion blade before going for the wall hanger sword that had actually been in your possession for a long time. Your subconscious and conscious brain would have conflicted and edited out the error by making you, for the time being, believe that the sword had always been about."

"Damn, ya would t'ink he was some sorta detective or somthin' like tha'." said Conroy from his place in his chair on the oposite side of the room. His comment caused him to catch Cassi's glare for a moment. "Whut! Y'listin' to the same damn speech I am angel?" He asked before he crossed one leg over the other unashamed of the kilt, the very picture a celtic punk godling sitting upon his upholstered throne in miniature.

Cassi shook her head and turned away from Conroy before looking back at me. "So during Hannelore's stare thing I realized what she was doing and when I touched your amulet I saw..."

"The horrible actions of a deceived young man before I joined the Initiative." I interrupted glancing about me to the spectators. My past was far from clean, Cassi knew that much at least, and the last thing I needed was to have my sins advertised to those I was supposed to keep within the law. "The same thing I see most nights when I sleep."

"Ok." Cassi said taking a deep breath and nodding her head. "One more important thing on the list Will, at least for right now. The one that's underlined. It's been in my head all day."

I sighed with relief before getting the whole of my weight under me and leaning over to grab the Colt and put it back in its holster. Sitting to my knees, I looked at the list and scanned it over. We had gone over a couple of items in the standoff but the one with the underline made me laugh out of reflex. "What are brownies? They are chewy, gooey and, delicious with milk." I said shrugging my shoulders. "We can go get some after we get out of here if you want." I said shaking my head. Maybe the stress of the last couple of days had gotten to her worse than I thought.

Cassi gave the last remnants of a heated glare before it melted into a grin, then a chuckle before finally dissolving into a laugh "That isn't what I meant. At least I don't think."

"Y'where probably talkin' 'bout the fair folk tha' made tha' sword o' your's angel." Conroy said taking a long pull of his freshly delivered beer as he wrapped his arm about the waist of the svelte beauty near his own height, quite impressive for her people, with light green skin and long violet hair.

She wore, well she wore nothing. A wild flower turned playboy bunny and the only flaw on the creature was an elaborate calligraphy "C" tattooed on her hip. It wasn't the first time I'd seen Nyx, but there was just a certain disarming power in the presence of the fairy. Granted it could have had something to do with that fact that despite her obvious non-human features, or the fact that she was just as immortal as Conroy, Nyx still looked far too young and far too... gown up at the same time to be walking about naked. She just waved and smiled. Like most of her kind I suspected Nyx had not bothered to learn a language sine Latin. Like most of her kind she rarely spoke, or at least that's what pixies want you to think. I think. I think they think. I....no that's just a dangerous cycle of thought.

"Oh those Brownies." I said as I looked to Cassi's sword as I stood up fully. "They are the smiths of the fae. Masters of the forge and various other crafts. They say no art they put their minds to can be rivaled by mortal men."

"Not really a fair contest. Most o' their works take longer t'an a human life ta make." Conroy said. "E'pecially ta creation o' one o" the Claiomh Solais."

"A sword of light?" Cassi asked before she realized she was translating Gaelic again.

"I thought there was only one of those." I said looking to Conroy shaking my head. "It was supposed to have been wielded by a king of the Tuatha Dé."

"The people of God?" Cassi asked. "You mean... angels?"

"That's still up for debate." I said shaking my head. "Some say it was a tribe of devout worshipers, some worship them, some say it refers to angels, and some say it is talking about the Nephilim."

"What?" Cassi asked, she and Conroy both looking at me.

"The children of the sons of God and daughters of men. The Bible mentions them in Genesis." I said looking towards the two. "What?"

"It says that in the Bible?" Cassi asked.

"Ye be readin' tha Bible?" Conroy asked causing Nyx to giggle presumably at his tone of voice and not her understanding of the English he was speaking.

"Yes and yes." I said as I looked toward the others in turn. "Conroy do you mean there are multiples of that sword?"

"Always 'ave been, just haven't been called by their given name. I'm sure half a dozen brownies would try ta claim ta have brought a hammer down o'er tha piece of steel tha' became Excalibur. I know for a fact tha' Miyamoto Musashi wielded a Claiomh Solais for a while after he won it in a duel t'ward tha end o' his life."

"So it is less a term for a magical sword and more a term for magical swords in general." I asked.

"More like a honorific for a class o' magical weapons." Conroy responded.

Cassi who had recently redrawn the blade to look over its surface in fascination as we talked about it spoke up. "And if I won it off the man who came to kill me with it?" She asked looking toward Conroy before looking back at me.

"T'would make it your's, Angel." He said with a grin and a wink. "Not many mortals 'ave ever laid claim ta such a weapon. Use it well and be careful. While such t'ings oft find themselves on tha path of those wit' great destiny, it very rarely finds it way t'ere for no reason. The life o' one who wields a Claiomh Solais is oft' fraught with danger."

"A life destined for danger. Newly found physic powers. I've taken the arm off my enemy? And now I have a freaking 'light saber?'" Cassi said with a grin as she turned the blade about in a repeat of her salute and dropped the blade home in the scabbard. "I. Am. A. Freaking. Jedi."

As soon as we could get the couch turned back over for the leprechauns, Cassi and I made our way back out to the truck. Evening was starting to fall over the world from the east. It was chasing the sun during the last leg of its journey over the sky painting over the bright yellows and oranges of the sunset with the dark blues and purples of twilight with a thin stripe of star lit blackness in the far eastern sky. By the time the two of us climbed into the truck Cassi's demeanor was mostly back to the way it had been before the scene I'd managed to start in the house. Still, I knew better than to think that it only took about an hour to be forgiven for pulling a gun on a friend.

"So, immortal elf assassins are starting to work in the area. We don't know what greater motives they have, but they killed a werewolf pack's alpha female. They also seem to be after me. I can't speak for your werewolf friend Will, but I haven't ever been involved in anything that would get the attention of normal hit men much less killers from another plane of existence." Cassi said, as she set the sword beside her in the seat before she started to giggle. "I really don't do anything half way."

"I noticed." I said with a nod and a grin as I flipped through a few local radio stations looking for some sort of news. I hadn't gotten any updates from my own resources about Gregorie's situation, but that just meant that nothing major had actually developed that got caught in the information mining the Initiative did. With any luck someone was monitoring things closely enough not to miss anything, but it wouldn't have been the first time.

Things looked all clear until I settled onto a station that was broadcasting a low official voice with only a few vague signs of an

East Texas accent. So far groups of hunters had started patrolling the area looking for anything that fit the description of the leaked pictures. Apparently a couple of pigs and a large dog had been shot in cases of mistaken identity. As of yet no people had been caught in the cross fire, but there had been several conflicts with local land owners and law enforcement over trespassing. It wasn't a good situation, but it wasn't as bad as I had expected when a photo of "Big Foot" got released into the media of East Texas during the heart of hunting season. Turning the radio back to my classic rock station, I leaned back in the seat of the truck as I drove down the road.

"Thinking of the next step?" Cassi asked a few words after an Iron Maiden song started into full swing.

I nodded my head in response.

"Not quite used to talking shop in public?"

A shake of my head marked my response this time around.

"Well you're supposed to talk out problems on occasion. I hear good things about that."

A shrug crawled up my shoulders as we turned onto the highway.

"You're just doing this to mess with me now aren't you Will?"

I nodded. The smile creeping across my lips almost managed to stay hidden.

"Very funny." Cassi said dryly before leaning back in her seat. "So whatever we have coming up next, how about we make part of it food?

I couldn't help but to nod my head and grabbed my phone and waited for the voice on the other end to let me know I had called Howies Pizza and that he would be, despite the tone of his voice, happy to help me. "Yeah I'd like to make an order for delivery." I replied as I closed in on the street that led toward my house.

Thirty minutes or less later we were sitting in the living room over a large pepperoni with a beer for myself and an impressively improvised iced coffee for Cassi, considering it had been her first endeavor in my decidedly bachelor kitchen. "Do you think the elves think I'm a threat? A threat they want to strike down before I become a real issue."

"It seems a bit far to go out of their way unless they have special information like a prophecy or the like." I said, grabbing a slice of pizza for myself before leaning back onto the couch.

"Prophecy?" Cassi said with a quirk of her brow. "I guess at this point I shouldn't be surprised. Still you're talking about people who can see the future."

"It isn't an exact science or anything. If that was the case we would have a continuous streak of lotto winners. An event has to carry a certain gravity to the person predicting the events in question."

Cassi sighed as she leaned back with her piece of pizza. "You must have an amazing benefits package to put up with all this, Will."

"The pay and the time off are great, but I don't really get much of an opportunity to take time or spend the money." I said with a shrug. "Health insurance is second to none, but that is more like the government protecting an investment. Men and woman capable of working this job aren't exactly a dime a dozen. They don't want us breaking down or becoming mentally unstable." I managed before taking another bite of pizza.

"So the illusion of the underpaid courageous public servant is just that?"

I couldn't help but to laugh. "Depends on how you look at it. My wage is a step or two above standard government pay grade for a highly educated FBI agent with five years experience and I have a yearly vehicle allowance and travel budget on top of that, but I also have to cover a large portion of my operating expenses due to the nature of my work. In the end, I still do really well for a bachelor after paying out for a lot of my equipment and extra travel expenses, but I won't be buying a yacht soon." Whatever Cassi was going to say caused her eyes to light, but the comment that gathered behind her eyes never got to see its birth before it was cut short by a knock on the door.

"Hold that thought." I said standing up and setting down my pizza slice on the open top of the box before walking toward the door and looking out the peep hole. "What the hell..." I started, before stepping back and motioning to and pointing to the door to my room with urgency. "Hold on!" I shouted toward the door.

A few second later after Cassi slid off the couch grabbed her coffee, another slice of pizza and her sword before slinking across the room and into the hall that held the door to my room. Seeing her disappear from my field of vision I turned back about and opened the door. "Sergeant Walters." I said with a nod. "I wasn't exactly expecting to see you directly. At least not until I came to track you down tomorrow."

The man looked like more of a hard ass out of uniform if that was possible. I had grown up knowing he was boot leather tough my whole life, but I'd never been the object of his ire. Worn working jeans and old boots with a button down black shirt and a matching felt cowboy hat. The permanent indention from his pack of cigarettes was still present in the shirt but the pack was long gone. Walters hadn't smoked in months. Those blue eyes seemed to bounce back a bit more light than they should have from beneath the rim of that hat.

"Yeah, well you're not exactly easy to find, Codex. As soon as the story breaks I go to the expert in the field with all this strange stuff and he is nowhere to be found." Walter said his face not changing from his neutral tone. "I call the number on that card you gave me and some Poindexter gets flustered then hands me over to an old warhorse who tries to bounce me around claiming that you are out cleaning up my mess." He said with a shake of his head. "Not good form Codex, not for the first time we crossed paths."

"Hey the desk jockeys can be a hassle in my office too. Be honest I didn't exactly look for you, that much of it is my fault." I said motioning my head inside. "Come on in have a slice of pizza and a beer if you're off duty. We'll trade notes." I said turning my back to the man and walking back to the table.

"Well, I can't do the pizza anymore, heartburn, but I'll take you up on that beer." Said the older cop as he followed me in. "You have much trouble other than that mess near Little Sandy?"

I managed not to show any of the surprise on my face, but I couldn't help but to be more than a little impressed at the deduction. "What gave away that I had anything to do with that?" I said motioning toward the couch before I walked into the kitchen to grab another beer. "I thought my clean up guys had that one buttoned up pretty tight."

"Yeah they did, but I noticed a few of the names on the accident reports we got from DPS and realized most of them frequented the same dive bar just outside of Lindale. The odds just got too high, so I got to thinking something was up." He said as he grabbed the beer I offered him.

"Oh damn Codex not you too. A friend of mine's kid drinks his at room temp too." He said with a shrug before taking a drink of the dark beer. "Anyway, I went by and asked about anyone else who ran with those boys. Dug up the name of their unofficial ring leader. Get pointed at a lowlife named Derik Marshall, and I come to find out he's hospitalized at one of the big hospitals here in Tyler. Animal attack they are calling it, saying he was trying to sneak onto the Little Sandy reserve to get a shot at "Big Foot". Couldn't avoid a nice big circle of clues like that. You might as well have signed your name to Marshall's forehead."

I nodded my head and sighed. Someone wouldn't have to have been smart to think through all that but they would have had to have been determined, know their patrol and that I was on the case to figure it all out. "Not bad, you track clues like you did that trail yesterday morning." I said taking a drink of my own beer and grabbing a second slice before taking a seat on my chair. "Doesn't explain how you got here. Last time I checked I wasn't in the book."

"Only thing I've been tracking longer than a clue trail is a deer trail kid. You're a bit harder to find than either, but a few guys in Tyler PD owed me a favor. I called in those markers and put out an unofficial bolo. Got a call about twenty minutes ago that you parked behind this place. I called off the dogs after that and headed on over." Walters said with a grin. "No worries, I know how things work. Your address is safe with me."

"Never doubted it." I said taking a long pull of my beer. "So, you get anything extra on those killings? My lab guys are stumped."

"Yeah, mine are saying it definitely isn't human." Walters said with a chuckle and a shake of his head. "Current horrible idea is that a bear got to them. In North East Texas we have seen them in the last few years, but that just doesn't stack up, bears leave foot prints."

"Just a wild theory. How would you track something that big if it could fly?" I said shrugging my shoulders and finishing off my beer.

"How many of those have you had, Codex?" Walters asked his eyebrows rising most of the distance of his forehead. "Giant killer birds?"

"If the shoe fits." I said with a sigh. "Can't be tracked moving over open ground, leaves tracks in the woods and it moves really fast. If you can't think of anything that makes sense, you go with the facts you have."

"Why is it every time I have one of these talks with one of you federal types things get weird?" The old cop said with a sigh. "Had to be …. ten years ago I guess. Got caught up in a case with some guy named Gideon. Damn tough son of a bitch, but he wasn't nearly as easy to get along with as you kid. The cold shoulder comes with time?"

"Wouldn't know, he must have been before my time." I lied smoothly. "What about that flying death machine of ours?"

Walters shook his head as he took another drink of his beer. "Hell, best I could figure was more of a Big Foot type. I know it sounds crazy, but someone who knows how to move over ground without leaving tracks could have pulled it off. Flying seems a bit crazy."

"Something that heavy would have a hard time of it though wouldn't it?" I asked. Gregorie could move through the forest without a trail if he made an effort of it, but that had more to do with his connection to the wild.

"Hmmm a hard time but it wouldn't be impossible. Still doesn't tell me what could pull it off, but I would look for entrance and exit points in the woods. Flying or moving careful, something that big would leave a mark in tight quarters." The old cop looked even older for a moment before he looked up toward me. "Look, Codex, I know you're not supposed to tell me some things about this case, but I know there are things out there in the night. I've been working this job for over thirty years. I also knew a few of those boys who you covered up the deaths of." he said locking those old experienced blue eyes onto mine. "They weren't the best of characters, but I'd been chasing a few of them since they were knee high. Don't much care what I have to do, but I want my shot at this thing."

I looked the man across from me over and couldn't help but respect that man who had come to my door, but despite the fact that he didn't remember it, I knew the Walters behind the badge. Good cops are more common than most people would like to think, but the Walters I knew came from a different generation of officer. He came from my father's generation. Men and women who didn't take up the shield because it was a solid career path or because it provided state benefits. People like Walters wanted to see right done and very rarely cared about the price.

A man who at one time shared the lease he and my father hunted on had fallen on hard times. Between the two of them they hunted every tag the two of them could and got a few other people who had no interest in hunting to buy a license to get them more tags to fill. Between one deer season and a few grocery trips paid anonymously ,they made sure that man kept his family fed. It was in the strictest sense illegal, but they had done what they saw as right.

I nodded my head. "Fair enough Walters, you're in." I said taking the measure of the man in front of me knowing him much better than he would ever know. "I got a few rules to go over with you, but the big one is that you take my lead on this. The trails I follow don't have things you know how to handle on the other end."

"Fair enough, Codex, but why don't you go ahead and call Miss Ross out of the back? She's up to her neck in this mess whether she knows it or not, and needs to hear what I found out about the murder she ran up upon." Walters added as he nodded his head towards the bedroom.

I turned about and raised an eyebrow. "What are you talking about, Walters?" I grabbed another slice of pizza.

"The car chase and motor cycle wreck last night. The attack in Longview and the fact that when I called up Tony, the medical examiner, he said Ms. Ross's car was picked up by an FBI office aide. Not to mention that the cop that called in that 'be on the lookout' said you had a passenger. And the spot I'm sitting in is still warm." Walters said with a grin. "The pretty little girl who gets her nose into things in her sleep and the mysterious federal agent. Hell I couldn't have wrote a more blatant set up if I was trying to write one of those old detective books."

I sighed and shook my head before looking toward the room and speaking up. "Story of my life. Ok Cassi, come on out, the grownup has figured us out."

A moment later the door opened and Cassi walked out with her hair freshly braided back, coffee in one hand, and sheathed sword grasped by the scabbard in her other hand. Cassi, the avenging angel of early morning sleepiness, looked to me for a lead. I nodded my head before she turned about and set the sword against the TV stand, not willing to let go of her coffee. "Hello, officer Walters." Cassi nodded before walking back toward the pizza box, grabbing a new slice of pizza and taking a seat on the other side of the couch beside Walters' and next to mine. "What is it that I need to know?"

The Sergeant removed his black hat as Cassi walked into the room. "Well, we've managed to get positive ID on the two victims, dental records. Ms. Ross, does the name Andrew Wilson mean anything to you?" Walters asked.

Cassi started to speak but stopped before shaking her head. "I.... I don't think so officer. Should I?" she questioned. "It....feels familiar."

"That would be because it is on your birth certificate." The man said flatly his eyes examining her reaction. "He was your father Miss Ross."

"Oh. Well I've never met him actually. He and my mother weren't together by the time I was born and he was nowhere to be found. My grandparents were well off enough that Mom never hounded him for child support. I don't really know anything about him" She said with a sigh. "When I was....they both..." Cassi said with a sigh before looking down. "The other man was my brother, my half-brother wasn't he?"

I exhaled as I leaned over and placed my hand on her back as I saw Cassi start to make sense of the vision she'd had prior to her involvement. It couldn't have been too long after Sue had been killed. If I hadn't been sent to respond to the call that far south I would have likely been at the scene when she ran up.

Wait a second. Sue died around the same time as the attack happened north of Tyler. Two supernatural killings on the same night and at the same time. That was almost too much to take in stride.

"From what we can tell Mr. Wilson had built another life for himself shorty after you were born and married Sharron Kingston, your brother's mother, a couple of years after you were born." Walter's said with a sigh. "Your brother, the second victim, had turned nineteen this year."

Cassi looked up from her hands and back toward Walters a furious wall of grey had already started to form behind her green eyes. She and I knew what had done this and she had stood face to face with it. With her father's killer. It had even spoken to her.

"Found you." The words bounced around in my head with hundreds of other facts that were starting to take shape. The Wendigo had killed Cassi's father. It had also gone after her. The elf from the Order of the Open Palm had also taken a shot at her. Could he have done so after following us to her home, after we'd out foxed his partner on the road? If I'd been wrong that he would stop and help his fellow attacker it would have been difficult yet not impossible to get back on our trail. A blacked out bike with no running lights would have been almost impossible to spot on the dark highway as well. That would mean that the same people that killed Sue were after Cassi and that they were likely after her for the same reasons. And if the elf that attacked Cassi was linked to the car chase it would mean that the order wanted her enough to send at least two assassins after her.

I caught Cassi's gaze as she looked up in my direction. Her eyes were full of grief and fear. She was quickly starting to fall into a downward spiral. You could see the cracks forming in her façade, but all of that ended in her eyes. Her brow was narrowed and her fists were clinched. She was standing at the edge and the world was starting to push her over, but she wasn't going without a fight. Not only was she going to press on, but I could tell she was churning through the facts in her head as well. Could she be coming to the same conclusions about the attacks that I was?

"Miss Ross, I can't say I know what you have on your plate feels like, but I know I don't envy you." Walters said breaking the silence. "But, I've dealt with more than one situation that didn't fall within the normal law before. Always been a few of us around here willing to step up and do what needs to be done and occasionally we are lucky enough to have one of these invisible government types around. Damn handy they are but the last one lived a little ways north of Houston as best as I can figure. Where did you go to school, Codex?"

"Sam Houston University, just a little ways north of Houston." I replied with a knowing grin. There is a whole language of not saying things you learn in certain professions, law enforcement officers at the local, state, and federal level are all masters of the secret tongue of exclusion.

Walters just nodded, a gesture that said more than the man would have ever wished to express out loud, and I seriously considered dropping a letter to Gideon to ask just how far he and Walters went back.

"What does the college Will went to have to do with anything?" Apparently it was Cassi's turn to break the silence. "Oh, I get it. This isn't your first rodeo is it, Sergeant?"

Walters just shook his head. I was definitely going to have to talk to Gideon when this was all over.

Cassi's eyes went wide and she looked from me to the old officer. "Oh don't start that silent head shaking on me!" She said pointing an accusing finger at me. "I just went off at this one about it!"

Two hours later, a while after darkness had fully fallen over the city, Walters had departed knowing the high points of the events of the last couple of days. I hadn't gone out and told him exactly what the Wendigo was, but I told him enough to know better than to go after the creature until we knew how to take it down. He'd also volunteered to take one or two things off of my 'to-do' list. He claimed I looked like the walking dead and that people his age barely slept anyway.

I mentioned that Cassi's attacker and the murders were linked in some manner, but it was no lie to tell him that I didn't know how yet. I didn't go into the reason why Cassi was the target but he didn't pry either. A guy like Walters didn't need to know why a young woman was being attacked by monsters and assassins. He just needed to know something was being done to stop it and that he was a part of that effort. He also didn't need to know about Sue's murder. Thankfully he was good enough not to question what had happened when I brought up the possibility of a ploy.

All in all, Walters had a kind of appreciation of the knowledge I could offer that could only have come from doing this kind of thing before. Generally you try not to throw the 'You aren't cleared to know this' line at a law enforcement officer. They begrudgingly accept it, but at best they are going to complain a good bit. At worse you lose an ally in short order. Walters knew better than to want to know too much. I couldn't help but be glad that I had the support of a man like him. Walters was good people. I knew from experience, whether he remembered it right now or not, that the old cop was a force to be reckoned with or without a badge.

As soon as the man had tipped his hat and walked out the door, Cassi looked toward me. "That guy is more than a little frightening." She said with a shiver. "He comes across all calm and still but just under the surface he is a wound spring. Always ready. Never resting. He is going to pack a punch, but I don't know if he'll survive it."

"The phrase we common country folk would use is that he isn't as good as he once was, but he is as good once as he ever was." I said with a grin as I locked the door before returning and sitting beside Cassi on the couch. "If it comes to that, Walters will give it everything he's got, and it might take him a while to pick himself up, but he'll get the pieces back together in good time after things settle. If he can't manage it, he'll spend the rest of his days fishing, hunting, and drinking cold beer knowing he did all he could."

"What if he doesn't survive it?" Cassi asked as she walked into the kitchen and started working more coffee maker magic.

"Then Walters would tell you that he would be spending the rest of his days fishing, hunting and, drinking cold beer. He would just be doing it somewhere else with the buddies that have gone on before."

Cassi stopped what she was doing and looked at me. "Wow.... I mean I guess it makes sense but it just hit me. With all these strange and magical things that exist, God must actually be real. I mean in one way or another. Maybe?"

I couldn't help but chuckle as I nodded my head after following her into the kitchen. "Yeah, stuff that far up the supernatural food chain is a bit sketchy, but the first time you see a man of faith bring that belief to bare against something truly evil, you can't doubt the existence of God anymore."

"I mean I always thought he was real. I mean I believe, but to know. I mean you don't see belief like that very often. Unless you get to see it I guess. You must be fairly die hard about religion if for nothing else for job security."

"Faith doesn't work like that actually. If you think it is hard for someone who doesn't know to believe imagine having to believe blindly while knowing absolutely. God is real. He could show up here right now and shake your hand if He desired. He could come kill the Wendigo. Convert the Order of the Open Palm with the sound of His breath. He could send down archangels to drive the horrors of the dark away and keep us all safe. But He doesn't." I said taking one of the pair of iced coffees Cassi set out on the counter. "He and I aren't exactly on speaking terms."

Cassi just stared for a moment before taking up her own coffee and taking a slow sip. After a quiet moment or six she spoke. "I see what you mean. Easy to believe. Hard to believe in." I nodded. Another long moment passed before she started again. "I think I still do."

"You should. Faith is good for the soul, and if nothing else, can be a damn powerful weapon in the world you've just begun to live in."

"What made you lose yours, Will?" She asked as we both walked back toward the living room and taking back our seats on the couch.

I looked toward the girl sitting across from me once we were settled and hesitated before I dared to speak. "What did you see when you grabbed my amulet?" I finally asked leaving the question to hang in the air like a spontaneous lead fog had moved over the room and settled into place.

"I don't really remember." Cassi said right away as she brought her legs up in front of her and wrapped her hands about her knees one still holding tightly onto her coffee cup. An instinctive defensive position. Whatever she had seen, it wasn't good. "I mean...it was just flashes of things. Most of it was emotional. It was like I was locked in an embrace that smothered me with so much love I thought I would choke. Warming me so much that I thought I would burn to ashes. Incredible love, horrible fear, savage hate, and searing grief. What in the world happened, Will?"

I took a deep breath and wished there was something a bit stronger than coffee in my cup before I let sound cross my lips again. "It was about six years ago. I was working on finishing up school. My girlfriend at the time, Bethany, had gotten into trouble with something supernatural. She'd taken something she couldn't pay for. And the rightful owners were going to send their equivalent of collectors after her. Granted she was... under the sway of something and it had twisted her up pretty bad. I was young, pliable and in love. That is what you had to be to kill the enemies she had made. It was a defense mechanism. You had to harm them out of love, not anger or hate, in order to kill them. A sob story and few well done lies later, I marched into an Initiative safe house and killed anything that moved. She had told me that the changelings that lived there were horrible creatures that used an innocent appearance to take their victims guard down."

"What's a changeling, Will?" Cassi asked quietly from behind her cocooned form.

"They are, they were, the children of a now extinct race of old fae that could successfully conceive a child with humans." I said with a sigh. "Much older than the elves by all accounts, at least the fae parents of the changelings were. We haven't seen any of that race for a long time. The changelings were the last link we had to them."

"The last link as if, they aren't around anymore?"

"The only ones left that the Initiative knew about were in that safe house the night I hit it." "This was before you were a member right?"

I nodded my head. "Bethany's sob story involved letting me in on the supernatural world. I was just another overworked under slept college student before then." I took a long drink of the coffee.

"And you trusted her. … That bitch!" Cassi said before unfolding and standing to her feet then pacing across the room and grabbing up her new sword. As soon as her hand touched the blade I could feel the pulse of energy reverberate through the room banishing the heavy dark air that had gathered about the room. "That's just sick." Cassi said looking at her own hand holding the sword and grinning. "I don't think the sword likes her either."

I shook my head and tried to chuckle. "No, I guess not. Can't say I blame either of you. Bethany isn't to blame. She isn't herself anymore."

"Typical." Cassi said shaking her head. "What is it? Victim of circumstance or maybe the whole misunderstood thing? Oh no wait. Was she trying to do the right thing?" Cassi said rolling her eyes as she sat back down beside me and took her sword up by the scabbard lightly tapped the basket hilt of her sword on one of the growing collection of sore spots on my head. "Why are the good men so dense?"

Seeing Cassi suddenly stand up, take up a sword and go to my aid made something inside me warm, but that wasn't something that could be afforded right now, and all the old tropes aside it really wasn't Bethany's fault. "She's possessed."

"What? Like spinning head and pea soup possessed?" Cassi asked setting the sword aside.

"Not exactly, more like the spirit of an ancient Greek deity taking up residence in her mind kind of possession. Not as evil but just as dangerous." I leaned back against the back of the couch my empty coffee cup left on the table in front of me. "Some call it a mantle of power. A being sometimes old, always powerful with such a metaphysical presence that when its physical form dies the energy has to continue on. Each has its own line of inheritance or rite of passage, and they trickle down through the ages sometimes keeping the same persona for thousands of years sometimes taking on new names with the times, or in the case of some, with each new host."So, your college sweetheart is the vessel of a retired god?"

"Goddess technically. Nemesis, the goddess of revenge." I said with a chuckle. "All in all the worse ex a guy could ask for." I laughed. "I haven't managed a successful date in years. Last time she saw me out with someone she burned down the restaurant we were eating in."

"Why haven't you gone all FBI on her?" Cassi said punching my shoulder lightly.

"Honestly, I've tried. She is too good. All through school I was second place. Bethany was first. She didn't even try as hard as I did. You toss all that knowledge in with the experience and some of the power of what most people used to think was a god, I am going to have to bring a better game than I currently have to run her down."

"And she has something to hold over you if you try and miss." Cassi said answering her own next question. I would have tried a long time ago, but Bethany made no effort to hide the fact that if I came at her she would strike out at those close to me.

"That and the fact that only she, Gideon, and myself know the full scope of what I did that night. You know half of it now, that's more than most." I said looking towards Cassi who silently met my gaze before slipping across the couch, folding her legs beneath her and leaning her head on my shoulder before closing her eyes.

I was professional, not dead. I couldn't help but grin as I pulled my arm up and over the warm body laying against me and rested my head over Cassi's as I let my gaze linger over her delicate curving form. Soft beauty wrapped over a subtle strength. It was becoming painfully apparent that her presence was taking hold of me. My job didn't exactly have a history of making relationships easy. Not to mention the afore-mentioned revenge goddess powered ex. But even as thoughts of the danger continued to spin in my head the warmth of another next to me and the trials of the last two days started to take their toll on my eyes and before I had noticed it, they had drifted closed and for a few hours, the world and all its stresses disappeared.

Morning came an instant later. The sunlight filtering through the blinds, reflected off glass over a picture hanging in my living room and back into my eyes refusing to leave me alone until I forced my eyes open. My couch wasn't the most comfortable sleeping surface I had, but waking up on the uncomfortable leather couch wasn't so bad with a beautiful woman still laying against you.

At some point in the night I had leaned far enough down in the chair and my feet had laid up upon the table allowing Cassi to lay her head against my lap as she hugged her sword to her chest with one hand and let the other rest over her chest her fingers wound with my own. I started to shift my weight trying to find the best way out from beneath the sleeping beauty atop me without waking her. It took several moments but I managed to slip free and stood up before grabbing a pillow and starting to slip it beneath Cassi's head.

She growled as she grabbed at the pillow and pulled it beneath her. "Come back with coffee agent or don't come back at all." She mumbled from beneath her pillow.

"Yes ma'am." I said with a chuckle as I finished stretching my arms out and walking toward the kitchen.

"Good boy." Cassi said, with an audible grin as I disappeared into the kitchen to start coffee for the day.

I was halfway through the coffee when I heard another grumble back in the living room and the sound of two feet hitting the wood floor and moving toward the kitchen. A moment later Cassi walked into the kitchen her half shut eyes void of thought or emotion. She crossed toward me, grasped my shoulder, turned me about putting the small of my back into the counter, grasped my jacket lapels, pulled them aside, and ran her fingers on the soft cotton of my shirt studying the cloth with her fingertips. Then, much to my chagrin, she stopped and thought something over in her mind and stood on her tip toes and kissed me on the cheek before disappearing out of the kitchen and down the hall to my bedroom.

"What the hell?" I muttered before turning back around to finish setting up the coffee and turning to my freezer to grab breakfast.

By the time I was walking out of the kitchen with a large TV tray laden with coffee and Codex bed and breakfast signature microwavable sausage biscuits still more than a little bit confused Cassi walked out of my room.

Her dark jeans and boots from yesterday held one of my dress shirt skillfully tucked in about her figure with two buttons left undone leaving enough of a "V" in the top of the shirt to make you wish another button just happened to fall open but not so much that it looked like she was actually trying. "Thanks for the shirt." She said before closing on the tray, taking one of the cups of coffee and heading back to the couch.

"No problem, ever." I said with a grin before grabbing a seat in my chair, setting the tray down and grabbing my own coffee. "You make it look much better than I ever have." I added. My brain started trying to think of where to take things from here. I had a creature that moved on the wind and elves who worked for a league of assassins. None of my contacts had any real information on either of them. I couldn't think of a way to get a lead except to have it fall into my lap.

The universe decided at that moment to pay me back for some past crime. Glass shattered over my shoulder and an object of some form hit the back wall of my living room and bounced back to land in my lap. A moment before things went from bad to horrible I recognized the little silver cylinder sitting in my lap. A gas grenade.

"Move!" I shouted to Cassi as the room started to fill with the yellow gas that flowed from the metal cylinder that had been in my lap. I honestly don't remember tossing the grenade away to land near my front door, but my hand was red and swollen from touching the burning grenade. Another cracking sound started from the windows. Before I really had my thoughts gathered two fountains of canary colored gas had erupted in my living room and was beginning to fill the space at an alarming rate.

Cassi rushed by me and started running towards the back door of the house. I grasped her wrist and shook my head. I reached to the rack and grabbed my scarf. I had barely managed to catch her wrist before turning the black material about in my hands and slipping it over Cassi's face as an impromptu gas mask before pointing down the hall leading toward by room.

"Bedroom. Window. Go!" I shouted before pushing her in the right direction again. Traces of the gas started to fog my vision as I ran down the hall after her for a few steps until the air cleared a handful of feet later allowing me to take several deep breaths, the last of which stung with the familiar bite of tear gas before I pulled my coat free of my arms and threw it over my mouth and nose. They were trying to herd us outside the back door and I didn't have long until they would hear Cassi break the window. I could either risk walking into whatever trap they had set for us or do the stupidest thing possible and run straight at the threat I knew was outside the front of the house. So I went with my only sane option and did something completely insane. I ran back through the yellow atmosphere that was now my living room before jumping at one of the windows leading out the front of my house shoulder first.

Running blind through a cloud of tear gas, jumping through a window and, onto an open front porch is not the best plan that I have ever come up with, but doing it onto patio furniture is even worse. The weave of weathered wicker cracked under the sudden weight and the small table exploded beneath me as I came the rest of the way down onto the porch back first. Then I made the horrible mistake of tossing my jacket aside and opening my eyes.

When one is exposed to hazardous fumes the first instinct we have is to hold our breath, and it is a good one. The problem comes when you take that first, tragically deep, breath. I took in a partial lung full of gas that had started to leak from the hole in the window causing me to double over into a coughing fit as the gas attacked my body.

A voice somewhere masked by my tear blurred vision cursed in a language I almost understood. I had read enough elven to know the sound of it in my head, but my verbal training in it was sadly lacking. If I wasn't under duress I could speak it, but choking on gaseous fiberglass doesn't lean towards a calming thought filled state of mind. I stumbled toward the banister, grabbed at the Colt, and turned myself over the rail and fell to the ground before the figure holding a very big gun directly to my face.

I barely managed to hear the 'Thunk! Click!' of the firing of another round from the spring powered launcher hurtled in my direction giving me enough time to move and turn what would have been a two pound steel fastball to the chest into a blow to my shoulder. It hurt like hell and I knew it was going to for several days after the fact, but for now I couldn't let the injury stop me as I finished pulling the Colt free and turning it onto my attacker.

A boot heel appeared from nowhere and struck at the back of the hand holding my gun, knocking my gun off mark sending the round I fired off wildly into the background. I barely managed to lift my arm up enough to block a second kick from that leg, or one from its opposing twin, this one bound for my head. Instead it landed on the back of my upper arm and shoulder. I went to grab the leg that had struck me with my left hand to make a vague attempt but the offending appendage was already gone. Then a third foot, or maybe one of the first two, snapped across the side of my head. After that, the ground jumped up and hit me on the other side of the skull. For that first instant I caught myself thinking that the cold earth felt nice against my skull. Then it struck me I had more important things to do such as fending off men with grenade launchers before they kill me.

Despite the haze in my head, my own left leg reached out in a kick trying to return fire at my attacker. The strike moved a bit like a steam roller by comparison. The kick would have been easy to dodge if someone expected it but standing nearly six feet tall there was a lot of room for muscle on my leg. The kick might take a relative eternity to get where it was going, but if I landed it, people would know what I had been about. They would know in a big way as long as they were near human. I felt the kick strike across someone's leg, hopefully it was my attacker who had pulled the Bruce Lee impression. I hadn't expected the blow to land in all reality, but I would take what I could get. I would go so far to say it was my lucky day, but not after just having my home attacked by a Bruce Lee impersonator with a surplus of World War Two munitions. It was more like life had charged me a ninety nine dollar bar tab and made sure to grin as it handed me my single back. All the while I knew it was just expecting to get it back as part of the tip.

A curse spat in the melodic tones of the elven language shot down at me before I felt the barrel of the 40mm press against the side of my head. "The tiger I will pull if you do move"

"The Tiger?" I couldn't help but ask as I tried to look up toward my attacker, but I got as far as a blatantly steel toed boot and bike leather clad legs before the barrel pushed into my skull encouraging me to leave my head where it was. "You named your grenade launcher the tiger?"

"No the tiger...I will pull the tiger and the gun will....fire." the voice replied. Now that I had a second chance to hear it, the elf's English was horrible. "The girl where is her?"

"Not here the girl is." I snapped back before breaking into hilarious laughter at my own Yoda impersonation. I was bruised, bloody, and horribly pissed that the elf had cheated with the steel toe cover on her boot. Or his, nothing against the fair folk, but with only a few words and a bit of boot clad leg it was hard to tell. "Where she is I know not!" I barely managed to say through the laughter.

"You will die for not speaking!" The elf shouted back twisting the coke can sized barrel into my temple to emphasize the point.

"Go ahead pull the tiger!" I shouted. "If you strike me down, I shall become more powerful than you could possibly imagine." I cackled again the pain was obviously getting the better of my senses.

I felt the tension of the barrel against my temple ease, and I broke my cackling and struck while the iron was hot. I pulled my arms across my face brought the bottom of my balled up fist against the barrel of the gun, knocking it away from my face and turning my head to the side to look up as I brought my gun up and let it settle on the elf.

"Back off or I will pull the TRIGGER!" I shouted as I sat up onto a knee not letting the gun slip from the point I had it aimed at. "This is where you start hoping those things don't catch anything on fire in my home and we start talking. You try anything funny or I start smelling smoke and I'll start shooting."

The elf kept his eyes and his grenade launcher trained on me as I stood up completely. He was almost the very image of the elf that had been called up in the divination I had worked yesterday. Slightly taller than me with a powerful swimmer's build covered by a collection of black biker's leathers that more resembled armor than it did motorcycle clothing. He was covered from the toes of his boots to the closed neck of the outfit. His face looked to have something that could have been wrought from the same hands that made the others pretty boy features, but that artist had been in a worse mood at the time. Harsh but handsome features with offensively dark eyes that were so still and calm that they appeared to be glass sculptures instead of living organs.

"Good very, William Codex, talk we will. The girl you will deliver or we shall finish this we have started." said the assassin.

I sighed and shook my head before speaking up in the elven language. "Perhaps we shall continue this in your native language follower of the Open Palm." I replied before I lowered the gun to aim center of mass instead of at the elves head. Allowing me to keep the gun and my arm close to my side in case the elf tried another Return of the Dragon.

A moment later I saw movement from the corner of my eye. Another leather bound form moved around the house. I glanced about to see another lithe elven form this one definitively more interesting. Her boots reached up to mid-thigh and the pants where a much more fitting feminine cut. Her jacket wrapped just as completely over her athletic frame creating an impressive combination of intimidation, grace, and more than a small amount of sex appeal. Typically beautiful elven features and slender eyes of bright blue that glowed against lightly tanned skin. All in all this second elf was definitively female. Still the primary difference between the two elves was the nearly waste length chestnut colored hair the newcomer had. It matched the other elf's close cropped hair in color. Actually several of their features were similar.

Oh, and this new elf carried a large assault rifle snapped to a harness over her chest. The already large frame weapon was equipped with a scope and under-barrel grenade launcher. So, that was the surprise waiting for us at the back door.

"You will have to forgive my younger brother, Special Agent Codex. He spends far too much time studying aspects of human culture such as your weapons and martial arts. He has obviously neglected his lingual studies." Said a honey sweet voice that flowed from the elf woman like a chorus of silver bells. "None the less he is still very good at his job. I digress. We know the girl is under your protection, Agent Codex. My employer doesn't wish to incur the wrath of the Holzer Initiative or especially yourself. You have undoubtedly absconded Cassi Ross to a safe location. We will be satisfied if you simply walk away and allow us to obtain her on our terms so we will not be forced to target you and yours."

"Wonderful, your partner can't speak the language and you can't stop speaking it." I said with a shake of my head. "And, no I won't let you take Ms. Ross. It is my job to make sure that bad things won't happen to people. I'm pretty sure that giving innocents over to assassins fall within that purview." My gun stayed trained on younger brother as I kept his form in the edge of my vision while I kept my eyes trained on the elf who was speaking. "So, all things considered, it would be best for all involved that you just mark this up as a loss and get out of town. You don't have long before the backup I called...."

"You don't have backup." She elf chucked with her sweet voice giving me an audible idea of what razorblades dipped in honey would taste like. "The nearest proper Initiative agent is in Missouri unless you are talking about your local cleanup crew that isn't even allowed to know who you actually are much less what you do. Besides we've been monitoring communications into and out of the house for the last half hour. You haven't called for help, Agent Codex. And if you are expecting the mortal authorities to respond to any disturbance we have wards in place to discourage the perception of the land your house sits upon."

"Well damn." I grinned. "I guess I should have thought about setting up a contingency for a situation like this before hand." Then I leaned back against the side of the porch holding up my left hand and knocking on the porch rail three times before dropping to my knees.

No I don't actually have a powerful defense mechanism built into my home. This was actually the first time a case had followed me home like this. I promised then, that if I survived this, I would put one in place however. Mostly because that would mean that the next time I try something like this my would be aggressors would have been caught blindsided. This time however, I wasn't so lucky.

Both of the elves stared blankly at me not taking to the ploy despite my very convincing duck down and wince. "Did you think we didn't check for traps, Agent Codex?"

"Well I was kind of hoping you hadn't thought to check."

"You haven't been the target of this assignment, Agent Codex, but we do not move without as much preparation as possible." stated the loquacious elf. "Frankly I was against the taking of a job that had such a strong chance of leading us to cross paths with the Initiative. And you, especially given your past record for sowing the seeds of discord. However, in our profession, like most others, we don't always get what we want. I'd hoped, even after Miss Ross came into her gift, that my brother and I would still be able to keep up the contract after she so suddenly and aptly disabled my lover."

So, Cassi had taken the arm from she elf's boyfriend. "And so you called in your baby brother to help you finish the job." nodding to the first elf again. "Your boy isn't much good to the order right now on account of a missing arm. Your bosses aren't happy with him having lost a resource like the sword. I imagine he doesn't have long to live, if he is still alive." I could see her eyes narrow at my deduction and that told me I was onto something. I needed her to get mad enough to slip up, but I couldn't let it be sudden enough that she would just shoot me. When you kick someone over the edge into madness they strike out in a moment of clarity before the fall. If you slowly nudge them and wait for the right moment to tip them over? They'll be so shocked that they will give pause. "How long do you have to return the sword before they kill him?"

"Two days..." She elf said before doing something that had to be difficult. She stopped talking. Narrow blue eyes glared at me as she adjusted the gun to ensure her aim on me.

"And the job?" I asked careful not to let my gaze stray too far from the grenade launcher. "What is on the line for its completion?"

Her eyes sharpened to a point so deadly they matched her voice. "Oh your lives."

"Have you told your brother that yet?" I quesioned still speaking English She had spoken to me in English the entire time despite his obvious ineptitude. She was trying to hide details of the job. I was about to make things personal. The next question I asked in my very best Elven. "Has she informed you that if you do not complete this job, you will die? She has bet her brother's life on that of her lover's."

The male elf's eyes grew to nearly the size of saucers and his lip curled up as he shoved the barrel of the weapon closer to my face bringing it from eight feet away to six feet from the end of the barrel to my nose. "Her lover! That evil treacherous bastard!" The elf spat. "He was not Illish's love. He was mine!" Perhaps I might have stumbled on my way out of this situation.

She elf was every bit as shocked as her brother. Rather she was shocked about the fact that I had just spilled the beans or that her lover had apparently wanted to collect the whole family set. I didn't wait to find out. I had a moment so I took it.

I reached out with the Colt and closed the gap between me and the end of the grenade launcher by another couple of feet and a few more inches. I squeezed the trigger and ran forward closing the gap between the launcher and myself again. It would have been easier to just shoot the elf himself but that would have left me open to She elf and her assault rifle. I needed to cause a distraction.

By the time I felt the gun bark, the end of my barrel was less than a couple of feet away from the front end of the grenade launcher. When I thought of the idea during one of She elf, Illish's speeches, I was just hoping to ruin the large weapon and take it out of the equation. I hadn't accounted for the muzzle flash of my pistol. You see, firing a bullet into the end of a gas grenade isn't going to cause the round to explode. At least it won't do anything like that on its own. The bullet however will punch a hole into the round exposing the volatile chemical mixtures that cause the gas solids inside the round to ignite, burn, and disperse. If you are really close to the mixture of explosive substances you do run the risk of the pistol's muzzle flash igniting the grenade inside the barrel.

Thankfully, I was already running away from the elf when I heard the high pitched hiss of the round. I managed to jump out and roll away the instant a cloud of yellow smoke exploded from the end of the launcher consuming my two attackers in the rapidly expanding noxious yellow fumes. I finished my roll and turned about to bring the front sight of the Colt down against the two elves who were both currently doubled over coughing and stumbling out of the cloud.

Now, don't get me wrong, I am not a big fan of killing anyone. But, when I looked at the two elves choking in a cloud of gas in front of my home, as more of the same gas floated out of my windows I realized something. I was going to have to replace my new couch. I, William Codex, would have to go back to the furniture store, get swindled by some blond bombshell and, talked into buying another overpriced under comfortable piece of leather. Again. Suddenly I didn't feel especially forgiving nor did I think I would have trouble sleeping as I fired three rounds into the cloud. The first one struck one of the two figures in the leg, but after that it was obvious, if I had any reason left to doubt it, that the two elves were professionals. They fell as low as they could and still kept to their feet before diving to the side and out of the cloud of gas. They rolled over and back to their feet in near perfect unison during my one open shooting line before running toward the driveway where two very familiar bikes sat. Actually make that one.

One of the bikes had the large suspension and rough tires of the Enduro bikes I had run into the night before. The other bike was a low profile thing that looked to be out of a Japanese cartoon or something. All swooping black angles and sharp points. I guess it more resembled a snake or a shark or something smooth and deadly all at the same time. I guess I got caught up in my male instinct to ogle blatantly fast objects with wheels because as I heard the cry of steel on steel I was shocked back into the moment. The elves weren't as lucky.

Even the most professional warrior can't expect everything. Especially when you are struggling to breath and half blind from gas I suppose. Still, I would have expected the elves to notice the deafening metallic ring as Cassi's sword cleared its sheath. Or even if that hadn't caught their attention, I can't imagine them missing the bright silver blade flickering with violet, green and black tongues of flame. They noticed nothing until Cassi brought her sword down at the back of one of the elves as they jumped onto their bike tearing open jacket and flesh.

The voice I knew belonged to Illish screamed as the blade bit into her shoulder blades. Younger brother sped off onto the road almost causing an accident with his blind turn out into traffic. Not to be out done, or left in the lurch, Illish made a final sprint for her bike despite her injuries. She almost managed to drive away as well despite her injury. That was before Cassi screamed and brought her sword down again. This time the blade slashed across the bike's back tire. The blade sunk into the tire and, for a moment, considered not stopping at the rim before grinding to a halt nearly half an inch into the metal. However, as the bike continued to try to move away the blade filleted bits of the wheel and the rest of the rubber of the tire as the bike rolled forward. When it was suddenly without traction on the wheel that powered the bike, the whole collection of smooth black body panel and apparently heavy engine fell over onto Illish's leg.

To her credit Illish bit back the scream that I almost let out at the sight and grunted as she worked to push the fallen bike away before it was too late, but the crash was too quick. The elf was pinned. She struggled to push the bike away as Cassi closed in on her, caught up within whatever magic flowed through the sword and into her.

Cassi's own eyes reflected the multicolored light pouring from the blade as she raised the sword up over her head. Dazzling motes of light and shadow fell over Illish as she tried to pull herself free from the bike.

That would have been it for Illish had I not fallen victim to the same mistake that I pointed out in the elves as they ran from the gas. I hadn't even noticed the thin knife blade resting against my throat until its wielder pressed the blade into my neck applying near breaking pressure to my skin. A hand reached up and held up a single finger toward Cassi. "Miss Ross, I would lower the sword and step away if you want to see Agent Codex live through this." The fingers on the hand in front of me were skeletal and comprised of bright polished silver. Intricately engraved and interlocking silver plates made the top of the palm. In the collection of bright metal pieces I caught a reflection. It was that of the dark haired blue eyed elf that I had conjured the image of in my spell. "My name is Estan, and we have a great deal to discuss I think."

Have you ever almost cut yourself? Have you ever felt that intense biting pressure of a thin sharp surface against your skin threatening to violate you? Imagine that fleeting sensation brought to bare against your body and apply it against the pulse of your neck. Now stretch that pre cut threat of the knife's bite. Prolonged and left to tease with constant pressure resting millimeters away from your very life blood, the pressure will start to mess with your head in short order. Your pulse quickens and grows stronger only bringing you a breath closer to death against the blade of the knife with every beat of your own treacherous heart.

Well if you haven't, it sucks.

If a blade is set to your neck, there are ways to get out of the situation but few of them, at least among the ones I knew, give you better than even odds of surviving the seconds after you attempted your escape. Even then, those really counted on the fact that the knife holder wasn't a trained professional. You have to exploit an opponent's weaknesses in order to escape such a situation. There was little room for exploitation when an assassin with centuries of experience held a razor sharp blade against your carotid artery.

I stood perfectly still in my best statue impression trying to keep my breathing shallow without speeding up too much. I just kept concentrating on my breathing and tried to keep myself still and relaxed against the blade of the knife.

"Very good, Agent Codex. If you tense up or try anything, I might just slip. Then Miss Ross would only have herself to fend off the two of us." Estan whispered before looking back up toward Cassi. "She poses no threat to Codex, now Miss Ross continue telling yourself that and it will calm the blade down. And whatever you do, do not direct that ire toward me or that sword may kill us all before it is over."

Cassi continued to glare at Illish. For a moment it appeared that she wasn't even aware of Estan's voice, but after another moment she still hadn't struck and her breathing began to level and the multicolored shifting flames across the edge of the sword started to die down. By the time the bright silver blade dimmed back to its normal mirrored steel finish, violent shadows so subtle I hadn't noticed them at first, receded away from her porcelain skin. It was still another moment before the tip of the blade lowered from striking height and Cassi took two slow even steps away from Illish and her fallen bike. "Let him go." Her own voice shook somewhere between trembling sobs and a low growl.

I saw Estan's head shake the reflection of his hand. "Now love, that won't do us much good. If you're going to hold that blade you're going to need to get a hold of yourself." He said as he tilted the blade back and forth over my neck before nudging me forward into a slow walk. "Put the sword away and then we can talk."

"Bullshit!" Cassi spat starting to pull the blade back up turning instead to Estan as the sword started to brighten as she stepped toward the elf. "Pull the knife away!" Her voice shook with anger as tears started to roll down her cheeks. "I will kill you all!"

As Cassi stepped forward I felt the knife slide against my skin and press inward missing my life by a sparse fraction of an inch. The wince and the arch of my back to try to move away from the knife were completely involuntary. "Your connection with the sword is deeper than I expected Miss Ross. You need to separate your thoughts from it or Heartseeker is going to drive you to your doom."

"How do I know you will let him go?" Cassi said with her sword lowering again, but her stance widened as she split her attention between Estan and Illish. "If I put my sword away you can kill him and then me."

"I swear a vow upon the life on my beloved you hold in your hands." Estan said his gaze keeping to the sword more than Cassi. "I think you know the strength of that oath Miss Ross."

"Which beloved?" I asked in a whisper against the pressure of the knife. "Funny thing happened just before you showed up. You've been a busy boy, Estan." I said trying to keep my tone light and chiding both to appear confident and to keep my voice soft against the knife's edge.

Estan shook his head and chuckled. "You try living twenty of your lifetimes, Agent Codex. You will need to change things up from time to time. Illish was my first and shall be my last lover. All others pale in my eyes." Estan said nodding to the elf pinned beneath the bike. "I swear my oath on her because her life is worth more than my own."

"But, her brother?" I said with a shake of my head. "No offense to the man with the knife to my neck, but that is weird, even for an elf." Elves were known for having more open ideas on the subjects of love and sex. Come to think of it, I think we humans are the prudes of the supernatural world.

"To each their own, Agent Codex, but it isn't the most outrageous stunt Illish or I have ever pulled." The elf said as his chuckle broke into a laugh but his pressure with the blade never wavered. "I held the blade before you Miss Ross you know the value of such an oath."

Cassi closed her eyes for a moment, but as her gripped tightened about the sword handle, I questioned whether or not closing her eyes actually changed her perception of the world about her for the moment. "I....I can't explain it, but the sword trusts you." Cassi said a moment later before opening her eyes. "It doesn't like you or her, but it thinks your word is good." Cassi said taking a deep breath. "Pray the sword is right Estan, for your life and hers." Cassi said before flipping the sword about and sliding it home into the sheath with an almost professional emotion.

"May whatever god or gods you pray to have mercy upon you Miss Ross" Estan said as he loosened the pressure of the knife on my neck before stepping back and around me. The knife he had already been tucked away to whatever place it came from by the time I could see his hands. "I am glad to be free of the weapon and will pray you are strong enough to master it." He moved across the yard and pulled the bike up with a single easy pull of that bright silver arm. "You will be free of me and mine until the sun rises again. If the beast has not killed you both by then we shall settle this matter." Estan said as he held out his flesh hand to Illish still holding the bike aloft with the other. He didn't even appear to be straining. The pretty elf took Estan's hand and pulled herself up before pulling her jacket straight.

"I will see you at sunrise, Codex" Illish hissed in my direction, as Estan slipped her arm over his shoulder to take the weight off her leg as the pair walked down the drive.

"All things considered, the bike stays here and whoever is alive tomorrow night can pay for the repairs and keep the bike." The jest and the elf's smile somehow seemed more dangerous than Illish's open threat and glare.

I walked toward Cassi as the elves walked out into the street to a truck that had just pulled up to the curb. It matched a description of the truck Brandon saw driving away the night Sue was killed. It turns out it was green. It also had a pair of off road bike strapped into the bed. Estan moved with great care not to aggravate either of Illish's wounds as he guided her into the vehicle before stepping in and closing the door behind him. Once I neared Cassi I wrapped my arm over her shoulder as we both watched the car leave. "Well, looks like it is going to be one of those days." I said as I held a couple of fingers to the small flesh wound on the side of my neck. "You OK?

"I....I don't know." Cassi said as she finally leaned into my side partly burying her face in my chest and covering her other eye with her hand. "I jumped into those hedges you sent me into and hid until I heard the other elf talking. Then I started to move around the side of the house to get a look at things. I saw them running away and you were rolling on the ground." She said before her eyes narrowed causing a new run of tears down both her cheeks. "I thought you were hurt. After that it's like a vision. I can only remember it in flashes of images and strong emotions. By the time I remember things clearly I was speaking with Estan." Her voice started to shake and I instinctively pulled her a bit closer. "What the hell happened, Will?"

"I don't know yet and I know I've been saying this a lot, but we are going to find out. I promise." I whispered before I looked up as Cassi silently cried against my chest. The fact that she was in such a state angered me so much that something in my chest started to stir.

I looked about the yard and started to take measure of things. For some reason the Order of the Open Palm wanted Cassi dead. So did a Wendigo, but they didn't appear to be working together. At least Estan didn't think they were in bed with "the beast." For some reason the Order also wanted to kill Sue. Could they have actually gone after the werewolves as a red herring? Maybe I was wrong and little brother wasn't a pinch hitter for Estan. It looked like he was still in the game. Two of them went after Sue while a sniper was ready for Cassi. Taking care of one killing in Lufkin did keep me busy for several hours. Hoping it would be long enough for the trail to go cold by the time I got to the second crime that would have featured Cassi's body. Somehow the plan had been ruined. Cassi's sleep driving vision might have caused the assassin to miss their mark. Or maybe the Wendigo was the unknowing bloodhound. The monster so much as admitted that it was after Cassi during the fight outside of Gregorie's. Perhaps the third assassin knew that it shared targets with the beast and was following it, and it chased down the wrong person. Was it possible that the creature tracked down the object of its lust via magical lines? That would mean it could have sniffed up the bloodline too far and actually passed up the object it desired. If it came across an older direct relative of Cassi's with the same trait the creature had latched on to, it could have possibly gone after the wrong person. All of that aside, neither the Wendigo nor the Open Palm were the type to kill out of their own mechanization. Perhaps I was looking too low down the food chain to get any real answers. I needed to know who hired them.

"You have that look on your face again." Cassi said as she pulled herself away from me, after looking up toward me for a moment. "Mustard gas is floating out the windows of your house, you have a bump on your head the size of a softball and your arm looks hurt. Not to mention a well deserved bruise on the side of your face from a magical sword. Point being, all this is happening and you're perfectly calm staring off in the distance trying to gather up facts."

"Tear gas," I said shaking my head. "We would be a lot worse off if it was actual mustard gas. It gets died yellow for intimidation and so you can't tell it apart from mustard gas. Lots of it available in cheap black markets."

"Such an important detail." Cassi said rolling her eyes as she grabbed me by the arm and started pulling me toward the bike to apparently help her get it out of the driveway. "Point is, Will, I have to wonder if you actually ever get scared or intimidated."

"Whenever you see me get that far away look in my eyes and I start trying to think up the facts that would be the sure sign to know I'm afraid." I said as she leaned down and help pull up the bike. It wasn't too bad with the extra set of hands. However, pushing it up the hill that was my driveway with the back tire shredded was another story. "I think Mark Twain always said it best," I started as we pushed the bike past the fence to my back yard, "Courage is resistance to fear, mastery of fear, not absence of fear."

"Fear is OK if you use it?" Cassi replied nodding her head in thought. "Be that as it may, I don't want this to be my Monday through Friday." She said with a laugh.

"This time next week this whole thing can be a bad dream. You'll just need to study up on things a bit to learn to control your abilities and other than that you won't need to have any contact with this world." I said as we set the bike on its kickstand.

"Well I don't want that to happen." Cassi said looking up to me a bit of color growing over her cheeks. "I mean Hannelore is great and I haven't been in East Texas very long, so the only other person I know near Tyler is Bigfoot. I doubt he makes for good company on girls night out, all the screaming pedestrians and him dying inside a city and everything. Besides, I'd miss you."

"Or the fact that he has the wrong chromosomes for girl's night out?" I offered with a chuckle before I stopped. I looked up from the bike and caught Cassi's bright green stare. She'd done it; she was the first one of us to put a toe in the water. Well there was the kiss and the previous night on the couch, but those were acts of the situation. To actually voice the fact that something might exist was saying a lot. Hell, to voice that either of us would exist after the next day or so was saying a lot as well. "I wouldn't like it if you disappeared either, but..."

Cassi shook her head. "But, this is all sudden and you aren't one for commitment either way." She said with a grin. "Truth be told, me neither. I mean you might be the first guy I've met whose past relationships are more messed up than mine but that took a vengeful Greek goddess."

Cassi stepped around the bike and moved forward stopping only a half-step shy of an embrace. "Let's be honest, if we hadn't been in a car chase, if you hadn't come to my aid after an elven assassin tried to kill me, if we hadn't managed to fight off a giant monster, if we hadn't just not vowed to pistols at dawn with three of said elven assassins, or if we hadn't met at the scene of my father's murder we wouldn't be.... feeling a lot of this right now. You might have gotten over your fear of relationships enough to get my number and I might have given it to you. Even if I had, you would still be wondering if you should call me so soon. Honestly Will, neither of us gets into this type of thing blind, we both know better." She finally stopping to take a deep breath.

"I...well I couldn't have said it better myself. How long have you been thinking it?"

"Since the kiss. You?"

"Since I walked up to the police car and thought 'Damn, why did I have to meet her at work?'." That won me a laugh. A really honest laugh and it was an amazing sound. It was the kind of thing I was supposed to be learning about a woman prior to falling full on for her.

"I would have never figured the dark mysterious FBI agent to be a flirt." She said before draping her arms over my shoulders. "Thanks for understanding, Will." She whispered before kissing my cheek.

I grinned as I wrapped my arms about her waist. "Hey don't think you're off the hook. I know this great sushi place I am going to think about asking you out to for a few days after this is all over, before I manage to get up the nerve to call you." I said before leaning my lips down to hers.

That kiss was, unique. It started with all the heat and pressure that had built up over the last couple of days and languidly burned down to smolder for a long moment before we stepped apart, our lips finally parting as if the kiss had been a fleeting memory.

The very next moment, as Cassi started looking about for something to do, I reached into my pocket and tossed her my keys. "Go get in, start up the truck, and find some good road trip music. We are going to be driving to Lufkin and it is a bit of a trip."

Cassi looked at me for a moment before nodding. "What's in Lufkin? Is that where Q builds all your toys?"

"Nope, that's where I hopefully keep some Wendigo sized back-up." I said as I reached toward my phone and started to dial Brandon's number.

By the time we left the Tyler city limits and were driving south toward Lufkin I was sure that my radio was conspiring against me. I was driving to gather up allies for a life or death battle while sitting beside a beautiful woman who I had just agreed not to fall for until this was over and the first two songs out of my radio were "Highway to Hell" by AC/DC followed by "I Can't Fight This Feeling" by REO Speedwagon. The second song made it to the first go at the chorus before Cassi reached forward and turned down the volume, shaking her head, and returning to her white and green paper cup full off some kind of spiced coffee.

After a long moment, Cassi shook her head and started to find a new radio station. "So this is that whole calm before the storm thing you hear people talking about." She said before leaning back. Her hunt for a station fruitless, she was decidedly studying the ceiling of the car instead of the road ahead.

I grinned as I took a sip from my own coffee, a triple shot of espresso with just enough cream and sugar that it didn't erode the cup from the inside out too quickly. "If it helps any, we don't have until tomorrow morning until things get crazy."

"I thought the elves agreed to wait until then before they came after us?"

"I don't trust them." I replied as I flipped the local radio to the Auxiliary input. I grabbed my mp3 player and handed it over to her.

"The sword thinks their word is good." Cassi said with a shrug.

"I don't know the sword, so I don't trust it either. Besides, it is better to ere on the side of caution all things considered." I nodded toward the weapon leaning on the seat beside Cassi between her and the passenger side door. "So, the sword talks?"

"It isn't so much talking as it is really strong impressions. I read people. I don't think I realize how much I did it till a couple of days ago, but that doesn't change the fact. The sword speaks that language, better than most people and without the use of body language, which is more than a little bit unsettling." Cassi let one hand rest on the blade after she picked a song to play while her other went back to her coffee.

"So it remembers Estan because it used to be used by him?"

"Yes, that and more. It's really hard to describe but the sword bonded with him as he used its power. The more strongly you feel about something the more powerful the blade's reaction and the more powerful the connection the next time. When I defended myself against you earlier for instance. I didn't know what to think about the situation so the sword didn't know how to act. When I saw you rolling on the ground and those two elves running away, I knew what I wanted to happen so the sword could feed off the energy."

"The way Estan was talking made the whole thing sound dangerous."

"I think it is. The sword doesn't have much in the way of a regard for life, quite the opposite actually. It is a weapon made to kill and it wants to do its job. Once you allow it to start and all your ideas mix with its energy, it's a bit hard to hold everything back. It's tempting too. It kind of feels like riding in a really fast car. You know, dangerous, but fun."

"So, use with caution then?" I asked, taking a drink of my own coffee, trying not to let my worried expression come across too strongly as I drove us down the road. Whatever this sword was, 'Heartseeker' Estan called it, was not to be trifled with.

"Either way we have the Wendigo to worry about. That is what you were talking about right?" Cassi said as she played with the music player trying to find something to listen to. "Will, do you listen to any music that doesn't play on an oldies station?" Cassi had started looking through my music collection after putting down her coffee for a moment.

"Classic rock is not oldies. There is a huge difference between..." I stated before my phone started cackling in a typical mad scientist laugh along with declaring something was alive. I reached down, grabbed my phone, and accepted the call before putting it to my ear and speaking. "Hey Kevin what do you have?"

"Wow! No small talk from, William Codex. Things must be serious." Came the tenor voice on the other end of the phone.

"You find me a way to get CS gas out of my new leather couch and I'll be in a better mood. Did you get my email?"

"I actually might be able to help you with that. What you're going to need is... Wait why do you have tear gas in your living room?" The lab tech asked.

"Elves.... long story. You have anything on the Wendigo?" I caught Cassi chuckling out of the corner of my eye and turned to look at her but she stopped almost instantly.

"Yeah I got a bit of information for you but none of it is good. You sure you are dealing with a Wendigo? I mean they are rare even where they are native and it isn't like one could just hop into a car and drive down from Canada. I'm sure they'd ask for papers at the border or something." I heard Kevin say as he clicked away on a keyboard at the same time.

"Tall, dark, and mostly fury with big glassy eyes." I replied between sips of coffee. "Rode on wind currents like it was a leaf, but threw a leg it ripped off a guy so hard that it hit me like a fastball. Yeah Wendigo"

"Ice, the eyes are supposed to resemble ice. Then again, someone as far south as you would likely never realize that. I'm sending some
data to your email now. Along with a few reports from our agent who works in the northern states. He laughed when I said you thought you had a Wendigo, but he sent it anyway."

"How much would it cost to box ship a chupacabra up to Oregon?" Samuel Eagle-Claw, an agent from the far north thought I didn't have enough experience to be going solo in the field yet. In some ways he was right, but at the time no one else offered to take my region and Gideon had thought I was ready enough after he was injured in the third year of my five year apprenticeship. Besides, it wasn't like Initiative agents on opposite ends of the country actually had to deal with one another on a regular basis.

Kevin laughed. "I hear word of a breeder in Mexico, but I don't need to tell you how to get into trouble, Will."

"Yeah, yeah. Go ahead and give me the short version of how to kill a Wendigo and I'll let you get back to work"

"Long story short. Hasn't been done on record." Kevin responded causing me to spontaneously lean my head back against the head rest of my seat.

"What do you mean it hasn't been done?" I think my voice came out a little bit louder than I expected.

"I don't mean it hasn't been done. Just that the method used hasn't been recorded. A bunch of old Native American tales and bits of folklore, but not Initiative profiles or case files. They are really rare Will. No reliable record on one since the 1940's. Hell, that might be the one you are looking at going against. The best documents I could find weren't even in English. You know how hard it was to find a translator of ancient Native American text on this short of notice?"

"Thanks Kevin. I'll get my lovely assistant to look over the email while I drive." I hung up my phone to the sound of Kevin protesting about secrecy and how Cassi wasn't vetted. But, considering that I hadn't heard his exact words, I paid it no mind. "Here. Open up the email app and look for one from an account labeled mad scientist."

Cassi grinned as she tapped away on the screen of the phone. "Not terribly worried about State secrecy and all that are you, Special Agent William Codex?" She said before leaning back and letting out a sigh. "The government can't get you a faster connection?"

"Not out where it isn't available. If I get into something real deep and really need it, I've had Kevin task a satellite, whatever that means. All I know is that when he does it I can get all kinds of data, but it is apparently expensive and they want all kinds of extra paperwork after the fact. What does it say?"

"Let's see here.... The earliest Wendigo records can be traced back to the Oji...Ojibwa and ...the ...Saul.... various Native American tribes of what is now known as the northern United States and Canada. It is known as the embodiment of greed and is never sated in its hunger for human flesh. Older members of this species are said to grow more ravenous hungers for specific prey and occasionally have even been known to focus the direction of their lust for human flesh. Once human they are said to be...."

"Skip down to the tactics sections. We can study after this thing is dead. I can give you the short version of all that before we get to Brandon's" I pressed the accelerator a little bit further as we hit a seam in traffic.

"Ok ok." Cassi scanned down the document muttering to herself. "Ah ha! The Wendigo, being a spirit of greed can, in theory, only be killed by an opposing spiritual energy. It is said that even the most grievous wounds won't slow the creature for more than a few moments. A killing strike is the only way to take the creature down. The ancient myths say, in one way or another, that the only way to strike down the Wendigo for good is for one who "has what the creature truly seeks to strike with that the beast can't understand". No official record on an exact process, but the last confirmed kill is a verbal tradition from the Cree people from the turn of the nineteenth century." The silence that followed felt like it was going to sink into the upholstery of my truck and never come up, but eventually Cassi spoke. "No one has done what we are going to try to do in over a hundred years."

"Well, at least we know it's been done." I said with a grin. "We have just under an hour until we get to where we are heading now. Let me tell you what I know."

By the time I answered Cassi's questions about the Wendigo and we made it through a crash course on werewolf behavior and etiquette we were pulling up the driveway to Brandon's home.

A few miles off the beaten path between Nacogdoches and Lufkin, down a couple of miles of blacktop road, Brandon kept a home on about thirty acres of land that had been in his family as long as lycanthropy. It had been the pack's meeting place before the time that the Initiative had managed to help them set up the Upland Island reserve. It was an older home, built when Brandon's predecessors had first moved out here, but it had been well cared for over the years. A fresh coat of white paint set off the dark trim. It looked as though it had been added onto once or twice over the last half century. Brandon's personal contribution hadn't actually been to the house but instead had taken the form of a large sheet metal shop building a couple of hundred feet away.

It was from that building that the familiar guitar of ZZ Top played with enough volume to cause the windows of my truck to rattle. "What does Brandon do?" Cassi asked, having to half shout from the seat beside me.

"He does engine work to pay the bills for the most part, some restoration and stuff like that, but he claims his art is his primary career. Metal sculpture, really big abstracts and stuff like that." I opened my door and stepped out letting the full volume of the music strike me as I started walking toward the shop.

Cassi and I were about twenty feet away when movement could be seen in the shop and the music died leaving the world reeling in silence. "Codex, that you?" said that basso voice filling the void of sound. "Couldn't hear you coming till you got close, had the music up." Brandon's shadow swallowed the two of us before he was completely out of the building. Dressed in a white t-shirt and work blue jeans with equally distressed boots the man was every bit a giant as he always was.

Sometimes you wonder if people like Brandon are really as big as you remember or if they just have such a presence that their gravitas is something like a fishing story and the longer you go without seeing them the larger they become. In the case of Brandon it was more like memory didn't do the man justice.

"We noticed. Everything OK?" I stepped forward and offered my hand to the man who took it in a firm shake that swallowed my hand.

"As it can be. I was just trying to get some things taken care of before you got here and we could head out. Getting a couple of pieces finished up in case.... well in case the pack needs some cash if things go wrong." Brandon's gaze looked past me and toward Cassi and I turned to match trying to take in the sight Brandon took in.

That extra loose button I had taken such care to notice was fastened and Cassi's jacket was buttoned over her body giving the garment the impression of a black suit top to match her dark jeans and boots. She looked every bit the cold serious professional, and the sword draped across her hip only served to enhance the image. While we drove here she had traded out her single long braid for a much more complex looking weave that started on either side of her head pulling her hair back before the rest looped into a braid behind her. She stared back at Brandon's gaze careful not to show any sign of intimidation or admiration and not moving till the large man nodded his head in greeting. Cassi then allowed a small smile to cross her lips before she returned the nod.

"This is your new partner, Codex?" Brandon finally asked and I answered with a nod. "I thought you Initiative agents were supposed to have a couple of years' experience."

"She isn't Initiative. A local player that has business with these guys, just like you, Brandon." I turned to look toward Cassi. "Cassi, this is Brandon, Alpha of his pack and world famous sculptor."

"I noticed." She said as she walked past either of us and looked up to the sculpture reclining in the middle of the large shop. "Who is she?"

I instantly recognized the figure. Sue, as she last lay in the clearing in the forest where Brandon had found her. An abstracted form of hammered metal plates recreated the beautiful curved form Sue had held in life. An immortalization in steel only viewable from straight on otherwise she appeared to be a collection of randomly shaped and placed pieces of scrap. The only feature visible from all angles was her face. Her features had been hammered from a single plate of flawless steel. The molded image of Sue relayed more of her likeness than any photograph could even boast. Her confidence, her patience, her love of life all brought to life by the hands that knew them most. She didn't look dead like the corpse I had seen in the forest. Forever in a peaceful sleep with a small smile barely crossing her polished silver lips.

"That is Sue, she was my mate." Brandon said as he followed Cassi's gaze. "The form is still rough I normally don't work so quickly, but I've had a great deal on my mind for the last two days. There has been very little time for sleep." The large man said as he started picking up some of his tools. "If the next day goes well, and I get the chance, you will have to see it when it is truly completed, Miss Ross."

"Brandon. Mind if I grab that bag I keep here and steal your shower? I got tear gas in places I currently wish I didn't have." I said walking toward one of the large cabinets on the wall of the shop and grabbing a black duffel bag out of it. Brandon and I had never been the best of friends, but I had learned from Gideon as soon as I started with the Initiative a long time ago that most people in our jurisdiction were willing to help us out and that it helped to have some spare gear tucked away in as many places as possible.

"Shower here is broken, but grab the industrial soap out of the one here before you head up to the house. If that stuff is anything like bear mace you are going to need it." Brandon chuckled turning to Cassi to get her take on the events of the morning as I stepped into the small, bare, but serviceable bathroom and returned a moment later with the gallon tub of orange smelling soap. Brandon was giving Cassi the tour of some of his work by the time I stepped out. I waited long enough to get a nod and a grin from Cassi as she patted the hilt of her sword before I left her with the werewolf and headed toward the house.

As I was walking up the steps toward the house the door pushed open. Stormy leaned in the frame and grinned at me. "Hey Will." She smiled as she stepped down the steps. She took her time and moved down the steps to make a show of the tight sweatpants and a workout top only one step removed from a being a sports bra. "I was just about to go out for a run. Care to join?"

"Work's in the way. Besides, you wouldn't get a workout if I was holding you back." I said as I stepped up the stairs beside her. "Let Brandon know you are going out. Things are going to get interesting in the next day." I said before walking to go past her and into the house.

Stormy stopped and turned about. "You found them." she said lightly sniffing the air as I walked past. I hadn't even seen her arm move as she reached out and grabbed hold of my shoulder. "Who is that?" Stormy turned about and looked at me inhaling sharply twice. "Who else is here?"

"Brandon and my...friend Cassi." I replied as I stepped away pulling Stormy's arm with me.

"A friend who has been all over you in the last couple of days." A trace of accusation welled up in her tone as she set those light blue eyes to mine. "You reek of her."

"First of all, you must be mixing Cassi up with the tear gas. I wouldn't say Cassi reeks. Secondly, I will smell like who I want to smell like." I said as I jerked my left hand out pulling the amulet and its chain free before catching it in my hand and stopping before I brought my hand back down on Stormy's forearm.

The young werewolf recoiled and let my arm go as she jumped down the rest of the stairs before looking up at me a snarl forming over her face. "You wouldn't dare. You owe me!" She shouted as her last steps back took her into a defensive crouch.

I know that threatening a wolf with silver is not something you should do lightly, but Stormy had gone from peaceful seas to her namesake in a couple of seconds. It was really my own fault I had coddled her and let her in too closely after I saved her. I was new at the job and tired of being looked at as an anonymous officer of the law instead of a person. Stormy, while she had been useful in providing information, was the first client I had in my time with the Initiative that had taken the time to learn about William instead of, Agent Codex. That made what I had to say hurt even more.

"Listen Stormy. I don't owe you anything. And as soon as you think I do, you can drive yourself across the state and back to your old pack. See what they think of you now." I said as I slipped the amulet back into my sleeve. "Get that idea out of your head right now." I said stepping down from the steps toward her. Our own height difference was enough to let me look down to her, but add a few steps into the equation and I towered over the blonde girl. "The day you want to challenge me is the day I am no longer your friend. Am I clear? We can either keep on being friends or I will go so big bad Initiative agent on you the moment you try to stand across the line from me that you won't be able to smell anything but silver and burnt hair for a week. Go for your run, get back here and hole up till Brandon gets back." I said before turning around and walking up the stairs into the house never looking back behind me. I had a serious case of shower tunnel vision.

By the time I stepped out of the shower, I felt like a new man. Granted I felt like a new man that could use some pain killers and a week's sleep, but it is still amazing what fifteen minutes under a hot shower will do for you. That abrasive orange scented soap stripped away worries, stresses, and thankfully tear gas from the last couple of days. The water washed away pains and relaxed my muscles in its warmth. I could have spent hours in that shower, but I knew I had already taken too long by the time I stepped out. Thankfully the bag I had on hand held a change of clothes and a few of the necessities. I shaved and dressed before stopping to look at myself in the mirror.

I was never going to be accused of being especially tall, but with a good pair of boots, I stood just over six feet. Heavy duty dark blue denim covered my legs and fell over the tops of my boots. It wasn't the thin pre-worn fashionable material you see in everyday clothing now. These were originally designed to be worn while riding a motorcycle. It was the type with Kevlar woven into the heavy grade denim. A plain white T-shirt rode against my body to protect it from the bullet resistant vest I strapped on next. A dark grey button down shirt covered my vest before I pulled my black leather holster rig back on over my shoulders and attached it to my belt. I checked for the Colt and my spare clips to make sure, yet again, that all the magazines were loaded and that the gun had a round in the chamber. It was a ritual I had committed to memory over the last several years, and the last bit of my petty concerns faded away as I twisted the silver chain of the amulet about my wrist before tucking it away into my shirt sleeve. I pulled the black sports coat on over my arms before I took a pair of black leather gloves from one of the pockets and stretched them on over my hands. A quick hand through my mostly dry hair and I took the whole image in.

The fact that I hadn't seen the sun in too long was made obvious by all the dark clothing, but that had always been a curse of living at night and having dark hair. I wished I'd packed more than a single disposable razor in the duffel as I felt most of a five o'clock shadow on my face where a goatee would be in a few days if I didn't get to it by then. The side of my face was still red and slightly swollen from the beating of the last couple of days, but that was my only visible wound, so for the time being it was all that mattered. My own grey eyes stared back at me in an honestly rehearsed stare. William Cunningham had bucked against the system as much as any other child, and perhaps even more than most by the time he was in college. Special Agent William Codex was a singularly unquestionable authority that existed above the laws of the land. He dealt out mercy and justice just as often as he did punishment, and when the time came he never hesitated to kill. William Cunningham was strong. Codex was invincible. The young man had thought he couldn't be defeated. The adult had been baptized by fire and knew that, in a horrible world, he would do all he could to beat back the darkness and if that wasn't enough, he wouldn't be around to regret it. Will Cunningham was human. William Codex was not. I could come back out tomorrow after this whole mess was done.

Prepared for the night to come, I stepped out of the bathroom and slowly walked down the stairs with Brandon's soap in one hand and my repacked duffel in the other. Once I was halfway down the stairs I heard the front door opening and dropped by duffel before reaching for the colt by the time Brandon and Cassi walked in. My hand relaxed its grip and I leaned down to grab the duffel bag back up as I nodded to the pair. "Brandon, did Stormy stop by to talk to you?"

Brandon nodded his head. "You could say that. She was in quite the mood, Codex. What did you do to set her off?" Brandon walked in the door so he could hold it open for Cassi who tried to hide her grin as she walked into the house. She was failing miserably.

"Something she smelled on me didn't agree with her I think." I said with a shrug as I set down the bottle next to the bag and looked down to the two of them. "Nothing horrible happened?"

"No, not at all." Cassi grinned as she looked about the living room. "I think she attempted to start a battle of wits, but she brought a knife to a gun fight." Cassi closed the distance between the two of us, stopped and looked me over before pulling something tied about her waist loose. "You're missing something." she said before she wrapped my scarf about my shoulders. "There." she said before returning to her feet pulling the scarf straight down the front of my coat as she went. Once she was flat on her feet again she walked around to explore the room about her.

"Woman like that can be your greatest ally or your worst nightmare, Codex. The good's worth ten times the bad, as long as you stay on her good side," Brandon said with a nod as he patted my shoulder. "I bet you'll be finding out how little what you choose has to do with anything before too long." The man laughed as he watched Cassi look over the pictures on the mantle.

I shook my head and looked back to Brandon after his whispered comment. The werewolf grinned and nodded toward Cassi. "I ...well yeah maybe but anything that crazy is a long way off."

"Stop assuming you have a choice in the matter, Codex. It'll be easier on you that way." "Right now I'm on the job." Brandon rolled his eyes as I said the canned response, but then something at the back of my mind jumped forward. "When I first got here I introduced Cassi by her first name. How did you know her last name was Ross?"

If Brandon ever answered the question I wasn't aware of it. My train of thought was broken as Cassi let out a blood curdling scream.

Brandon and I both sprinted across the room toward Cassi as she grasped one of the pictures from the mantle, sank to her knees, and began shaking back and forth grasping the picture to her chest openly sobbing.

I slid to a stop beside Cassi before kneeling down, wrapping an arm about her, and trying to get a look at the picture. I caught a questioning gaze from Brandon as he looked from the mantle and back to me. "A picture of Sue after her first successful change. About fourteen years ago."

The werewolf wasn't telling me everything. I knew that much. What he wasn't telling I couldn't decipher, I would address that later, for now I held Cassi for a few more moments before she relaxed and the picture she held tilted forward and I was able to see it.

It was an old photo obviously pre-digital and the corners were slightly yellowed. The frame about the picture was polished steel, Brandon's medium of choice. In the picture was a woman who was obviously a younger Sue. She looked up from where she knelt near a small campfire in the clearing the pack uses out on the Upland Island reserve. She was thin, far too thin actually, like she hadn't eaten properly in some time. Her skin was slightly greyed and her eyes were a bit red, but some of that was standard fare for a wolf after their first change. There was still something more behind those eyes despite the obvious wear the ordeal of the last night had had on her. She smiled that beautiful smile I had always known her to have. I had never spoken to Sue about how she had come to join the pack, but she had always hinted that her life beforehand wasn't good for her and that she had no desire to go back. Even in this glimpse into the past, when she was new to the pack, it was obvious how much she loved her new life and perhaps the man behind the camera. Something in her gaze smoldered with emerald embers that would one day grow to be something much more. It was familiar somehow, but I had most certainly never received such a look and smile from Sue. Then it hit me. The hair was slightly different as well as a few of the facial features but that smile and those power laden green eyes were the same I had known to belong to Cassi.

"Mama, mama... mama..." She repeated over and over again as she leaned into me. I don't think I could have been more disoriented if I'd been hit over the head. I glanced up from the dumbstruck woman toward Brandon who looked down to me and nodded in confirmation before speaking.

"She was camping deep into the reserve hiding from someone, we never got much in the way of details. One of the new wolves in the pack caught her scent. He hadn't changed in the whole span of the cycle and wasn't the most sterling of pack members we had ever had. I heard Sue scream after she was attacked. I was too late to prevent the bite, but I saved her life. I had just taken control over the pack from my father, but he guided us in what to do. We got the wound treated and contacted Gideon. By the time Sue came to, it was obvious that the curse had taken her. She was the first I had ever known to call it a blessing."

He had known from the moment he had seen Cassi. Now that I was looking at the woman in my arms and the past picture of Sue it was obvious especially when I thought more about the healthier Sue that I had always known. The two women couldn't have denied one another if they tried.

"She tried to raise us for a long time. Single mother with three kids. I didn't know then she was fighting addiction the whole time. My grandparents didn't tell me that part until I was older. I guess it didn't take much to push her over the edge. One day she was there, waiting for us to come home from school, the next she was gone." The words were strong but they came between deep breaths that worked to hold more crying at bay. "We never heard from her again. My grandparents told us several years later that we shouldn't expect to see her again, that she was most likely dead. We had a funeral. She has a marker in a cemetery in Dallas."

I gave Cassi some breathing room and relaxed my embrace, but I didn't stray from arms reach as we both looked toward Brandon for some explanation. "In a lot of ways, the woman that was your mother died. From her own accounts the drugs had purged a great deal of her mind. She remembered you, your name, that your eyes were the same color as hers. She missed you a great deal, but so much of her past life was blurred with her addiction that she was always afraid to go back home. She eventually found a life, we found one another. I know it is little consolation, but she did have a good life."

"I did some research once my grandparents told me the whole story. How did she survive with the addiction? They say you can't ever really get over it." Cassi continued to look at the picture as she spoke.

"That was why she called the curse a blessing. It killed the addiction. It killed the voices." The last part Brandon added in a soft tone as if some unseen force in the room might over hear him.

"Lycanthropy, the virus, rewires your brain. Particularly the lower brain where instinct and addiction is maintained." I added. "Theoretically, it could have gotten rid of any chemical dependency." Brandon's second admission stuck in my brain. "Psychic abilities are subtle and sensitive changes in a person's brain chemistry. It would take less trauma than turning into a werewolf to overload something like empathy, especially if it wasn't as pronounced as your own."

Cassi nodded her head, but she was obviously lost in the picture that was now sitting in her lap. Brandon and I exchanged a few glances. The werewolf was going to have a lot to explain. I hadn't even caught that he had known her last name until now. "Brandon, does she have... I mean do you have more pictures of her?" Cassi's statement interrupted my train of thought making it painfully apparent that I had lost my entire bad ass secret agent vibe.

"There are a few in an album on the book shelf." Brandon answered as he leaned down to take up that picture Cassi had found. "Go and look at them and find a few to keep. I'm going to go answer all of Codex's questions outside." With that Brandon nodded to me and turned to walk out of the house.

I stood and offered Cassi a hand up. Once she had clasped her hand in mine I pulled her to her feet and squeezed her hand lightly before sliding it free. We stood there for a moment looking at one another. The moment started to beg for something to be said, but quickly the air changed and we both just nodded. We had both verbally agreed to see this to the end, but if we had any doubt in what was going to have to happen between now and the morning, it was gone now. I nodded and turned to walk outside to meet up with Brandon.

As I walked outside, Brandon was waiting - leaning back against the porch rail. "So, Sue's murder is tied up in this whole mess?"

I nodded as I leaned against the house across from him using Brandon's gigantic shadow to block out the high sun. "Looks like it. I thought that maybe at first they took her out to fill out a second contract and to pull me away from Tyler. Make sure I couldn't get on the trail till it was cold. How long have you known?"

"That Sue had a daughter named Cassi Ross? For nearly the whole fifteen years she's been with me. How long have I known that Cassi was your woman?"

"She isn't my woman."

"Your friend...humans." Brandon said rolling his eyes. "I didn't know who she was until she walked in the door of the shop. It was fairly obvious once I saw her. I was hoping it would wait until this mess had blown over."

"Did Sue ever explain anything about the voices?" Brandon looked up at me, his not quite human eyes narrowing. "It might be linked to Cassi's gift."

"Only that they were driving her mad. It's what drove her back into her addiction. Heroin for the most part but she wasn't horribly picky toward the time she came across the pack. She had apparently stolen from a drug dealer and was hoping that she could camp on the reserve until the heat died down and she could make her escape."

"I never suspected." I just shook my head and pushed myself off the wall to work out the stiffness that was gathering in my shoulder. "It wasn't in Gideon's reports or anything."

"I suspect your mentor knew there was more than what we were telling him about Sue's situation, but he trusted my father and I. He took the report at face value." Brandon said as he judged me moving my shoulder. "You've done the same for the pack once or twice."

I had no choice but to nod to that. Most recently Phil should have had a full write up done on what happened, but the young wolf that bit him had been scared and didn't deserve the mark on his record and no one saw it so officially a rogue wolf attacked Phil while it was stalking the pack on a prowl night. I'd honestly not even gone down to investigate. Sue and I talked the whole thing out over the phone.

Cassi broke the silence as she pushed the door open. "Brandon, your phone rang and I let the answering machine get it. Stormy said she was staying at a friend's place this evening." Closing the door behind her she took up a spot of wall beside me. The two of us side by side were still able to hide behind Brandon's ample shadow.

"I'm not surprised." Brandon shook his head. "Her tail was tucked firmly between her legs when she left."

Cassi laughed. I don't mean a polite knowing little chuckle but a full on chortling laugh. I was fairly certain the reaction caught her off guard as much as it did Brandon and I, because she almost doubled over so far she flipped. "Sorry...just too much stress and...and.... she was so.." After a few failed attempts at the tale Cassi started to regain her composure and looked up to me with a grin. "You would have needed to be there, Will."

I looked to Brandon for some form of support or perhaps more information than that, but the big man just chuckled and shook his head. "Not my tale to tell Codex."

Outnumbered I decided to drop the issue at that, at least for the time being.

Cassi finally looked to have pushed past her hilarious over reaction to Stormy... well storming off to stay at a friend's. I couldn't get over how that woman kept having more weight thrown at her and kept going. Sure, she would stumble and pause to adjust, but a few moments later and Cassi was ready to go. Perhaps it was the empathic powers allowing her to absorb my own forced calm in the face of the situation. Perhaps it was the fact that she was strong enough to withstand such great stresses. Personally, I was starting to think that it was a combination of the two with a heavy leaning toward the latter. Still, I didn't want to see what happened when the walls around her mind cracked.

Brandon was the first to speak up after that actually. "Well that's enough remembering for now. What exactly are we up against tonight?"

"I was hoping just to explain in the truck on the ride back." I answered, before pushing back off the wall and motioning back toward the truck. "We want to get where we need to be by dark. I doubt our big problem is going to give us long after dark whether we are in public or not."

"Fair enough. Your back seat empty? Once you catch me up I could use a few winks." Brandon was already walking toward the truck as I nodded and looked to Cassi who took one more last deep breath and nodded, her face washed over with stone calm. We were as ready as we were going to be.

It had taken about an hour of driving to explain the whole situation as we saw it to Brandon. I'd been worried at first that he would have no interest in his job going against the Wendigo while I worked against the assassin's, but the werewolf surprised me. He wanted nothing more than to leave the beast alone and to rip the elves apart, but a few deep breaths and a knowing nod from Cassi seemed to have an amazing effect. Brandon accepted his role in the plan and leaned back to get some sleep. All considered, he wasn't going to get much rest. We had just over an hour to go until we got to the rendezvous point. The rest of our back-up would be ready and waiting to get started.

"So, where exactly are we heading?" Cassi looked up from the handful of pictures that she had been thumbing through since we'd gotten onto the road. One was a picture a Sue, a few months after the first change. The woman looked far healthier, and if it was possible, happier. The second was of Sue sitting on a porch swing at the house we had just left, drinking a cup of coffee. The sunset lit her hair on fire. Finally she had a picture that I knew was taken only three years ago. Sue laughed from her place around a campfire along with a younger Stormy who was being held in place, despite her dislike of the situation, by Brandon to pose for the picture. From the far side of the photo I grinned back at the picture taker.

I was three years younger and apparently missing nine years of stress. My hair was cut to about an inch long and buzzed on the sides. A horrible accident with a hand held flame thrower had lost me most of my hair and that was the only thing like a respectable haircut I could manage for the time. I had most of my eyebrows in the picture, so that meant it was after the second blow torch ordeal. I used my old favorite weapon to fight off an evil Native American spirit in Huntsville. I really had a thing for rule number five right after I started with the initiative.

"Just north of Tyler. Walters should be meeting us there to lead the way to the most promising 'Bigfoot' spotting." I said taking my eyes off the picture and putting them back onto the road where they belonged. "He was going to do some scouting about and see if he could find the start of a trail. All going well, we take down the Wendigo tonight and we don't have to deal with the elves until the morning if they are worth their word."

"Estan is. The sword told me that much." Cassi reached down and brought the handle of the weapon to her lap after setting the pictures into the center console of the front seat. "Did you reload the SIG?"

I nodded my head. "Yeah, has a round in chamber ready to go." I said. "There should be something for you in there as well. I was going to wait until we got to Walters but now is as good a time as any."

Cassi started digging into the console before pulling out a large bundle of black nylon straps with a black pistol handle. "Good lord Will. You really know how to impress a girl." she said as she unwrapped the bundle of straps to reveal a pistol that looked more like something from a comic book than from real life. The revolver style gun had an extra-long cylinder and the barrel was disproportionately short. "You know a goofy looking puppy is a cute gift Will. I really don't know what to think of a goofy looking gun. Seriously, what is it?"

"It's called a Judge. It's a pistol that fires several different types of ammunition. Either a forty five caliber pistol round like my colt .410, or a small shot gun shell that can be loaded for a variety of purposes." I grinned. "It's powerful, loud and ideal for someone who isn't quite sure what they are going to get into. The first round is a forty five caliber pistol round. Lots of stopping power, but I still wouldn't try anything at long range. The gun isn't designed for far off work. The next two rounds after that are homemade buck shot. Four large silver balls keeping in fairly tight group. The last two are called super flares."

"Super flares?" Cassi asked while she started to work out the nylon straps before pulling off her jacket and starting to work the fire arm on.

"More or less, they are flare gun rounds. They can be used to signal for help and blind anyone nearby that is light sensitive. A lot of things that see in the dark don't agree too well with sudden flashes of bright light. Keep your eyes down if you fire one into the air and you'll get a good head start."

"First shot a normal bullet, second and third rounds are silver ball bearings, fourth and fifth rounds are to get out of dodge or call for help." Cassi nodded in approval. "When did you find time to get this thing?"

"Well to be honest it is a hand me down, but all the best guns are." I said with a grin. "I've had that one in my arsenal for a while.

When I know I'm getting into a situation involving something that needs different kinds of special ammo I reach for the Judge. It's solid, reliable, and if you have to pull it out, and level it at something, anything smart enough to know what a gun is will stop and take note." I'd tossed the gun into the console on our way out from my house. Cassi was going to need more than the sword if things got ugly and a Judge was an ideal defensive weapon.

"I'll always remember this day as the day that a federal agent gave me a gun that was in no way legal for me to carry." Cassi chuckled.

"If that is what you remember out of everything else today, that'll be a good thing." I said looking toward her from the road for a moment. "Remember keep close to me, or Walters if we are separated. Lean on your inherited sword skills for defense and leave the gun play to the pros as long as you can manage it. You know by now that these things happen a lot quicker than they feel. Don't let yourself get tied up with the Wendigo no matter what." I said before putting my thumb over the seat and pointing toward Brandon. "All going well our muscle should hold him up and Walters and I can keep him busy long enough to see what works and then we'll kill him, regroup and wait for the elves. Hopefully when the three of them see that the two of us have grown a werewolf and mortal world law enforcement, they will back down."

Cassi nodded in agreement as she looked back at Brandon. "He doesn't want to live past tonight. That is why he is willing to go against the Wendigo, Will. I don't think I've ever seen anyone so sad. I mean I'm just starting to feel at home with this mind reading... I mean empathy thing, but two days ago I felt two men being torn apart by a monster, and it hurts more to look at him."

"Brandon was raised to be a pack leader. Outward emotions aren't his strong suit. I always figured that is why he went into art. It's a way to feel something without showing weakness to his pack. Sue...your mother and he were something special. I'd only known them for a few years and most of that was in just fleeting meetings, but it was obvious how much they depended on one another. Professionally, it is too soon to tell how well he will recover from that. The human half of him has seen a lot of trauma but knows he has people to reach out to. The wolf however, without such a valued member of his pack, won't cope as well maybe even worse for having a full suite of human emotions." I looked back toward Brandon for a moment and shook my head. "If we are out there and he loses it, the first round won't do you much good, but the silver is gifted and the flares will blind him."

"That's horrible!" She started yelling before following my brief gaze and lowering her voice again. "That's part of the job isn't it? Everyone you see has to be weighed and measured. You have to know how to kill Brandon if he snaps. You have to know how to kill Hannelore if she loses control of her gift. You have to know how....how to stop me."

That sentence hung in the air by the end of the theoretical dagger that had just ripped me open. I started to shake my head. I wanted to laugh and tell her that nothing like that would happen and even if it did I wouldn't be the one to do it. That we were free to explore whatever was happening between us whenever this was all over and that we wouldn't have to do so with the chance of that future hanging over our heads. I really wanted to lie to Cassi right then, but I couldn't. I hadn't even realized I was biting my own lip until I tasted the blood. After a deep breath I nodded my head.

Cassi nodded her head in return. I couldn't turn myself around to look at those green eyes, but I could feel their gaze against me for a long moment before I felt her fingers reach over the center console of the truck and pulled my right hand free of the steering wheel. Her other hand let her sword slip back down into the floorboard before wrapping about my hand along with its twin. She pulled my hand toward her lips and placed an almost ethereal kiss against my knuckles. Maintaining her perfect silence, leaving us with nothing but road noise, she set my hand down on the center console of the truck and wrapped her fingers inside mine.

Clouds were starting to gather above the already failing light of the autumn afternoon sky; making the world appear a few hours closer to darkness than it really was even for that time of year. Cassi had taken to the job of navigator without question and had guided us to the address Walter's had mentioned in a brief phone call, and we had made it to a mildly crowded interstate complex comprised of a gas station and a Dairy Queen.

"Leave it to the cop to pick a Dairy Queen." I said with a chuckle as I pulled the truck into a parking spot. "Free coffee for a local uniform or for an off duty cop that's been around as long as Walters I bet."

"Hell, where do I sign up?" Cassi chuckled as the truck rocked into park. After I unbuckled, I reached over and patted Brandon on the shoulders and jumped back as the giant werewolf stirred with a snarl and came out of his seat.

A few moments later we walked into the little Dairy Queen side of the building. Brandon trailed Cassi and me by a few steps to make us a little bit less conspicuous. Tubes of bright florescent light cast out all shadow in the eating area of the small fast food joint. White lines of reflected light glowed on all the brightly polished wood veneer surfaces and the linoleum floors. The place smelled of grease with a faint undertone of pine scented cleaner. A sullen looking teenager behind the counter shoved her cellphone back into her pocket as we walked in and plastered on a fake smile. "Hello. What can I get for you?"

"Well, we are looking for a friend actually, but I'll have some coffee and..." I looked back to the other two with me for their orders before looking back over the lobby for the old sergeant.

Walters was surprisingly difficult to spot. Dairy Queens don't exist everywhere in the country so for those of you that have never walked into one, trust me it isn't hard to find an old tough cowboy type in one unless you are trying to find a particular old cowboy. That is kind of like finding a needle in a stack of needles.

Cassi chuckled having apparently picked up on the trace of frustration I was feeling. "I'll find him. Be right back. Coffee." Cassi said with a grin as she turned and walked toward that back of the seating area where every Dairy Queen's restrooms are kept. Honestly, it hadn't been the first time I'd admired Cassi's walk but when she was trying her stride was downright hypnotic. An instant later I noticed that I wasn't the only one taking notice of the shapely young redhead walking across the room. A handful of eyes looked over coffee cups and exposed the side of their faces till one eventually stopped in his gaze and looked upwards before shaking his head and looking back toward the counter and made eye contact with me.

Walters grinned from beneath his hat and tapped the side of his head. A couple of cups of coffee and a Styrofoam cup the size of a compact car full of soda for Brandon later, the werewolf and I made our way across the room where I sat across from Walters. "Dirty trick Codex, using the girl like a bird dog. Ruined my whole mysterious persona." Walters nodded toward Brandon who had just sat in the booth beside him. "This your heavy you're bringing in? I talked to a guy I knew and just managed to get these in by the way." Three new pistol clips full of forty five rounds slid across the table at me. "We can settle on what a gun smith charges for custom hollow points after this whole mess washes over, but if they are as effective as you claim we can call the materials you gave me payment."

"No we can't." I quickly said back shaking my head. "What I gave you was a gift. I'll pay you back for what you paid the smith in full. The silver won't work if it isn't given." I said before taking the bullets and pulling them to my side of the table and tucking them under my coat.

"This thing doesn't like silver?" Brandon asked he carefully watched the bullets change hands as if one might jump out and try to bite him. "So you're both going to be shooting gifted silver at the thing I'm going toe to toe with?"

"That a problem?" Walters asked as he looked toward Brandon.

"Not unless you miss." Brandon said. "I don't feel like getting a silver bullet in my back."

"Most people would be worried about bullets in general. At least most humans would." Walters eyed the man sitting beside him.

"I thought you said your other shooter was in the know." Brandon said to me with a shake of his head. "Whatever you do fighting this Wendigo thing, you'd better make sure you don't hit me with one of those bullets. OK?"

Walters nodded his head as he looked from Brandon back to me. "So am I going to have a hard time telling the monsters apart?"

Brandon started to stand up from his seat before he saw Walters grin. The big man just shook his head. "My hair is darker. Weather shaping up as it is, and with human eyes, I'll be the shadow making the monster scream." Brandon said with, well, a wolfish smile.

Cassi slipped into the booth beside me and smiled as she picked up her cup of coffee. "Hello, Sergeant Walters." A polite smile played across her lips for a moment before she took a sip.

"Miss Ross. We're breaking the law together. The least you can do to not make me feel old. Just call me Roger." The old cop said with a grin before taking a sip of his own coffee.

"Fair enough, Roger. The big guy is Brandon. Since no one else bothered to tell you." "How did you?" Walters started double taking between Brandon and Cassi before shaking his head. "You know what, I'm better off not knowing. Aren't I?"

I just nodded after a long pull from my coffee cup. "Ok, one more time from the top. We follow Walters out to where we think this thing is holeing up and we track it down. Brandon, you'll take point once we make contact and keep the Wendigo tied up. Walters and I will fill it full of holes and Cassi will have the sword in case it gets in close. We'll see what works best and we'll do it till it stops moving long enough to take the normal insurances."

"Normal insurances?" Cassi questioned from over the top of her coffee. "Dismemberment and the judicious application of rule number five." I said with a wink.

"Rule number five?" Walters asked.

"Everything hates fire." Cassi and Brandon answered in almost perfect unison. Brandon chuckled before looking toward me and said, "You still teach Gideon's rules. Good."

I nodded my head before another drink of my coffee. "Well then let's get moving. Brandon you're up and moving with Walters, he has a bigger truck than mine."

193

"How did you know...? No I don't want to know why the feds know what I drive. You can ride with me and we can give the kids a few minutes." Walters and Brandon both nodded before getting up. "I'll lead the way to the patch of woods Finsen pointed me to earlier today. It's as good a start as any by what we could find."

Cassi and I gave the other two a head start before we got up and followed them out, jumped into the truck, and followed them out onto the road.

We'd had enough time to finish off the cups of coffee before Walters pulled off the interstate onto a small back road closer to the site where the Wendigo first killed in the area. After a couple more miles we pulled onto a small dirt drive and into a pasture surrounded by the tall pines so typical of East Texas. This pasture however had never seen use as a cattle field or the like. Judging by the tall, tangled uncut grass, this field hadn't seen any use in quite some time. Walters waved us over as he pointed something out to Brandon.

"Finsen got called out this way early today for some horrible sounds in the forest that a hunter said sounded like human screams. We never found a body or any evidence of one, but I couldn't help but notice a few little details. There were some scattered tracks in the forest but none in the field. An area where something had bedded down. Something way too big to be any animal that belongs down in this part of the world. There was also a squatter camp out in the woods. No sign of a body there either."

"As good a start as any. Thanks, Walters." I said with a nod as I looked about me out of habit and pulled the Colt free of its holster before ejecting the previous clip and sliding one full of silver core rounds into the gun before pulling back on the slide and releasing the non-silver round in the chamber. "Ok we stick together until we make contact. Walters, you're in charge of the tracking. I know my better when I see it."

"Hell kid you're better than most your age." He said with a nod. "I got it. Just keep that nail driver of yours ready to go.

"The guy who trained me wouldn't like it if he heard you complimenting me." I said with a grin. I'd gotten rusty since my last trip into the woods with Walters and my father, and the old Sergeant had never paid me a compliment on the skills he had helped teach me.

"Sounds like a good guy." Walters nodded before starting off in the direction of the forest. I'd started to chuckle at that statement but my grin never got the chance to become audible.

As we crossed on the border into the forest the wind picked up and a roar of air washed over us from somewhere within the darkness provided by the trees. All the mirth I had in me was picked up and thrown back on that sudden gust of wind that dissipated as quickly as it had come.

Walters' gun had seemingly teleported from his hip to his hands in a draw so quick it hadn't even registered. Cassi's sword rung free of its scabbard coming to rest at the ready in her right hand as she fell into a naturally defensive stance. The old quick draw and the 'would be' lady knight and her silver sword aside, Brandon had taken the cake for battle field preparedness. Where the bulking Native American man had stood a moment ago a black four legged furry Abrams tank now stood. Bright pale too human eyes glowing dim blue in the dark with a maul full off dagger like teeth bared toward the unseen foe.

I had thought for a second that I was finally going to see the edge of Roger Walters' sanity. He slid back several steps and started to bring his service revolver around to face Brandon in his wolf form. Still, even in the seconds that panic had started to spread over his face, Walter's eyes remained cold and calculating taking the hard facts that started to grow vague as panic set in to most people. The pile of half discarded and torn clothing scattered about the form. The fact that none of it showed signs of blood. I'd bet the last detail was the not quite animal eyes staring back from the wolf. The same eyes, that when Brandon was in his public form, hadn't quite seemed human.

"Son of a bitch." Walters said as the panic started to disappear from his face. "This would be the kind of thing I would like to know about beforehand." He said before looking toward Cassi and her sword. "And I'm still trying not to think too hard about that." He said with a shake of his head before walking back into the woods, Brandon stalking on his right and one step behind. I followed on the left and Cassi kept her sword free and stood between Brandon and I, her own eyes danced about wildly filled with anxiety that hadn't been taken care of with her quickly absorbed knowledge.

The wind inside the forest gathered and swirled about us wrapping about the trees and sometimes seemingly came at us from two different directions at once. That rushing air sounded like distant howls dancing about the forest occasionally reaching volumes too high or pitches too varied to be created by simply passing between the trees. Between the tree cover, the clouds, and the ever late hour the forest was already starting to get too dark to see. It wasn't exactly like trying to see in the dark but the shapes of the trees and the growth of the forest itself seemed to blur into an ever intimidating mirage of changing shadows and figures.

Walters and I moved through the forest with practiced stealth. I had the benefit of youth, slightly better vision, and a profession that had caused me to spend more than one night sneaking through dark places. The old hunter who had taken over the body of Walters, the deputy, moved through the trees in whispered silence with the type of attention to detail that came with a long life of living in the forest. I knew from my everyday life that Walters was a woodsmen and tracker, and that those skills brought a certain amount of stealth. With the extra tension provided by the moment Walters moved more like a specter than a man. Cassi had the benefit of a lighter step by lack of body weight alone, and to someone who knew the details of her gift it was obvious she was moving through the forest with skill she borrowed due to her close proximity. I wasn't even sure she knew she was doing it. Brandon on the other hand, was in a class of his own. His black hair, his wolf form, and his increased animal instincts caused me to lose track of the over four hundred pound wolf despite the fact that the beast wasn't standing more than five feet away from me in the forest.

As we moved deeper among the tall shadowed pines, the winds about us picked up and the howling started to grow to a loud tornado wail sounding like a freight train rolling toward us on two or three different sides at a time. The trees added creaking cries of stress as the winds picked up. Waves of pine needles and dust flew across the game trail we followed throwing hundreds of distractions across the trail. Motion blurred at the edge of my field of vision and my right arm brought the colt up across my view and my left arm reached up to block Cassi from walking into my line of fire. Walters stopped and held his hand up signaling all to stop before pointing into the forest ahead of us and slightly to the left with his revolver. An instant later Walters let out a loud whistle and a flourished point of his finger to signal Brandon to move in the direction. The wolf allotted a fraction of the second to send a contemptuous glare toward the bird dog signal before diving into the forest directly to the source of the movement we had all spotted.

"Give him a few more seconds and get ready to follow quickly. If that blur was our mark, we aren't going to be able to lead a shot on it until Brandon stands that thing up." He said before nodding his head and taking a few deep breaths. "Miss Ross, if you would cover this old man while we let Will exercise those young long limbs of his."

Cassi looked to me, confirmed something I hadn't even realized, and nodded her head. Walters nodded his head in agreement and I was off to the races.

I wouldn't say I'm especially fast, but I've got long legs, grew up in a forest just like this one, ran cross country in high school, and back in college I ran through the hills, valleys, and pines of Sam Houston State Park to ward off the freshmen fifteen. I couldn't keep pace on flat ground with anyone who ran track but uphill, over log, and in most non-prime conditions I could move at nearly top speed and not break my stride or my neck.

As fast as I was, through the overgrown pine forest Brandon was barely visible as a disturbance in the forest far in front of me. I ducked beneath a tree limb and leaped to the side to move around a fallen log before running back down the trail toward the sound of a growl over the next rise.

When you are forced to act in a high stress situation a lot of things happen in your brain. The hypothalamus responds to the perception of danger triggering a dump of adrenaline into your system starting multiple chain reactions throughout your body. These chemical reactions lead to things like increased heart rate, respiration, and sweat gland activity all working to keep the body moving. Sympathetic nervous system reactions cause the five senses to pay greater attention to detail while sacrificing the larger picture. For instance, a widening of the pupil increases light sensitivity and, a slight bulging of the eye, creating the infamous tunnel vision effect.

With that knowledge and the mental training that I had acquired from Hannelore, I consciously worked to keep my vision wide without sacrificing my attention to detail. I can't say that concentrating on preventing my eyes from bulging actually caused my eyes not to swell, but the argument could be made that it helped keep my anxiety response from going out of control and as a result helped prevent tunnel vision.

As I topped the next rise I started looking about to see any sign of Brandon. My eyes scanned the clearing as I stopped near the top of the hill and brought the Colt up to eye level and looked down the glowing green dots of my tritium sights. The light provided by them wasn't so much to ruin my night vision but it was enough to draw my eyes down the barrel of the gun and help me focus in the dark.

Brandon stood on all fours hackled and snarling toward the tree line. I ran two or three steps before stopping and sliding down the hill working to keep my core centered over my hips and stay upright until I reached the bottom of the pine covered hill.

That had at least been the plan. Once I was half way down the twenty foot slope, automatic gunfire roared from the far edge of the clearing lighting up the dark of the forest with bright flashes of fire. Surprise rocked me back and off balance, instinct must have kept me from tumbling down the hill out of control. Instead I managed to fall flat on my back with my arms out to my side to control my slide. Bullets whistled over my head each one crashing against the ground and creating geysers of dirt every shot growing closer as the gunmen started to draw a line on me.

Brandon ducked low and ran toward the forest as the guns trained and fired on me. On the last few feet of my downhill slide I shifted to my side and rolled down the hill. While I rolled down the hill I could hear shouts, scattered burst of gun fire, and a loud basso yelp.

By the time I stopped rolling and pushed myself up to my feet I managed to get my bearings and find the tree line. I tried to track the burst of gun fire, but the shooters knew how to operate in the dark. Short controlled bursts would ring from part of the shadows before another blast came a few seconds later constantly rotating and constantly moving. As best as I could track the three shooters were in the thick growth now occupied by Brandon. It looked like the elves had broken their word.

I could hear Brandon growl from somewhere deep inside the forest. A werewolf in the woods against three humans, even with the judicious applications of firearms, would be no contest. Brandon was faster, stronger and in the dark his senses were in a whole different league.

Elves however were a different story. While their hearing or sense of smell wasn't as strong as Brandon's their eyesight was nearly equal to his in the dark. The fair folk are stronger and faster than humans. Not to mention the fact that each of them was packing some serious heat and knew what it would take to hurt Brandon, once they figured out what they were fighting. Hopefully they hadn't expected me to bring the werewolf into play and they wouldn't have the silver they needed to take Brandon down quickly. However, they could still bleed him out with enough vital hits that his ability to heal couldn't keep up. Or they could just shoot him in the head. Then it wouldn't matter what the bullets were made of.

I tried to listen back toward the direction that Cassi and Walters would be coming from but with the howling wind, the bursts of gunfire, and the relative elevation the idea of hearing them this soon was wishful thinking. "Not my best move ever." I thought to myself before I ducked low and moved into the woods to back Brandon up.

I was actually hoping to use a lack of speed as a weapon. I knew inside the forest that the elves and the werewolf would be playing a high speed gambit to out flank and stay ahead of one another. I wouldn't have to worry about Brandon attacking me and with any luck the three elves would be attacking on the run trying to stay ahead of the wolf. They wouldn't be looking for someone to be crouched down moving slowly through the field of combat waiting for the right moment. So that's exactly what I did. I kept low to the ground and moved through the forest slow enough to keep as silent as I could. I had to take advantage of the occasional burst of gun fire to move closer to the fight that had now moved several yards into the forest. I tried to look ahead toward the flashes of light and the bursts of moving shadow, but in all honesty it was far too dark to tell much about the fight. All I could hear was quick shouts in elven and gunfire followed by the inevitable crashing sound or growl. Normally after Brandon made his move it was followed by more screams and shouts.

I don't know exactly how long it took me to get a good view of the fight in terms of time, but I know that it took four bursts of fire before I finally slipped up to the edge of the clearing that Brandon was apparently stalking about. The three elves, all now bearing crimson scratches, stood back to back to back near the center of the clearing each scanning the edge of the forest frantically.

"The beast lied to us." Illish snarled in elven from behind the sights of an M-16 with one of those under barrel grenade launchers. "I knew it hadn't been hired by our employer. It made no sense"

"First of all that beast is not our concern at the moment love." Estan snarled from behind his own weapon, a small carbine automatic with a large suppressor. "And treachery doesn't mean he wasn't hired by our employer. We are not getting the rest of the payment until the job is done. Perhaps the Wendigo decided it stood a better chance killing us than beating us to the mark. You must not underestimate its kind."

"Why is the werewolf here with Codex!" Shouted Illish's younger sibling whose name I'd never gotten. "You told me that killing the wolf had nothing to do with the other case." The younger elf half growled. "I knew you took that cheap bounty for a reason. You were only going to pay me for the one job!" He said taking his eyes away from the forest and glaring at Estan. "This is your doing isn't it? You took me with you to kill the wolf while Illish stalked the beast as it hunted the girl."

"You fool! Keep your eyes up!" Estan shouted as he shifted about to cover half of their surrounding instead of a third. The warning had come too late however. Four hundred pounds of solid shadow dove from the forest directly into the new gap in the elves' defenses. The younger elf was torn to the ground as Brandon bit into his left leg and started off toward the other side of the clearing to finish the kill in the cover of the forest.

Illish however wasn't going to let her younger brother fall so quickly. The female elf drew her gun down in the direction of the werewolf and pulled the trigger letting go a quick burst of gun fire. Two of the three rounds stuck Brandon in the center of his back. The jacketed rounds ran Brandon through and through each letting off a burst of crimson and a clean exit wound on his side.

Brandon yelped before shaking his head cracking one of the bones in the lower part of the younger elf's leg before leaving him and making for the forest, leading a trail of bullets supplied by Estan and Illish while the third elf rolled about on the ground clutching his injured leg.

As far as I could tell, from my hiding place in the edge of the forest, Brandon's wounds hadn't been caused by silver. A wolf of his age and power would barely have to acknowledge the injury after a couple of moments. He could likely tear into the middle of the unprepared elves and rip them limb from limb, but that would have been a quick death. Brandon had picked up on the scent of the elves and broke after them, lost in his animal instincts. His human side only clung on enough to know that he wanted the death of his mate's killers to be slow and painful.

Estan kept his smaller weapon in one hand and pointed toward the forest while moving forward and Illish covered his back. His silver hand reached out and grabbed the young elf by the collar and pulled him back across the earth toward the center of the clearing. I'd now seen him pick up a motorcycle and pull an armed and armored body across uneven terrain with that arm. I officially made a point not to let him hit me with it.

More frightening yet was the way the two older elves worked together. They had no need to communicate as they set up the third where he could take up a defensive post, his gun pointed to the forest, thankfully away from me. Illish and Estan covered one another's every movement as they looked for the wolf and kept their injured companion protected all without any sign of speech or signal. The two assassins had simply been at the game so long, likely working as a team that they didn't need to speak. They simply thought as one.

I kept the colt down and tried to think invisible thoughts as I waited for a shot. Not only did I need to wait until I didn't risk being spotted by one of the elves after I shot the first of them, but I didn't know where Brandon was and if I put a round in one of the elves only to have it pass through to the werewolf I would be in a worse place than if I was spotted. I'd loaded the colt with silver rounds to slow down the Wendigo they would be more deadly against Brandon than they would be against their intended target.

People would like to tell you that gun fights are dramatic battles somewhere between a game of chicken and a martial arts movie. If someone tries to tell you that, they have never been in a gun fight, don't believe them. One moment I was crouched waiting in the woods as the elves circled around trying to find their target. The next moment I caught Brandon to the left at the edge of my field of vision. In the next, Estan, who had been searching for Brandon in my general direction, looked where the injured elf pointed off to the right. Illish was about to use her moment to turn and cover the other half of their circle. But that was my moment. In that moment I stood, brought the Colt up, took aim, and squeezed the trigger. An instant later a large portion of Illish's chest blew out her back.

The sound of the gunshot technically came before the bullet hit, but the shot was at such close range that the crack of the large caliber round in the air sounded more or less in step with the crimson explosion that painted the two remaining elves.

I hadn't been counting on such a speedy counter. Illish's brother screamed, turned on his side and fired wildly in my general direction until the clip in his rifle was empty forcing me to dive back into the brush. Illish's body hadn't had time to hit the ground yet. Estan however, wasn't so foolish.

"Codex!" Estan shouted, turning about and keeping his gun bared in my general direction. The small carbine balanced easily in one hand. Despite his drawn attention, I was confident that if I moved he would catch me in his peripheral vision and open fire. "I had been regretting coming to take your young lady friend. Now I think I am going to enjoy it. As a matter of fact, I am going to make sure of it."

I knew better than to jump up at the ploy. No matter what he was going to do or how he felt about it. If I stood up and gave away my location, I was going to get what was left of the clip in that carbine assault rifle of his delivered throughout my body. Then I wouldn't be around to help Cassi. Not to mention that I really, really didn't feel like dying from high velocity lead poisoning.

Most likely the only things keeping me alive at the moment was the fact that Estan knew that I was pinned. Also that if he stopped looking for Brandon for the instant it would take to kill me, the werewolf would take advantage of it.

Illish's little brother finally found the clip for his weapon that he'd been looking for and slammed it into the larger, more intimidating fully automatic weapon strapped to his chest. "Silver" he said in elven as confirmation to Estan who returned the nod. With two of the elves looking about it was only a matter of time before I was spotted. Estan was starting to look around more carefully now that the other elf was looking for the wolf.

I didn't move as I scanned the forest about me looking for a sign. I wasn't going to get out of this by standing up to two elves and three automatic weapons. The younger elf was forcing himself up to one foot as he scanned the forest with his gun barrel. He was hobbling and his stance was awkward at best. That would have been of value had he been in arms reach. I wasn't fast enough to rush him however and Brandon would have silver reigned upon him if he tried. And since the elves weren't speaking in English he wouldn't even know it was coming.

I couldn't stand back up and give away my location. Estan was just as likely to shoot me down as he was to stand and talk. Besides, that wouldn't give Brandon any information. The opponent Brandon and I stood around was too strong for either one of us to attack. We were going to have to out fox our enemies, or out wolf them rather.

I grinned as I thought back to the other morning where I saw Brandon standing in a middle of the circle of children each waiting until another attacked and drew the large werewolf's attention before they went in to take the towel from Brandon. I thought back and tried to remember the instinctual rhythm to the attack and defense that caused the circle to inhale and exhale chaos and calm. To the warrior with the towel in hand at the end of the day went the honor of the game, but it could not be won unless someone stepped out first. Brandon was an alpha; he had won the right to the kill in each contest years ago because of his proficiency at killing. He could finish this, if someone gave him an opening.

I let the muscles in my legs tense as I took in a deep breath. I locked my eyes on my target as I exhaled. Another deep breath and I set silly concerns like personal safety and a well-deserved fear of bullets aside while I continued to compress my body. Then I watched for the tip of the young injured elf's gun barrel to drop before I broke hard to the right before running out into the clearing and directly at the barrel of the gun.

Eight feet isn't normally a relative distance, but when it comes to times like this everything changes. Eight feet is a mile to the man running at the gun, but it is only a couple of inches to the man with the gun watching as some idiot rushes them. The elf had to be thinking that I was crazy. In all reality I think that by running at the gun I was more confirming the fact that I was crazy. That moment of hesitation most likely saved my life, or at least prolonged it by a few more seconds.

By the time Estan started to turn about to face me and the other elf started to pull the trigger I had dove hard to one side to avoid most of a spray of bullets. Thankfully I had already started forward again when I felt a tear and a hot explosion of pain in the meat of my left arm, or I would have likely fallen off course. Instead I stumbled through my last steps as I crashed into the younger elf.

The gun went off again as we crashed onto the ground and rolled. The elf tried to hit me in the side of the head with the butt of his gun, but I imagine that was the last thing on his mind as I reached down and sank my thumb into the bite wound on the outside of his leg near his knee. The gun slapped lightly against the side of my head more pleading than aggressive as the elf screamed. A second blow across my head was a bit more noteworthy and my grip on the elf's leg ended and my arm covered the side of my head in time for the butt of the gun to crash against my forearm. I brought up the Colt and brought the bottom of the handle of the gun down against the side of the elf's head.

"The bond. It was the bond. The bond made us to kill the bitch." The elf tried to say against the threat of unconsciousness still trying to struggle away from the tackle as I placed the gun underneath his chin and twisted it to drive the point home.

"Say it one more time but in your language." I slowly said in my rough elven accent as I kicked up to my feet letting the Colt hold its mark between the elf's eyes. In all honesty my understanding of the language was much stronger than my command of it. Someone was going to crack eventually

"I said that it was the..."

"Shut up Edrin!" So that was his name! I saw Estan out of the corner of my eye as he afforded Edrin a glance. Both the automatic barrels turned and lined up on me and I honestly couldn't help but grin. "Any last words, Codex?"

"How about... Got you Estan." I said looking past him at the dim bluish glow of eyes moving silently from the edge of the woods.

The elf's eyes widened as he turned about to face the charging werewolf. He struck Brandon across the side of the face with a brutal right hook from his bright silver arm. The blow sounded with a dull echoing thud and a flash of bright white light that sent Brandon's wolf form across the clearing hard enough to make the first tree the wolf hit snap and fall. There was another loud crack as Brandon hit a second tree but this time the trunk showed no signs of damage as Brandon slid to the ground.

"Illish swore on her life to have the order replace my hand Codex. And thanks to you my love proved she was prepared to lay her life down in the process of fulfilling that bargain. She sacrificed a great deal don't you think?"

Edrin was still half dazed by the blow to the head so I ran towards him to confuse Estan's line of fire as he brought his gun about and let out a roar of bullets. I turned about and raised the Colt and let Estan's kneecap fill up the sights of my gun before squeezing the trigger to hold him off as I passed Edrin and made for the edge of the clearing. My shot went wide thanks to the funny firing angle and the fact that I was on the move.

My arm was starting to burn as the initial shock of the gunshot wore off. The wound was shallow and the bleeding was slow. It was going to be sore and I might need a few stitches before it was all said and done, but the shot had missed any major arteries. I would live.

Estan's gun started clicking empty right before the trail of bullets reached my new holdout point in the woods. The elf cursed as he dropped the gun and fell to his side to pick up Illish's assault rifle and brought it to bare. Thankfully that had given me enough time to run back into the woods and a bit further around the clearing. By the time I could get my eyes back on the clearing Edrin was getting back to one knee and leveled his gun on the forest.

Right then another gun went off. The loud crack sounded of a non-suppressed pistol and a thirty eight caliber service revolver to be exact. Walters' shot hit the younger elf in the side and exploded out the other side of the elf's ribcage. Edrin fell over on his side, a pool of blood already forming beneath the gasping elf. He was a corpse; he just didn't know it yet.

The assault rifle Estan held started to turn about to face the direction of the new attack right as Cassi broke though the edge of the clearing. She closed the gap on Estan's back with her sword raised over her shoulder the bright silver blade ignited with those familiar prismatic flames.

Several things happened all at once after that. Estan turned about brought up his silver arm to block the sword. The collision of the two enchanted weapons unleashed a flash of opalescent light that ignited the clearing in full color as if the sun broke through the night sky and the trees.

As the light from the magical collision was fading Brandon broke from the forest and sprinted across the clearing behind Estan taking a bite from the back of the elf's leg. Estan tried to turn about to strike at Brandon with his silver hand as he brought the gun up and pulled the trigger in Cassi's direction, but she had already turned away from Estan's reach and was about to jump back into the fray again. Walters, now a few steps closer, let off another round from his pistol putting a round in Estan's chest just inside of the left shoulder.

Estan looked back toward the last remaining elf before looking back up toward Cassi as her blade started to crash down toward him. Cassi had the elf dead to rights but at the last moment Estan placed his new hand on his chest and muttered a word. By the time Cassi's sword fell, it moved harmlessly through a semitransparent form of bluish light as Estan faded from this world.

Walters and I both closed in on the clearing with our pistols still raised. The older cop didn't know what had happened and was likely thinking the elf could come back, but I knew better. Estan was gone. Nor would he be coming back anytime soon and that was if he survived his injuries or worse yet the wrath of his order.

By the time I turned about, Brandon the black wolf was ripping at the throat of Edrin. The elf's leg kicked in dying reflex, but his chest was no longer rising and falling with breath by the time the werewolf looked up.

The forest grew quiet as the cold dark fully grasped the world about us in its frozen grip. Cassi's sword saved our ability to see thanks to the dim but far reaching flickering light. "That was intense." Cassi said between ragged gasps as her sword dipped to the ground.

"That was not the plan I had described." Walters said as he limped into the clearing his bad leg obviously bothering him worse after moving through the forest. "You were supposed to get his attention not bum rush him."

"The sword wouldn't let me....I mean I couldn't just stand there and watch." The dimming flames of the sword danced in time with Cassi's quick breathing. "Damn that sounds weird."

"You're telling me, Miss Ross" Walters said as he opened the cylinder of his revolver and started sliding new bullets into the gun. "I can't tell you much about magic swords, but anything that makes you think different than you know you ought to isn't good."

Cassi started to speak up but never got the chance. The wind at my back picked up and whistled through the pine columns about us. That whistle grew louder and louder turning from a high pitched wail to a deafening roar that vibrated and shook us all to the bone.

Brandon backed out of the forest and barked into the coming wind his ears laid flat against his head his tail standing straight out against the gale. Even his powerful low growl was barely audible among the cry of the wind.

"This the big one, Codex?" Walters shouted over the wind to me as he pulled the gun up to ready.

I nodded my head. "Yeah let Brandon stand him up and take any shot you get. We still have to figure out how to kill it." I doubted much of what I said was even heard over the cry of the wind at this point. I would just have to have faith that everyone remembered what needed to happen. My own gun followed the same line as Walters' pointing directly into the wind. Things were about to get serious.

Normally, in situations like these, you expect time to slow down. However, it barely seemed that Cassi, Walters, and I had time to brace ourselves against the wind before Brandon howled silently into the oncoming roar and charged forward. The black wolf moved so quickly and low to the ground that he looked more like a living shadow moving beneath the wind. Something on the wind, perhaps a scent, gave Brandon a hint as to the creature's location. Because, an instant before the wind stopped and the creature started to form out of wind, the great wolf pounced into the air.

It was wielding a freaking motorcycle. One of the blacked out off-road numbers that the elves had likely ridden to the meeting the Wendigo had set up. The giant beast comprised of hair and muscle would have made the bike look comically small if it had been riding it. Instead, the fact that the beast was wielding the bike like a large club was more disturbing. In a grand gesture to prove that big and hairy didn't mean big and stupid, the Wendigo laughed as he used the motorcycle like a fly swatter knocking Brandon to the ground. It was a good plan. Hell, it was a really good plan because when you looked at it, the beast had most likely planned to have the elves meet him here knowing they would run into us and half its work would get done. It had out thought all of us.

Just to emphasize the point, the beast landed on the ground a moment after Brandon fell and swung the bike down again to literally press the werewolf into the ground. After a third hit he left the bike to rest on Brandon before looking at us, taking a deep breath and speaking.

"I have bested your beast. I shall take your woman. I will see you and the old man dead. Run now and I may forget about you in my pursuit of the female." That deep voice growled the words more slowly than needed as if he was speaking to children. It stepped forward onto one of Brandon's legs eliciting the crack of bone and a half growl half cry from the dazed wolf. Upon hearing the noise the Wendigo twisted its foot.

"What do you want me for?" Cassi shouted bringing the sword up to bare against the beast. "I've done nothing to you!" Walters took advantage of the moment to step up into the clearing leveling a pistol on the creature.

"Your blood carries great power. It is power not born through your father's line. It must have been through your werewolf mother. I will have this power. It will be mine once I devour you."

I'd heard of cannibalistic beliefs that said the person who ate of their victim's flesh gained some portion of their power. And, according to what little theory of magic I had learned from Hannelore, it could work if done in the right way with the right state of mind. Perhaps that is why it had been so long since anyone had killed one of the creatures. If someone was capable of taking on power like that, and if they got their hands on the right victims turned meals, they could acquire all kinds of tricks, like traveling on the wind. Things like that would make a creature like the Wendigo much harder to track and to kill.

A Wendigo's first kill had to be out of pure greed, prime the proverbial supernatural pump. After that greed, such lust for power could give it enough metaphysical vacuum, to take upon itself some small portion of the traits of it victims. If such a creature got a hold of Cassi, an empath who could absorb practical knowledge from those she formed her psychic bond with, they would increase their ability to steal power exponentially.

I really hate figuring things out at the last minute. I glanced back to Cassi before looking to the Wendigo shaking my head. "Not going to happen." I said. But, I imagine it sounded something more like "Not BANG BANG BANG BANG happen." as I started to unload the Colt into the creature's chest.

Walters followed suit and started unloading his revolver at the Wendigo as he stepped backwards toward the edge of the forest for cover. Cassi settled her sword in a defensive stance across her body and started backing up as the blade of the weapon started to take the light from the about us, tearing it apart, and reflecting it back in its individual colors as fire. The Wendigo stumbled back against the rain of bullets as the rounds bit into flesh and bone with little to no resistance.

None the less, the Wendigo roared back against us sending forth a torrent of noxious air that nearly took me off my feet before I managed to drop to a knee to get below the bulk of the wind. Cassi however wasn't quick enough. The wind took her from her feet and sent her flying back toward the tree line, her sword falling from her grip as she flew out of the clearing and into the trees in the direction Walters had gone. The blade sank halfway into the ground and the fires and silver light of the blade faded back to well-polished steel.

Less than a minute into the fight and the Wendigo had managed to take out my heavy hitter, separate Cassi from her most powerful defense, and take Walters out of my line of sight. This was not going well in the least. I started stepping back and looking for an opportunity to put the last couple of rounds in the Colt into the beast as he started to charge forward.

Thankfully, Wendigo's aren't sprinters. When it traveled on the wind it was untouchable and had unearthly speed, but I imagine the economy of energy didn't work out in the short leaps. While I wouldn't want to try to outpace the creature once it got up to speed, the beast had a lot of weight to move with furry legs that weren't as large as they appeared to have to move all that weight upon. So, it lumbered forward raising its large right arm in preparation to separate what would likely be a large portion of my body from the rest of me. I tried to pick up the pace running backwards and putting the last two rounds I had in one of the creature's legs.

The Wendigo stumbled a bit but a couple of large pistol rounds into the leg of something like this beast didn't do much to slow it down. Thankfully, between his meager acceleration and what little good the last two Colt rounds I had time to act. I managed to back away quickly enough to drop the clip inside my gun, grab the second one, and slam it home. By the time I chambered the first round however, the Wendigo was all but upon me.

The beast leaped into the air on its better leg with a roar, challenging me to do what little I could with the gun before it was too late. I did the best I could to take aim as the Wendigo eclipsed what little light that was left for me, and right as I was about open up with a hopeless barrage of bullets a couple of pistol rounds hit him in the neck from the edge of the forest. After those two bullets hit, the jump was turned into more of a gurgling stumble instead of a roaring stomp. A roaring stomp I could manage to dive out of the way of. The Wendigo fell to the ground crashing onto a shoulder, rolling over, and was already starting to push itself up.

"First time I dropped a speed loader in years and it had to be in the woods at night. And with a load full of silver bullets!" Walters cursed from the tree line as the wind died with the sound of the Wendigo's roar. The creature bled from its neck and while the wounds were already starting to close, the more delicate parts of the creature's throat were apparently taking longer to heal than muscle or thick bones.

"Just in time either way." I said before pointing across the field toward Brandon who was pushing the bike off himself. "Get the big guy on his feet." I said before squeezing the trigger of the Colt twice while aimed at the Wendigo's leg and once again at the neck to try to keep the creature from healing up too quickly. "This is a war of attrition we can't win. We'll run out of bullets before he runs out of energy. Did you see Cassi?"

Walters nodded as he ran towards the bike. "She nearly flew into me. I managed to grab hold of an ankle as she went by. Brought her back down to earth. Hit ground about ten feet past me. Looked hard but not bad. How are we going to kill this thing?"

"Someone has to possess what it seeks and kill it with what it can't understand." I said with a shout as I backed away toward the sword reminding the Wendigo I was still here with a round to its shoulder as it started to get up.

"What kind of clue is that?" Walters grunted as he pushed the bike up. "Oh God Codex. This thing tore him apart." Walters looked up to me and back down to the mangled body that was Brandon in his wolf form. "He's breathing, damned if I know how, but he is."

"Not silver, now that the bike is gone he can start healing the wounds. Get ready Walters. I'm almost out of ammo." I replied as I put two more rounds into the Wendigo's body before putting one in its back and the last bullet in the base of its skull. "I'm out." I shouted as I reached for my last clip of silver ammunition. The sheer number of bullet wounds was slowing the Wendigo, who was even now pushing himself up to his feet. While none of the rounds were tearing the creature's body apart like they would a person's, it had to be slowing from blood loss if nothing else. That however was quickly diminishing despite the new round that Walters put in the beast.

"Crap, the wolf is getting up." I heard Walters say, as I chambered the first round of my last clip of silver ammo. Walters had rounds left in his gun so that made maybe a dozen shots between the two of us. Brandon was back up on all fours and heading for the fight an instant later. He blurred across the clearing and tackled the Wendigo, who was just standing back up, like some sort of furry obsidian wrecking ball. Built for speed and the same weight as a bear, Brandon literally knocked the beast back several feet. "Remember, don't hit Brandon!" I shouted toward Walters as I started trying to strafe to the side of the beast.

Have you ever watched a nature documentary where two male lions fight? If not, imagine two large angry creatures throwing all of themselves into a conflict with no care for their personal safety but instead completely concentrating on how badly they can harm the other. Now imagine that they were both smart enough to utilize a moderate amount of martial arts. Every hit landed by Brandon or the Wendigo resulted in the other being ripped open and sending a fount of dark blood across the clearing.

Despite the Wendigo's surprise attack, our tactics and numbers were starting to get ahead in the fight, but that wasn't going to help us if we couldn't figure out how to kill the beast. Brandon could stand toe to toe with the beast, but didn't have the means to take it down in the end. Walters and I could fill it with holes and harass it, but without knowing how to do the job we would run out of bullets before much longer. Cassi, well Cassi could run out to the edge of the woods, pull the Judge from the holster and put a completely ineffective lead round in the creature's back bouncing the shot off its shoulder blade harmlessly. Then I grinned knowing what was coming next.

If I'd had any doubts about how I was starting to feel about this woman they vanished as Cassi ran, half ducked, across the clearing to where her sword rested. The Wendigo knocked Brandon back and tried to turn at one point, but Walters and I pounded the beast with two silver rounds each to distract it.

Cassi, or rather a beautiful mad woman disguised as Cassi, slid to a stop, pulled her sword free from the ground, and screamed. The blade came to life in her hand brightening to a silver sheen and igniting into that prismatic fire that seemed to draw its brightness from about her. It cast the light outward leaving Cassi shrouded in semi darkness. From there she grinned, raised the pistol she held in her other hand and pulled the trigger again.

The first round in Cassi's pistol, a traditional lead forty five caliber hollow point, had next to no effect on the beast. That was the only round of its kind in the gun however. The next time she pulled the trigger the gun released a handful of silver buckshot and let it fly into the back of the Wendigo. The beast screamed as the shot buried into it. An instant later Cassi screamed before she fired another round into the beast, eliciting another yell, and charged.

Time seemed to slow as Cassi ran at the beast. Her auburn hair had apparently escaped most of its braid during her flight and now danced in her wake as she sprinted the remaining distance across the clearing. She was nothing but a blur of dark clothing, red hair, bright green eyes, and the dancing lights of her sword as the gap between her and the Wendigo disappeared. The sword fell right as the beast was turning about to face its attacker. Silver edge bit and tore into the Wendigo's flesh and slid across the monsters ribs with little to no resistance. The light cast from the sword flared as it dug into its prey letting out a sizzling sound as the beast's side was flayed open.

The Wendigo turned about and raised its arm to back hand Cassi. As if the time dilation of the moment wasn't bad enough, it got worse as I watched that giant hand come crashing down toward her. I vaguely remember yelling as I emptied my clip at the beast aiming at its shoulder. Out of the mostly wasted five rounds I had left three of them connected with the Wendigo's shoulder. Don't let anyone tell you that running and/or screaming as you try to fire a handgun is ever a good idea. Out of the three hits one of those rounds had been a solid enough hit to bring some pause to the Wendigo. The others might have gone wide like the other two. Way too close and out of options I threw my Colt to the ground, reached into my shirt sleeve, and flipped out my amulet.

Objects from the past that carry energy like sacrifice with them carry a limited amount of that energy. Most the time when such an object is used it is the radiance of that stored energy that causes any external effect. Think of it like a form of radioactivity. Or you could think of it as a form of supernatural battery. Now whether or not Hannelore is right or not about me being a warlock, I can discharge supernatural batteries.

Stepping in front of the attack I screamed as I mentally wrenched myself into focus on one central point of the amulet pouring all the desire I could generate into that location as if I was trying to pop a bubble of energy around the amulet with a needle of willpower. The whole world started to warp around that one point as I struggled to gather my will and apply it to my target, a task that I normally spent half an hour or better preparing myself for. Literal seconds and relative hours later, I felt the confines of the well of

Brian Raif

energy within the silver pendant break and time reeled back into order about me.

The clearing went from night to day in an instant and kept brightening until the whole world turned blindingly white for a moment. The air vibrated soundlessly and as part of the wave of power bounced back. I was forced back into Cassi. While she and I fell back, it was obvious that we had fared much better than the Wendigo. As the light faded, I watched from on my back beside Cassi as the Wendigo was sent flying backwards through a pine tree causing an explosion of splinters. Two more bursting trees later the ground shook as the beast hit the ground.

I shifted my weight on to my side and looked over Cassi who laid flat on the ground next to me. She had a cut over her left eye that had already left a trail of crimson down the side of her face. A wound she must have acquired from when the wind blast had knocked her back into the forest.

That however looked to be the worst of her collection of bumps and bruises. "Can't say I don't know how to show a girl a good time."

Cassi laughed as her brilliant green eyes opened as she pushed herself up. "If this is your idea of a good time, we are going to have to start some re-education." She said before looking me over in return. "Is that a bullet wound, Will? Oh God." She suddenly started pulling my coat away from my shoulders to get a better look at the wound.

As she looked over my shoulder I looked around the clearing. Walters still had his gun up and pointed in the direction the Wendigo had flown, but his head was trying to shake off the light that was still dancing in his eyes. Brandon was lying face down in the clearing in his human form breathing in gasps, his dark olive skin was several shades more red and looked devoid of hair except that which was on his head. I moved to stand up while cursing beneath my breath. I'd completely forgotten about the werewolf.

"He will be fine." Cassi said as she pulled me back by my shoulder. She opened the leather pouch on her belt and pulled out a roll of gauze and started wrapping the wound.

"First aid kit?" I asked as Cassi set to work.

"It was in there the whole time I.... well I remembered I guess." She said with a sigh. "It's fading actually. That sword blow was sloppy. It's like something I should know how to do is a fading memory." Cassi started to chuckle. "I guess it was too much to ask to be a master swordswoman overnight."

"Suppose so, but the knowledge is out there if you want to get it back." I said as she tapped off the wrapping that would slow the bleeding until we could get my arm looked at. Most of my shirt sleeve was soaked. Brandon was starting to push himself up from the ground and Walters was walking toward the first of the broken trees

"Remind me to never threaten you in front of the pack again, Codex." Brandon said shaking his head. "I didn't know warlock was part of your resume." The large naked man walked toward the path that the Wendigo's flight had carved into the woods.

"I am not a..." I started but, Cassi placed a finger to my lips and smiled before standing up alongside me as we started toward the beast. By the time I knelt down and grabbed my gun from the ground, Walters spoke.

"Codex, we got trouble. This thing is breathing." The old cop shouted from a few feet into the forest. "Doesn't anything in your line of work know how to die?"

I checked my gun over and Cassi raised her sword as we moved toward the edge of the clearing at a jog. By the time we arrived Brandon was taking several deep breaths and rolling his neck about. "I don't know how it stood up to it at ground zero. I wouldn't have." Brandon said, before stretching out and moving to crawl along the ground on all fours. By the time it would have looked strange, Brandon was gone and the mountain of black fur was back.

Twenty yards into the forest from the edge of the clearing, Walters stood at the beginning of a new ditch that had been plowed into the ground. Another ten yards ahead and half buried about four feet into the ground was the Wendigo. Its breathing was rapid and most of the beast's hair was burned away leaving the majority of its skin covered in cauterized scars. As I watched, the scars began to fade and hair started to grow back, the Wendigo looked up and growled. "I...will ...not be stopped ... Initiative. I will sate...... my hunger. Then.....I....will.... kill...you." The beast's wide spherical eyes looked up toward me now foggy orbs of white and gray.

"I am tired of being talked about like I am a happy meal. Let's see how it talks without a head." She said stalking forward until I grasped her shoulder and held her back.

"We won't get another window like this. We have to figure out how to kill this thing and make it stick." I said looking toward Walters and the Brandon making sure they knew the statement applied to them as well.

"What was the clue again, Codex? The one you told me earlier." Walters said as he lowered his gun but still kept both hands locked on it.

"Someone who has what it wants has to kill it with what it can never understand." I repeated shaking my head still not able to make sense of the riddle.

"It's greedy right? That's how you described it earlier. 'Never satisfied.'" Walters repeated some of my own words back to me as he slipped his gun into the holster at his hip as he started rolling up one of his shirt sleeves. "Can't understand things like sacrifice and love."

"We've been hitting it with silver the whole time and I unleashed the amulet at it." I said shaking my head.

"And the sword. I don't really understand it yet, but it works off... well emotional attachment. You have to want to do something because you believe it or because you believe in someone." Cassi chimed in beside me.

Walter's nodded his head. "Figured as much, I saw you draw that sword and then I saw you run in at that thing when Codex was in a tight spot. Y'all both had what it can't understand to hit it with, but neither of you have what it wants. Neither of you can be the one to do the deed."

"It wants power though..." I started but Walters shook his head.

"No, it wants fulfillment. Greed isn't the want of power. It's just want. Ya got to not want anything out of life. Brandon could've killed it if he had the right power behind him. He came here to die, but that means he doesn't have any power it can't understand. It knows hate."

"What are you getting at, Walters?" Cassi asked as Brandon let out a growl causing us to look back toward the Wendigo whose breathing was back under control and most of the burns were gone. We didn't have long.

"Well Miss Ross, if you would be so good as to let me borrow that sword for now. You can have it back once I'm done." Walters said his second shirt sleeve up revealing a sun savaged arm still heavy with wiry muscle that only seemed to have grown more defined with age.

"Walters what are you thinking." I asked shaking my head putting a hand on Cassi's sword arm. "That is a cornered injured beast capable of tearing you limb from limb. I can't let you do that."

"I think we moved past chain of command a while back, Codex." Walters beckoned for the sword from Cassi again. "It can't understand the power that drives the sword and I've got no wants in life. It's been a long happy one. Saw my wife grow from the pretty girl I married to a beautiful woman and I've seen my daughter follow suit. Even got to see my granddaughter graduate high school this last spring. More would be good, but I want for nothing." The old cop said with a nod. "Best I can figure that's what you have to be to kill this thing. You got to accept that you're going to give it all up to do it."

"Allow me. I might survive its counter attack" Brandon said standing up holding his arm out for the sword while his unclothed self stood next to us. Walters was already shaking his head.

"Don't know much of why you feel the way you do son, but you've got time to heal and still enjoy your life." Walters said as he wrapped his hand over the hilt of the sword holding Cassi's hand by proxy as her eyes started to well up. "Last thing I'd like to go down in the books saying to a pretty girl is that she should give a fed a chance, but they do make good money Miss Ross. Least you could do is milk the guy for a few dinners before you found a local cop to settle down with. Just let me take care of this one."

The sword's silver sheen grew a tone brighter and the flames took on more of the blue and green tones of the prismatic fire as Walters took control of the blade. Cassi nodded and loosened her grip letting the old deputy take the sword before wrapping her arms about the man.

Walters returned the embrace after he fit his left hand into the basket hilt of the sword. It was a few moments before Cassi finally let go and stepped back from the man and nodded.

"Things aren't supposed to go like this." I said shaking my head as I walked the next few steps with Walters.

"Hard to ride off into the sunset with the girl if you go and get yourself killed son." Walters said with a chuckle. "Look, I need you to get a message to a friend of mine. Names Evan Cunningham works Sheriff's Office a couple of counties over in Rusk county...."

"My name is William Cunningham." I interrupted the man before I even knew what I was saying.

"No you're not Codex you're... Will? Son, what the hell are you doing out here. I..." And then things started to fall into place for Walters. You see, when someone's perception of me had been blurred by the name switch they can't draw conclusions about one name based on information about the other. Once they've heard both names however, if the evidence is strong enough, the connections can be made by a strong enough mind. We are warned not to let it happen if at all possible normally.

"Son of a bitch. So this is pencil pushing for the feds eh?" Walters laughed as I could see it all come to light. "I knew you were too much like your daddy, Boy. Look, you remind him we made a deal years ago and he's gonna be keeping an eye on Mae till she gets back on her feet."

"Walters.... Roger. You can't go and do this."

"Like hell I can't, Son." The old cop said with a grin. "You just tell your daddy to keep his word and that he ain't ever gonna top this one."

"I can't tell him anything about this. You know that much."

"You give that old man time, he'll figure things out and you'll get a bit of leeway. If he knew what you were doing he'd be damn proud, not that it would change anything actually, but it'd be a different kind of proud. You keep an eye on Miss Ross as long as she'll let you. Hell, you aint gonna do better. Never much liked that prissy little girl you brought out to the lease a handful of years back. Bad feeling about that one. Beth or whatever her name was."

I just laughed and nodded my head. "Last chance Walters. We'll find another way."

"Not before it hunts down someone else." Walters said before holding out his right hand for a shake that I returned with a quiet nod. "Now remember, tell your daddy he isn't ever going to top this one as soon as you can." With that Walters took another step closer to the Wendigo and I stayed back and watched with the Colt ready to go just in case. Looking back now I realize that I was holding an empty pistol at the ready. I hadn't even noticed anyone walking behind me until Cassi wrapped her arm about mine, the Judge held in her free hand as she looked on. Brandon stalked a few feet behind back in his wolf form looking on from the underbrush.

The old cop turned cowboy, adjusted the black Stetson one more time before he closed the last few feet between himself and the Wendigo who had started crawling on its hands and knees toward us. All the while he was watching Walters close in. Exploded muscle and burned flesh stitching itself together as he struggled forward. "Old man..." started that controlled growl of a voice. "You think solving a riddle will kill me?" The Wendigo started into a putrid laugh.

"Yeah, I reckon so." Walters said raising the sword over his hand and arching the silver blade through the air leaving a trail of blue and green fire in its wake as it cut through the Wendigo's raised arm with no resistance before crashing down into the beast's head. Splitting it open with a sickening crushing sound as the Wendigo screamed and struck out with its remaining arm. Its hand grabbed at Walters' chest and ripped apart flesh and ribs with ease even as part of its head fell loose from the beast, as the sword bit down into its shoulder. Walters narrowed his eyes and kept the sword bared on the beast even as the sword flames ignited the Wendigo and started to fall over the old cops own arms. The two figures were both starting to burn in prismatic flames as the Wendigo closed its grip around the heart in Walters chest letting out a horrible scream as smoke began to rise from the wound as Walters body began to attack the Wendigo's.

The old man didn't even know he was dead yet as he ripped the sword further down into the creatures chest like it was some type of chain saw, instead of a sword, sending bits of charred Wendigo flesh and fire in every direction. As the two figures stood there in the forest staring at one another, they were both set on fire. It became obvious however that the fire was only consuming one of them.

The Wendigo screamed as the fire grew so hot that its skin and what little fat on its body melted as the scent of burning meat and hair filled the air. Walters' stare was ice cold and completely empty for several seconds before his body finally lost balance and fell over dragging the sword along the Wendigo cutting the screaming form open before he fell to the ground. Whatever life was left in the body on the ground was biological reflex. Walters had left as soon as the Wendigo struck the killing blow.

The Wendigo's death was more of a whimper as the creature's form began falling apart in large chunks of ash about Walters' corpse. The old cop was surrounded in a small circle of black ash as the blade of the silver sword that had shone brightly in the night started to fade along with the last bit of light in Walters' eyes. All that was left was Walter's body, untouched by the flames, and a blade of dull soot covered steel.

That night Brandon and I carried another body out of a forest, and Cassi cried without sound as she followed us in a silent funeral march. The blade of the sword in her hand was still covered in ash as we walked through the forest back toward the duo of trucks left in the pasture. The only sound was the crunch of pine needles beneath our feet during our procession. The forest looked as though it had been hit by a storm however. Broken limbs and old downed trees bore witness to the Wendigo's summoned winds, but now the strong tall mourning pines swayed silently in the gentle breeze of the aftermath.

By the time we arrived at the truck a black van was waiting in the distance with only its running lights on. I'd placed the call before we had started out of the forest. The black suits would clean up the elves and the mess left by the Wendigo while we took care of Walters' body. I would call in a few favors to get the stories lined out. The official report would say that Sergeant Roger Walters was killed in the line of duty by the same cult that murdered Cassi's father and half-brother earlier in the same week, but that his call for back up to the corroborating federal agent led to the capture of the cult before they could take another life.

By noon the next day rumors were already flying through the net that the reports of a cult in the area were just a government cover up for murders committed by an actual rogue Bigfoot that had been killed by authorities and was now being shipped to a secret research facility to be studied. When I went to check on Gregorie that evening, he expressed his sorrow for Walters' death and confided in me that he was helping spread the Bigfoot rumor on his twitter account and on a couple of forums. He thought the whole cover for a cover up situation was rather laughable. I tried to explain that by helping, it was going to take longer to squash the rumors, but that just egged Gregorie on.

Another day, being the fourth after Susan's death, after Brandon had the chance to recover from the majority of the burns caused by my amulet, the werewolves and a few close friends of Sue held a memorial service in the clearing on the Upland Island reserve. Brandon said a few words as Cassi and I watched on from the edges of the crowd. Once the service was over the alpha werewolf took her around to some of the pack members and introduced her as Sue's daughter. Not that many of them needed the introduction. I wasn't the only one that saw the resemblance between them now apparently. For my part I stayed on the edge of the crowd during all this. While I'm sure it wasn't missed that I had arrived at the service with Cassi, I wanted to be sure that her reputation with the pack was based on Sue's time with the werewolves as much as possible. Much better than by her association with the local law enforcement, even to this pack. To them I was a good guy. Sue had been a mother.

As I sipped a cup of coffee near the edge of the table I spoke with a few of the wolves and their supernatural neighbors that were present, assuring them that the threat had been neutralized and passing out new copies of my contact card.

"I thought I heard Brandon asking on the phone just last night if you knew who was behind all this." Stormy had apparently been behind me during the last conversation.

"Not that my conversations with the pack's Alpha are any of your concern, but that situation has been contained and precautions are being taken."

"What exactly does that mean? Considering my likely placement as alpha female in the near future I'd like to be kept well informed." Stormy said as she dismissed the two wolves I'd been talking to with a glance. I don't know if Sue had known about this part of Stormy when she had taken her under her wing, but the girl was right, she was one of the most qualified to take up Sue's old position.

I couldn't help but to run my eyes over the gathered crowds and make sure I could see a safe Cassi before I answered. "The Wendigo and the assassins that killed Sue have been dealt with." I repeated my statement. "All things considered no one has cause to bring that fight back your way."

Stormy's tone had changed completely over the last two times I had seen her and I feared I knew why. "Cassi has no ties to the pack now. If the people who were after her wish to continue after this ordeal, they have no reason to look this way."

"I couldn't care less." Stormy poured herself a cup of coffee from the large urn on the table I stood by. "If she puts the pack in danger once I am alpha female. I will..."

"Call me and let me know just like you are supposed to." I looked back to Stormy and shook my head. "I don't want to get a phone call like the one you made on Fenrir back in Odessa." I said as I took a long drink of my coffee, set down my empty cup, and pushed myself off the table. As I walked by Stormy her glare followed my hand. I reached into my pocket and pulled out the little piece of paper she had written her note for me on. "Keep this as a reminder. I don't owe you anything." And with that I walked back into the crowd toward Cassi and Brandon.

It had been only a couple of hours after I had called Norm about Walter's death that I had gotten the call from my father telling me that Roger had died in the line of duty. It hadn't technically been the case, but we had managed to make the situation look legitimate so Walters wouldn't go down as a vigilante, insane Bigfoot hunter, or anything like that, despite the fact that the truth laid somewhere between the two.

Walters had died while protecting and serving. He died a hero, so he was buried with full honors outside of Tyler in the same church cemetery in which the rest of his family before him had been laid to rest. I actually pulled out the dark suit and shades of the standard federal agent for the funeral. The outfit served as appropriate attire and as a silent statement to who I represented. My father stood in the honor guard in dress uniform talking with several old friends from different counties or departments before the service began. Each dressed in the unmarred and finely pressed uniforms of browns, blues and greens all of them holding a white cowboy hat. I spotted Finsen and a hand full of other younger officers standing several yards away prepared to fire off the salute.

As was standard with the Initiative, I wasn't allowed to claim my position as an officer of the law in public. So, instead of taking my place in the guard, I stood in the crowd of those gathered to see Walters off with my mother to one side and holding a place for Cassi at my left. She'd spotted someone she knew at the service and went to say hello once we'd gotten to the grave site.

"Honestly William of all the times to bring a woman around." My mother whispered to me as the crowd from the funeral service had started to gather.

"I'll make sure to let Roger know how disconcerting this all is for you the next time I see him." I suppose to some it would have been considered morbid to make such a joke at a funeral, but it had always been the way of my family to look at death with a light heart.

"Oh don't think dying has got that man out of my reach. I'll send word to Mr. Walters this very evening." My mother chided as Cassi neared from having stopped to talk to another attendee she'd known. "Oh Cassi dear. I was just telling William how he should have brought you out to dinner the other night when I invited him. Bringing a beautiful young girl around for the first time at a funeral?"

"Well I haven't known Will all that long Mrs..." "Samantha, please dear." My mother said with a grin.

"Thank you Samantha, but like I was saying, I haven't known Will that long. I'd actually met Roger shortly before. My family was victims in the case he and Will were working on and..." The story she was about to tell was close enough to the truth that Cassi's eyes had started to water apparently because my mother pushed me aside, reached across me, and wrapped Cassi in an embrace.

"Don't worry about it dear. Will had said he met you through work, and I knew he was doing some profiling in this area. You don't need to talk about it now, but if you want to later don't hesitate."

"Profiling?" Cassi looked toward me as she returned the embrace a knowing grin growing over her face.

"William's job is profiling criminals for the FBI." My mother answered as she looked to me, curiosity starting to cross her face, as Cassi put a hand over her lips from behind my mother's back. Her eyes wide in silent apology.

"It looks like they are about to start." I responded giving Cassi a wink as I patted my mother on the back so she would know it was time for the service to start. That had been too close. One slip would have led to another and before I could have gotten a hold of it Cassi would have called my mother Mrs. Codex, and that would have led to a lot more explaining than a slip on my job. Not to mention that if my mother said the words correctly Cassi could have instantly forgotten that I was me. I was going to need to make a phone call to Norm to get that worked out.

Norm had arranged for one of the Initiative's floating agents to cover my district for a couple of weeks while I recovered from my injuries. Most of the time I still spent working behind the initiative's back. I knew now that Cassi's parents had been killed to draw Cassi out so someone could have her captured by the elves. Then someone turned the Wendigo onto her presence. Someone wanted Cassi captured for something. Worse still, someone else wanted her dead and to top it all off, I didn't know who had recruited either of them. How much Cassi was starting to mean to me aside, someone was starting to make power plays in my sandbox and Gideon had taught me that you never let something like that go on. You let someone pull one over on you and before you know it two more are stepping up to kick you while you are down.

"You don't put a bucket under a drip in the ceiling. You climb up to the roof and fix it. Otherwise, next thing you know the whole storm's going to come down on your head." I might not be able to get much done while I waited for a gunshot wound, a minor concussion, a cracked rib and a collection of muscle strains to heal, but I wasn't going to just sit around. Besides, Cassi had a wonderful idea for my physical therapy about a week into my vacation mainly moving boxes and furniture.

With no job in Longview she was going to lose her apartment soon, so Cassi had found a place to stay in Tyler. Hannelore had actually offered one of the upstairs rooms at her home. I was a bit taken aback for a moment when I first heard about the idea. I think that was more for fear of the beating my self-esteem would take, now that the two of them lived in the same house, than for anything else. The two women got along wonderfully.

Between funerals, recovery, and getting Cassi moved it was nearly two weeks before I finally did call and ask her on a proper evening out, and thankfully it was surprisingly normal. We went to a little sushi place I liked and Cassi did her very best to laugh at my horrible jokes while I did the best I could not to stare too hard at her in the little black dress she had worn. We talked about colleges, home towns, favorite ice cream flavors, and anything else either of us could think of that didn't involve murders, assassins, monsters, or anything under the umbrella of the supernatural.

It'd gone so well in fact that by the time we had closed down the sushi bar, the movie we were going to try to catch was a distant memory. So, instead we drove back toward my place for a late night of coffee and Netflix. The good start of the evening should have been a big clue that something was going to go horribly wrong.

Cassi was curious when she saw the woman sitting on my porch waiting for me. I on the other hand was furious. A first date never goes off without a hitch when your college sweet heart is host to the power of the ancient Greek goddess of revenge.

"I thought work didn't follow you home often." Cassi asked as I made to step in front of her blocking line of sight between her and Bethany. A second later I felt a familiar psychic tickle at the back of my mind that I had learned over the last couple of weeks was Cassi trying to apply her gift. "Oh... that's her isn't it?"

I just nodded and walked toward the porch before reaching around beneath my jacket and flipping open the strap on the holster of the SIG. I really wished I had the Colt on me but the large semi-automatic didn't make for good dinner wear compared to nine millimeter's concealable size. Cassi rested a hand at the small of my back as we both moved up the stairs that led to my front porch and the woman waiting beside the door.

"William. It's been too long." Bethany greeted as she stepped up from the door frame. Despite my opinion of her, only a handful of words described my ex. Gorgeous, eloquent, sexy, devious, and trouble were a few of the ones that always crossed my mind. She stood near my own eye level with dark ebony hair that framed beautiful, strong, but soft features that were more often seen as part of iconic statues of a goddess instead of living flesh. Full bright red lips spread into a wide ivory smile. Most of her lightly tanned skin was covered by an obviously well cut suit that managed to glide over every curve of her form but cling to none. The only prominent exception was the hypnotically low neckline of the jacket that barely hinted at the idea of a shirt or something like one at the end of an impressive amount of cleavage and skin. Resting near the center of that distracting neckline was a silver amulet in the shape of a griffin perched on top of a silver disk. The disk had a cross engraved on it, but the creature sitting on the symbol brought on a whole new meaning. It was the icon of Nemesis dominating over the top of the wheel of justice.

I looked at the woman standing in front of my door staring directly into her hazel come hither stare. "Come back during business hours Bethany. The office is closed and you can't come in." I said before reaching for my door.

"And you can't either. I'm afraid the door won't open while I'm here William. I had to make sure that I got the chance to speak with you and your friend. An Initiative agent and a practical empath seen in public together as much as the two of you have been? That causes quite the buzz in the supernatural community." I still checked the door despite her warning and while the knob turned as if it was unlocked it would simply not budge.

I glared at Bethany and reached toward my back but Cassi's hand on my back stopped me. "It can't hurt to hear her out if it gets her out of our way Will." Cassi whispered loud enough for everyone to hear. "She'll just continue to throw a fit otherwise."

Bethany started to talk as I let my hand drift away from the SIG as I nodded. "I suppose you're right. What is it Beth?" I let my irritation overflow my voice as I turned to look back to Bethany.

Her hazel eyes seemed to lighten to pale blue in the span of a few seconds as she narrowed her gaze at the pair of us. "I came to call so I could let you know how dangerous that sword she carries is. Heartseeker is not a child's toy."

"Nor is it yours." Cassi said as she stepped closer to me keeping behind me to my right rubbing slow calming circles into the small of my back. "If that's what you came for you can leave. I know better than you how dangerous the sword is."

"She's protective William. That's a good thing. You always had poor defenses when it came to women." Bethany said as she looked from me to Cassi. "Has she told you that the sword talks to her? That if this..." She started motioning to the two of us. "... goes anywhere the sword and her gift will drive her mad if one or both of your intentions are anything but pure? Are you sure you want to place that big a bet on someone who got attached to you by picking up on my emotions from when she touched the amulet Willaim?"

Hearing a reminder of her visions while she was attached to the amulet was enough to widen Cassi's eyes. Her teeth clenched before she smiled and spoke. "Are you going to try to keep this going all night?" Cassi asked trying to calm herself down as her impromptu massage on the small of my back started to speed up.

"Not hardly, just 'til William realizes how dangerous you are. I can take you home after that. Will tends to be pretty grouchy without a good night's rest."

"That's ok. I'll most likely stay here all night." Cassi said with a grin pulling herself closer to me.

"I suppose you would serve as a distraction. It might actually do the two of you some good." Bethany said as she walked towards us from her place near the door. "I suppose I will have to put up with whatever sub-par entertainment he decides to use until he comes around." She said as she quite literally looked down the edge of her nose at Cassi. "Face it dear, he's killed for me."

"Funny he has done that for me as well, and he knew he was doing it at the time." Cassie grinned back. "Have you ever killed for him? With all your divine power you must be nigh invincible. What kind of risk is that?"

Bethany shook her head. "Very astute and correct of you on both counts. I haven't killed for William, yet. But, once my employer has lost interest in you I will be more than happy to." Bethany started to speak again before Cassi interrupted her.

"Me first." Cassi grinned as her grip tightened on the SIG at my back, pulled the gun free from beneath my coat, leveled the sights on Bethany's face and, pulled the trigger. By the time any of us had seen it happen she had fired two pistol rounds into Bethany's face.

The dark haired woman screamed and clutched her face as blood poured forth from her nose and fell onto the porch of the house. Bethany started to charge at Cassi. Before I knew it, the beautiful woman with me fired another round, this one hitting Bethany right between the eyes.

"Bitch!" Bethany cried this time stopping and looking over the hand she had clenched beneath her eyes at her obviously broken nose trying to stop the bleeding. The bullets hadn't so much as punctured Bethany's protected skin but the force of the blows had been enough to cause more than a fair amount pain.

Cassi waved good bye as the woman ran past us continuing her cursing.

"How did you know shooting her wouldn't hurt her?" I asked shaking my head as Bethany tripped away into a shadow and disappeared. I grinned as my new front door slowly pulled itself open.

"Would you believe I didn't?" Cassi said with a laugh before slipping the gun back into the holster at the small of my back and grabbing me by the hand and pulling me into the house. "Before you say it Will, I know I've started a fight with a bigger fish, but I won't be told who I can and cannot spend my time with. Especially if I am thinking I want to spend a lot of time with them."

I couldn't help but nod and smile in agreement as I closed the door behind us. Once I locked the door, closing out the one problem that evening had brought, the rest of the night went very well in fact. We still never actually got around to watching that movie however.

Acknowledgments

I love telling stories, but what should I say or not say when baring my soul to the reader and singing the praises of all those who have helped me get this far? I think that somewhere in the back of my brain I never thought I would have to do this part.

First and foremost I must thank my parents Craig and Jo Raif who even when I was making up stories about having to draw crayon wires under the living room table they just nodded and asked why. I suspect it would have been different if the crayon wires had been drawn on the top of the table in plain sight, but as far back as I can remember they have encouraged my creativity. If I could find the words to properly thank you two, they would be outdated in a day because I would understand all you've done for me that much more.

Next, the two women who brought this story out of me. Leigh Harrison who gave me the three word primer that ended up being the first ever William Codex short story, and Ginger Grant who as a dear friend and kindred creative soul told me to, "Just shut up and write the book already." You two have been the little angel and devil on my shoulder through this. I'll leave you to fight it out to see which is which.

I can't forget the beta readers. My dear friend Chris Bannon, my brother in all but blood Chris "Chaos" Martin, my relatives and roommates Daniel and Chelsea Heron, and once again my mother. Without your encouragement and patience I wouldn't have survived this process.

My eternal gratitude to all of you and all the others I regret not having the space to mention.

William Codex: Knight of the Silver Sword

Edited by Alyssa Bledsoe

Cover art by Matthew Hogan Photography

Interior art, eBook formatting and amazingness provided by Jessica Ross

A special hidden thank you to the spectacular Tina Wall

All Art owned by Author of this work